The Frontiersman
River of Blood

The Frontiersman
River of Blood

William W. Johnstone
with J. A. Johnstone

PINNACLE BOOKS
Kensington Publishing Corp.
www.kensingtonbooks.com

PINNACLE BOOKS are published by

Kensington Publishing Corp.
119 West 40th Street
New York, NY 10018

PUBLISHER'S NOTE
Following the death of William W. Johnstone, the Johnstone family is
working with a carefully selected writer to organize and complete Mr.
Johnstone's outlines and many unfinished manuscripts to create addi-
tional novels in all of his series like The Last Gunfighter, Mountain Man,
and Eagles, among others. This novel was inspired by Mr. Johnstone's
superb storytelling.

All Kensington titles, imprints, and distributed lines are available at special quantity discounts for bulk purchases for sales promotions, premi-
ums, fund-raising, educational, or institutional use. Special book
excerpts or customized printings can also be created to fit specific needs.
For details, write or phone the office of the Kensington sales manager:
Kensington Publishing Corp., 119 West 40th Street, New York, NY
10018, attn: Sales Department; phone 1-800-221-2647.

PINNACLE BOOKS, the Pinnacle logo, and the WWJ steer head logo,
are Reg. U.S. Pat. & TM Off.

ISBN-13: 978-0-7860-3949-4
ISBN-10: 0-7860-3949-3

First printing: August 2015

10 9 8 7 6 5 4 3 2

Printed in the United States of America

First electronic edition: April 2017

ISBN-13: 978-0-7860-3604-2
ISBN 10: 0-7860-3604-4

Chapter One

Breckinridge Wallace ran for his life.

Behind him, an enormous bear lumbered after him, moving with shocking speed despite its great size.

The same could be said of Breckinridge, who stood several inches over six feet, making him close to a head taller than most men, and whose shoulders seemed to be as wide as an ax handle. Bundles of corded muscle in his arms and shoulders stretched the buckskin shirt he wore. He was a giant among men, and he sometimes joked that he was still young and hadn't gotten his full growth yet.

He wouldn't get much older if he wasn't able to outrun that damn bear, he thought as he raced across a flower-dotted mountain meadow toward a line of trees.

The scenery surrounding him was beautiful, and he would have been able to appreciate it better if he hadn't been running for his life. Snowcapped mountain peaks loomed majestically over the lush meadows on the lower slopes. Off to Breckinridge's right, a fast-flowing stream bubbled down from the heights, seeming to laugh and sing as it raced over its rocky bed. Towering pines reached for the deep blue sky.

Those pines offered Breckinridge his only real hope of escape. If he had to keep running, sooner or later the bear was going to catch him.

He had to climb if he wanted to live.

Mentally, he cursed his foolishness. Even though he hadn't been in the Rocky Mountains for very long, common sense alone should have told him that it was a bad idea to have anything to do with a bear cub. Having grown up in the Smoky Mountains back in Tennessee, he knew good and well that messing with any animal offspring was dangerous.

The fuzzy little thing had been so doggoned adorable, though, as it rolled around in the wildflowers, and Breckinridge hadn't hurt it. All he'd done was pick it up . . .

Then the mama bear had exploded out of some nearby brush with an ear-shattering roar, and the race was on. Breckinridge had spied some trees in the distance, so he dropped the cub and lit out toward them.

Bears could climb trees, of course, but a man could climb higher—or at least so Breckinridge hoped. All he had to do was stay out of reach of that maternal rage until the mama bear got tired or distracted and moved on.

Assuming, of course, that he was able to make it to the trees before she overhauled him.

His long, bright red hair flew out behind him as he ran. Some Indians he'd run into in the past had dubbed him Flamehair because of it. He was running so fast now that it seemed like his hair might actually catch on fire because of his speed. Breckinridge knew that was a pretty fanciful notion, but it crossed his mind anyway.

He looked over his shoulder, saw that the bear had gained on him, and tried to move even faster. That wasn't possible, though. His long legs were already flashing back and forth as swiftly as they could. He covered ground in great leaps and bounds. His salvation, in the form of those pine trees, drew ever nearer.

But so did the bear.

Breckinridge was still carrying his long-barreled .50-caliber flintlock rifle. He tossed it aside to lighten his load. A few steps later, he pulled the pair of flintlock pistols from behind his belt and threw them aside, as well. Breck hated to discard his weapons, but they were only slowing him down. He could always pick them up later—if he survived.

For a second, when the mama bear charged him, he had thought about shooting her. He'd abandoned that idea pretty quickly for a couple of reasons.

One, he wasn't sure he could bring down the bear with a single rifle shot, and he didn't figure the pistols would do much damage to her.

And two, he didn't want to deprive that cub of its mother. The little varmint might not survive without somebody looking after it, and it wasn't the cub's fault that Breckinridge was such an impulsive galoot.

The bear was so close behind him now that the earth seemed to shake under him every time its ponderous paws slapped the ground. He thought he felt the creature's hot breath searing the back of his neck, but that was probably just his imagination. If the bear was really that close, it would have already laid him open with a swipe of the razor-tipped claws on its paw.

He was only a few yards away from the closest tree now. He saw a likely branch about eight feet from the ground and barely slowed down as he leaped for it.

His hands slapped the rough bark and closed around it with a desperate grip. His weight and momentum swung his body forward. With the athletic grace he had been blessed with since childhood, Breckinridge kicked his legs upward, continuing the swing and twisting in midair so that he was able to hook a knee over the branch, as well.

Below him, the bear roared and reared up on her hind legs to swat at him. Breckinridge felt the claws rake through his hair. That was how close he came to having his head stove in like a dropped melon.

He reached up, grabbed a higher branch, and the powerful muscles in his arms and shoulders bunched and swelled even more as he pulled himself higher in the tree. The pine's sharp needles jabbed at his face, but he ignored the discomfort. It would be a lot more painful to fall into that bear's not-so-tender embrace. He got a booted foot on another branch and pushed himself up.

Below, the bear stopped trying to hit him and started climbing instead. The branches were close together, though, and the beast had trouble forcing herself through the dense growth. Breckinridge, even with his broad shoulders, was able to twist and writhe as he climbed, making his ascent easier.

The branches got thinner the higher he went, and so did the trunk. Breckinridge felt the tree start to sway a little from the combined weight of him and the bear. He started to worry that the tree would lean over so far the bear would be able to get at him easier.

For a second, he dropped his right hand to his waist

and closed it around the bone handle of the hunting knife with its long, heavy blade. If he had to, he would draw the knife and try to fight off the bear with it. Cold steel against fang and claw. He still didn't want to hurt the bear, but he would defend himself if it became necessary. His instincts wouldn't let him do anything else.

He climbed until he was a good thirty or forty feet off the ground. The view from up here was spectacular, he thought briefly, but he was more interested in what was directly below him by about fifteen feet.

The bear had stopped climbing, perhaps sensing that the trunk was getting too thin to support her. With her claws dug into the rough bark, she roared in anger and frustration and shook the tree. Breckinridge had moved in closer to the trunk himself, so he was able to throw his arms around it and hang on for dear life as the pine tree rocked back and forth.

That went on for several minutes, long enough that Breckinridge felt himself getting a little sick to his stomach. Finally, though, the bear stopped shaking the tree. Making grumbling, disgusted sounds almost like a human, the huge, shaggy beast began climbing back down.

Breckinridge clung to the trunk and tried to catch his breath. His pulse was pounding inside his head like a blacksmith's hammer beating out a horseshoe on a forge.

The bear dropped the last few feet to the ground, then started pacing around the tree. From time to time she looked up and bellowed at Breckinridge. He wondered just how stubborn she was going to be about this.

She wasn't showing any signs of wandering off like he'd hoped, that was for sure.

So for the time being, he was stuck up here, and as it did every time he was trapped in enforced idleness, his mind began to wander. His thoughts went back to the way he had come to the Rocky Mountains in the first place . . .

Chapter Two

Trouble had a way of finding Breckinridge Wallace. It wasn't that Breck ever went out looking for it . . . well, maybe he did every now and then . . . but for the most part he was a peaceable young man.

True, he had a thirst for adventure, for new places and new experiences. That fiddlefooted nature surely would have led to him leaving his family's farm near the town of Knoxville, Tennessee, sooner or later. He knew his pa and his four older brothers could take care of the place just fine without his help.

It wasn't like he'd ever been that diligent about carrying out his chores anyway. As far back as he could remember, every chance he'd gotten he would run off to the woods to hunt and explore and just be out in the world, enjoying it.

Now and again those adventures had landed him in trouble, of course, like the time those four Chickasaw renegades had tried to kill him. That had gained him a bitter enemy in the person of the scarred, vengeful warrior called Tall Tree.

Tall Tree was dead now, but Breckinridge Wallace

had other enemies in the world, through no real fault
of his own.

Take Richard Aylesworth, the son of a wealthy
merchant in Knoxville who had been Breckinridge's
main rival for the affections of the beautiful Maureen
Grantham. Of course, as it turned out, the rivalry hadn't
really amounted to much. Maureen had chosen Aylesworth over Breck without really hesitating. Aylesworth
was handsome and rich, after all, a polished and so-
phisticated gentleman, instead of a big, redheaded
galoot with none of the rough edges knocked off.

To be fair, though, Maureen hadn't married Aylesworth until after Breckinridge was gone from the area,
having taken off on the run from a dubious murder
charge that, when you came right down to it, was
Richard Aylesworth's fault.

Fleeing the law, away from home for the first time
in his life, Breckinridge had fallen in with assorted
shady characters, found himself in and out of danger,
lost everything he had, fought river pirates and Indians,
shot a man in St. Louis who had it coming, scouted for
the army, and made a good friend, Lieutenant John
Francis Mallory, with whom Breck had made a pact to
go west to the Rockies, known by some as the Shining
Mountains, and become fur trappers.

Mallory hadn't lived to see that day arrive, but to
honor his friend's memory Breckinridge had followed
through on the plan they had made. After a disastrous
trip home, back to Tennessee, Breck had hired on with
a party of trappers headed up the Missouri River.

That just led to more trouble, of course, since it had
a way of finding Breckinridge. Trust had been betrayed,
lives had been lost, old scores had been settled, and
four survivors from the party had continued on west.

In addition to Breckinridge, the other men were Morgan Baxter, Roscoe Akins, and Amos Fulbright. Baxter was the son of the man who'd financed the expedition, and as the sons of rich men usually were, at least in Breck's experience, he was a real jackass starting out.

The hardships and tragedies they had suffered along the way had forced Morgan to grow up a mite, though, and Breck had come to like him.

Akins and Fulbright were typical trappers, rough, stolid men without much education or imagination, but you could count on them when the chips were down, and out here that was perhaps the most valuable quality of all.

After the violence that had shrunk the group to its current level, the four men had pushed on upriver, into the heart of the Rockies, until they found this long valley with its lush meadows and numerous streams.

This was prime beaver country, Breckinridge thought, although from everything he had heard back in St. Louis the beaver weren't as plentiful anywhere as they had once been. Trappers had been coming out here for more than twenty years, and their efforts had shrunk the beaver population.

Breckinridge and his companions meant to give the business a try anyway, so they had set up camp and gone about running traplines along the creeks in the area. Every day they split up to check those traps, and that was what Breck had been doing when he spotted something that made him curious and wandered away from the creek to look at the little bear cub . . .

And that was how he'd come to find himself up a tree with a couple of thousand pounds of furry rage pacing around below him, waiting to tear him apart.

* * *

The mama bear was nothing if not stubborn. She stalked around and around the tree for what seemed like hours while Breckinridge waited up in the branches. He was starting to get hot and thirsty, but he didn't have any water with him. He tried not to think about it, but that didn't always work.

Morgan, Akins, and Fulbright were elsewhere in the valley, probably within a few miles. If he'd been able to fire a shot, they might have heard it and responded to see what was wrong, but his rifle and pistols were lying out there in the meadow. The guns might as well have been back in St. Louis, for all the good they could do him right now.

He had his powder horn, though, along with steel and flint. Maybe he could start a signal fire . . .

And burn the tree down around him. Yeah, that was a fine idea, Breckinridge told himself caustically. He needed to do a better job of thinking things through. If he'd done that in the first place, he would have stayed far away from that bear cub and wouldn't be in this fix now.

No, he was just going to have to be patient. There wasn't any other way around it.

Once he had come to that conclusion, he decided that he might as well put the time to good use. He used the rawhide strap from his powder horn to tie his left wrist to a sturdy branch, then wrapped his legs around a lower branch, leaned against the tree trunk, and went to sleep.

Breckinridge had no idea how long he sat there dozing, but after a while he heard shouts that jolted him out of his slumber. He lifted his head and shook it to clear out the cobwebs of sleep. He heard a chuffing and growling below him and knew the bear was still maintaining her vigil.

"Breckinridge! Breck! Where in blazes are you?"

"Hey, Breck! You around here?"

Breckinridge recognized the voices of Morgan Baxter and Roscoe Akins. A moment later Amos Fulbright joined in, calling, "Hey, there! Breck Wallace!"

The three voices came from slightly different directions. Breckinridge figured they had returned to camp from checking the other traplines, then when he didn't show up, too, they had come to look for him. They knew which direction he had gone when he left that morning, so it wasn't difficult to follow his trail.

He untied his wrist from the branch and looped the powder horn strap around his neck again. Standing up carefully, he balanced on a branch and parted some of the other growth to look out across the valley.

His keen eyes spotted a man wearing a buckskin jacket and a broad-brimmed hat of brown felt about a quarter of a mile away. That was Morgan Baxter, Breckinridge thought.

He held on to the tree with one hand and cupped the other to his mouth as he shouted, "Morgan! Hey, Morgan! Over here in the trees!"

Morgan's head lifted, telling Breckinridge that he'd heard the shout. He turned and called to the other two men, then started loping toward the trees, carrying his rifle.

"Morgan, don't get too close!" Breckinridge yelled. "There's a bear!"

He kept calling the warning until Morgan slowed down and waved to the others to be careful, as well. Morgan came to a stop about a hundred yards away and cupped his hands to shout, "Breck, where are you?"

The bear's head swung toward him. Folks said that bears couldn't see very well, but that they had excellent senses of hearing and smell and relied on them to locate enemies. Breckinridge didn't know for a fact that any of that was true, but this bear heard Morgan, no doubt about that.

"Stay back!" Breckinridge called again. "Don't come any closer!"

"Good Lord!" The exclamation came from Fulbright. "That griz has run him up a tree!"

"Breck, are you all right?" Akins called.

The bear's head swung back and forth as she tried to figure out where all the humans were. The way the voices were coming from different directions seemed to have confused her. That gave Breckinridge an idea.

"Boys, keep yellin'! Whoop it up!"

The three trappers followed Breckinridge's suggestion. They whooped and hollered and created a racket that echoed back from the hills at the edge of the valley.

At the foot of the tree, the bear lurched one way and then another, growling and occasionally bellowing in frustration. She wasn't sure which way to turn because she had no way of knowing which of the humans represented the greatest threat to her cub. Her exasperation led her to rise up on two legs, paw viciously at the air, and let loose with a tremendous roar.

Then, muttering almost like a person again, she dropped back to all fours and started toward the creek. Breckinridge figured she had decided her best course of action would be to return to her cub and forget all about these crazy two-legged critters.

Morgan, Akins, and Fulbright waited until the bear was several hundred yards away before they approached the tree Breckinridge had climbed. Breck was still up there in the branches, gazing off into the distance.

"You can come down now," Morgan called to him. "The bear's gone."

"Or are you stuck?" Fulbright asked with a grin on his whiskery face.

"No, I ain't stuck," Breckinridge replied with a little annoyance of his own. "I just noticed somethin'. Looks like somebody else heard all the hollerin' that was goin' on."

He lifted a long, muscular arm and pointed at a thin, broken column of smoke rising in the distance.

Smoke signals. Indians were talking to each other over yonder . . . and Breckinridge had a pretty good idea what they were talking about.

Chapter Three

Since the battle that had left most of the party dead on the way out here, Breckinridge and the other three survivors hadn't had any more trouble with the Indians. They had run into a few Crow, but the word had spread through the tribe that the man they called Flamehair was considered a friend.

This wasn't really Crow country, though. From what Breckinridge had heard, the most common tribe around here was the Blackfoot—and they were ornery varmints who didn't consider anybody a friend except themselves, neither red nor white.

The smart thing for the four trappers to do would have been to stay together all the time, as a war party was a lot less likely to attack a group of four well-armed men than they were a lone trapper.

But doing that meant it would take them four times as long to gather the same number of pelts, and that was just plumb wasteful. Besides, they hadn't seen any Indian sign in this valley, so it had seemed safe enough for them to split up whenever they ran their lines.

Until now.

Luckily, the four of them were together at the moment, and they needed to stay that way. Breckinridge shinnied most of the way down the tree and then dropped to the ground. His hands were sticky from pine sap, so he started wiping them on his buckskin trousers.

"Is that smoke what I think it is?" Morgan Baxter asked worriedly.

"I reckon it must be," Breckinridge replied. "I don't know for sure, havin' never seen smoke signals myself, but I can't figure what else it could be."

Akins said, "They're smoke signals, all right. I was out here a couple years ago, and the bunch I was with saw smoke like that for a couple of days before a bunch of Arikara jumped us. Did good to get out with our hair, we did."

"Not that you had a whole hell of a lot to lose," Fulbright said, referring to the thin blond growth on Akins's skull.

"This is no time for joking," Morgan said. "We were told this was Blackfoot territory, so if anybody's responsible for those smoke signals, it's probably them. They're hostile to whites."

"And to everybody else," Breckinridge added. "We'd best get back to camp. If we're in for a fight, we want to have as much powder and shot at hand as we can."

What he said made sense. He trotted out into the meadow to pick up the rifle and pistols he had thrown aside when the bear was chasing him, and then all four of them moved quickly up the valley toward their campsite.

A bluff topped with trees and rocks reared up next to one of the creeks, and that was where they had made camp when they reached the valley a couple of weeks earlier. The location was handy to water, and the trees and rocks would provide cover if they needed it. The height advantage, although it wasn't dramatic, wouldn't hurt anything, either.

The four men reached the stream on which their camp was located and followed it, trotting along the grassy banks. The creek twisted around a bend up ahead, dropped down a short, rocky waterfall, and then traced a fairly straight, level course across a mile-wide meadow to the camp.

As the trappers entered the little cut at the top of the waterfall, Breckinridge spotted something and threw out an arm to stop the others.

"We're too late," he said. "They're already over there."

"How can you see that?" Akins asked sourly. "The camp's a mile away!"

"I've got good eyes," Breckinridge said simply.

It was true. He had been blessed with exceptional sight, hearing, and smell. He figured that was the Good Lord's way of outfitting him for the perilous existence in the wilderness he now knew he was meant for. He had never felt as much at home as he did out here in the high country.

"Can you tell how many of them there are?" Morgan asked.

"Not for sure. At least half a dozen, I'd say. They're movin' around, though, so it's hard to get an exact count."

"What're they doin'?" Fulbright said.

"Just rummagin' around right now."

"They're going to steal our supplies," Morgan said.

His voice was bleak. "The damned thieves. They'll probably take all our pelts, too."

They had several dozen pelts already dried and rolled up for transport, and four or five more scraped, stretched out, and pegged down to dry. Not enough to make or break anybody, but still worth a significant amount of money. Enough that Breckinridge didn't want to lose it.

His eyes narrowed in thought. After a moment he said, "Here's what we're gonna do. You three fellas stay out of sight, circle off to the west, and then come at the camp from that direction. There's a considerable amount of trees and brush over there, so maybe you can get fairly close without those varmints noticin' you, especially since they'll be busy lookin' at something else."

"What are they going to be looking at?" Morgan asked suspiciously.

"Me," Breckinridge said. "I figured I'd walk across that meadow beside the creek, big as life and twice as ugly, so they'll watch me and not pay any attention to you boys."

"That's crazy," Morgan argued. "As soon as you get close enough, they'll just shoot you."

"Maybe not. From everything I know about Injuns, they're a curious lot. They'll want to know why a lone white man is walkin' in like that, bold as brass. They may think I don't know they're there, in which case they'll lay low and let me get closer 'fore they make themselves known. Anyway, I'm gonna keep 'em occupied so you fellas can sneak up on 'em."

"White men sneakin' up on Indians," Akins muttered. "It's supposed to be the other way around, ain't it?"

"Most of the time," Breckinridge admitted. "But if it's good enough for them, I reckon it's good enough for us."

Morgan rubbed his chin and frowned in thought. After a moment he nodded slowly and said, "It might work. What happens if we're able to get up close?"

"Wait until they come out in the open to jump me, and then you can cut loose at 'em," Breckinridge said. "That'll take 'em by surprise and give me a chance to run in and start whalin' away on 'em."

"This may be pretty unlikely, but . . . what if they're friendly?"

"Well, then we won't kill 'em, of course. There's always a chance they ain't Blackfeet. Might be Shoshone or some such. In which case we might even be able to do some tradin' with them."

Fulbright scratched at his thick black beard, grimaced, and asked, "How will we know whether or not they're friendly?"

"You'll be able to tell," Breckinridge said confidently. "If they ain't, there's a good chance they'll be doin' their damnedest to kill me."

Chapter Four

Breckinridge waited until the other three men had waded across the creek, moved down the slope, and headed off to the west, crouching and using every bit of cover they could find as they trotted along.

Once they were out of sight, he canted his rifle jauntily over his shoulder and marched down the hill in plain sight. He followed the creek across the meadow, strolling along as if he didn't have a care in the world. He even whistled a little tune, although he was still too far away from the camp for the Indians to hear him.

When he was a little more than halfway across the meadow, he noticed that the interlopers had stopped moving around. He looked close but couldn't see them anymore. That lack of activity convinced him that the Indians had noticed his approach.

Either they had hidden and were watching him as he came closer, or they had decided to leave. He didn't think the sight of one lone white man would have spooked them, so he was betting on the former.

He glanced to his right, where Morgan, Akins, and Fulbright ought to be working themselves into position.

He didn't see them anywhere, which was good. It meant they were staying out of sight, and if he couldn't see them, neither could the Indians.

It suddenly occurred to Breckinridge that if anything happened to his three friends, if they were delayed for any reason, he could easily be walking into an ambush in which he was greatly outnumbered.

In that case he would just have to make the best of it. He still couldn't think of any other plan that would have been better. He and the others couldn't afford to abandon everything that was in the camp. Their continued survival depended too much on it.

Breckinridge had fallen silent, but he started whistling again as he came within earshot of the bluff. He veered to his left, away from the stream and toward the game trail that led to the top of the shallow rise.

Something flicked through the air toward him, causing his instincts and reflexes to take over. He twisted aside as fast as he could, which was barely fast enough to keep from being impaled by the arrow that flew past him. The shaft came so close it brushed the fringe on the front of his buckskin shirt.

Well, that answered the question of whether or not the Indians were hostile, he thought.

More arrows flew toward him. He dived forward so the deadly missiles sailed over him and buried themselves in the ground behind him.

Whooping and howling, the savages leaped out of their hiding places and charged down the game trail toward him. Since he had successfully dodged their arrows so far, they must have decided it would be better to finish him off at close quarters.

Breckinridge pushed himself up on one knee and lifted his rifle. It was already loaded and primed, so all he had to do was pull back the hammer as he socketed the curved butt against his shoulder. He settled his sights on the chest of the warrior who was leading the charge and squeezed the trigger.

The rifle boomed and kicked hard against him. The Indian went over backward as violently as if he had run full-speed into a low-hanging branch. Breckinridge knew the heavy lead ball had found its mark.

The Indians were still far enough away that he thought he had time to reload before they could reach him. He set about doing so, making an effort to keep his nerves under control and remain calm and cool as he measured a charge of powder from the horn.

He didn't look at the Indians but instead watched what he was doing. As long as they were letting out those bloodthirsty yells, he didn't have to see them to know how close they were getting.

More rifle shots suddenly rang out from across the creek. Breckinridge knew his friends were joining in the fight. As he used the flintlock's ramrod to tamp a patch-wrapped ball down the barrel, he glanced up and saw that a couple more of the warriors had tumbled to the ground.

That left half a dozen of them on their feet, however, so he still had a fight on his hands.

Pistol shots boomed now as Morgan, Akins, and Fulbright charged out of some cottonwoods on the far side of the creek. Breckinridge primed his rifle and raised it again.

The nearest warrior was about thirty feet from him. The man let fly with a tomahawk just as Breckinridge pressed the trigger. That caused him to duck and threw his aim off a little. Instead of hitting the Indian in the chest, the ball blew away a fist-sized chunk of his skull above the left eye. Momentum made the man race forward a few more steps, already dead, before he pitched face-first to the ground.

Either way, the Indian was a goner, Breckinridge figured.

He set the rifle on the ground and pulled out his pistols as he rose to his full height. He leveled the guns and fired.

One of the warriors went down with blood fountaining from his throat where Breckinridge's shot had torn it open. Another staggered, his right shoulder shattered where the ball had struck it. He stayed on his feet, though, and used his left hand to pluck a knife from his waist as he closed with Breck.

Steel rang against steel as the Indian stabbed down at Breckinridge, who used the barrel of one of the empty guns to turn aside the blade. With his other hand, Breck swung the other pistol against the side of the man's head. Bone crunched under the smashing impact and the warrior's legs folded, dropping him into a limp sprawl.

Another warrior slashed at him with a tomahawk. Breckinridge twisted aside and kicked the man in the belly. As the Indian doubled over, Breck brought up his right knee and smashed it into his jaw. The warrior went down, knocked out cold.

By now, Morgan, Akins, and Fulbright had splashed across the creek, and they launched themselves into the thick of the melee. Fulbright carried a tomahawk like the Indians, and the big, black-bearded man wielded it efficiently, shattering a warrior's skull with it. Akins used the brass-plated butt of his rifle to batter another of the Indians to the ground. Morgan Baxter fired a pistol into the chest of a third man.

That left Breckinridge facing only one of the warriors, but this one was a big, strapping fellow who drove him backward by viciously slashing a knife back and forth. Breck dropped his empty pistols, timed his move, and suddenly lunged forward to grab the Indian's wrist. He dropped backward, planted a booted foot in the man's stomach, and levered him up and over.

The warrior let out a startled cry as he found himself flying through the air. He crashed down on his back with enough force to knock the breath out of his body and leave him stunned.

Breckinridge rolled over, snatched his own knife from its sheath, and leaped at the fallen warrior. The knife rose and fell, late afternoon sunlight winking on the blade as it did so. Breck plunged the knife into the warrior's chest. The man spasmed, kicked, and died.

That left only one of the Indians alive, the man Breckinridge had knocked out a few moments earlier. Breck pulled his blood-dripping knife from the corpse of the man he had just killed, pointed with it, and warned his friends, "Keep an eye on that one. He's still breathin'."

"We can do somethin' about that," Fulbright said. He leaned over and split the Indian's skull with one swift stroke of his tomahawk. The warrior would never regain consciousness now.

Breckinridge grunted in surprise and said, "I didn't figure you'd kill him."

Fulbright wrenched his 'hawk free and straightened.

"What'd you expect me to do?" he asked. "Did you plan on torturin' the varmint to death, like they might've done to you if they'd caught you?"

"Of course not!"

"Well, we couldn't let him go. He'd have run right

back to the rest of his bunch and told them where we are and that we'd killed a bunch of his friends. We'd have had to move our camp, and that probably wouldn't have done any good. They'd have tracked us down to settle the score anyway. I can tell from the decorations on their clothes and the way they wear their hair that they're Blackfeet. Those varmints *never* forget a grudge. I've heard some of the old-timers say they still hate white men 'cause of somethin' that happened when ol' Lewis and Clark came through here thirty years ago."

That was the longest speech Breckinridge had ever heard Fulbright make. Morgan said, "I'm afraid Amos is right, Breck. We couldn't afford to let any of them get away."

Breckinridge wiped the blood from his knife and stood up. Since he had killed more of the Indians than any of the others, he supposed he didn't have any right to complain. And looking at it from a practical standpoint, the others were indeed right.

"So what should we do with them?" he asked.

"There's a ravine up in the hills about half a mile from here," Akins suggested. "We could dump 'em in it and maybe throw some rocks down on top of 'em. Nobody'd be likely to find the bodies that way."

Morgan nodded solemnly and said, "That sounds like a good idea."

It sounded like a bloody, unpleasant job to Breckinridge, but he didn't have anything better to offer. He said, "We'd better get at it, I reckon, if we want to finish before dark."

Chapter Five

The grisly task took most of the rest of the day, as Breckinridge had predicted. He did the lion's share of the work, using his great strength to haul two of the corpses at once on the long walk to the ravine.

It took him, Akins, and Fulbright to shove enough rocks over the bodies to protect them from scavengers and, more importantly, keep them from being discovered. Morgan, who was more slightly built and not as strong, kept watch while the larger men labored.

When it was done, the four men returned to their camp and made sure there were no more signs of violence there. The Blackfeet had pawed through the trappers' belongings but didn't appear to have stolen or destroyed anything.

"If we hadn't come along when we did," Fulbright said, "chances are they would've gone off and hidden somewhere close by, then snuck back to ambush us later."

"Why do you think we haven't seen any of them until now?" Morgan asked.

Breckinridge said, "From what I've heard, Injuns

tend to move around a lot. Could be they're just startin' to drift back into this area. They might've spent the winter somewhere else, then started this way after the spring thaw."

That explanation made sense. Akins, who had the most experience out here on the frontier, agreed that it was likely.

They put all their supplies and equipment back where it was supposed to go, then built a small fire inside the stone cooking pit they had erected when they made camp here. That kept the flames from being visible, which was even more important now that they knew there were hostiles in the area.

As they ate supper, which was coffee and salted meat from an elk they had killed a few days earlier, Morgan said, "We'd better not go out alone anymore. Might be a good idea to stay together instead of splitting up."

"That'll slow us down and means we'll be out here even longer before we get a big enough load of pelts to take to one of the tradin' posts," Fulbright argued. "Doesn't that just increase our odds of runnin' into more trouble?"

"Maybe we ought to split the difference," Breckinridge suggested. "We can run the traplines in pairs. That way one man can be keepin' an eye out for trouble while the other checks the traps. And if we do run into any more Blackfeet, two men'll stand a better chance against 'em than one."

Fulbright shrugged his beefy shoulders and said, "I reckon I can go along with that. Although two men won't have much of a chance against a Blackfoot war party, either. I got to tell you boys, we were mighty lucky to come through that fight like we did today. By all rights, those redskins should've killed at least one of us."

"Luck's got nothin' to do with it," Akins insisted. "We just outfought 'em, is all."

Morgan sipped his coffee and said, "What I want to know is . . . how did you wind up getting treed by a bear, Breckinridge?"

That made the other men chuckle and put a grin on Breckinridge's face.

"It's my own damn fool fault," he said. "I got carried away by how cute a little bear cub was and went to pet it."

"Good Lord," Akins said. "You *are* lucky to be alive."

"I know that," Breckinridge said. "Luck has always sort of followed me around."

What he didn't mention was that most of the time, it was *bad* luck . . .

The dark-haired young man who stood at the sideboard in the luxuriously furnished room, pouring brandy from a cut-glass decanter into a crystal snifter, was handsome, expensively dressed, and appeared to have everything in the world a man might want.

But there were three things he didn't have, and their lack gnawed intolerably at him.

One was a wife who loved him. He was married, but she despised him.

Two was the child they should have had by now.

And three was revenge on the man he blamed for those other two things.

He tossed back the drink, and then as he thought about the man he hated, his fingers tightened on the snifter. He had to force himself to set it back on the sideboard carefully, or else the delicate crystal might have shattered under his grip and sliced his hand open.

A soft step on the stairs made him turn his head in that direction. His wife paused about three-fourths of the way down the staircase and asked, "Richard, are you coming up to bed?"

Most men would have answered quickly in the affirmative. Maureen was petite, slender, and very beautiful and alluring in a blue nightdress that set off her fair coloring and dark hair.

Richard Aylesworth just shook his head and said curtly, "I'll be up later. I still have some business to attend to."

Maureen just nodded and said, "All right." Dull acceptance was in her voice. She didn't even pretend to be disappointed any longer. The fire that had once been between them was gone, snuffed out by tragedy.

Of course, most people wouldn't blame her for feeling that way. After all, he had shot her and caused her to lose their child. He could have just as easily killed her, too.

But they were the only two people who knew that, and anyway, it wasn't his fault.

He'd been trying to shoot Breckinridge Wallace.

As Maureen turned and went back upstairs, Aylesworth looked at the brandy and considered pouring another drink. He discarded the idea. He had spent too many nights sodden with liquor, slumped in one of the overstuffed armchairs, lost in half dreams of vengeance and hate.

He wanted to be clearheaded tonight, because he was finally taking a step he should have taken long before now. He was going to do something about what had happened besides brooding about it.

He went into his study, filled his pipe, and smoked it while he waited for the visitor he expected.

After what seemed like hours—the lamp had burned low and Aylesworth felt like he was about to wear a hole in the rug with his pacing—a quiet knock sounded on the door. It opened to reveal a liveried maid standing in the hall. The slave had a worried frown on her face.

"Mist' Aylesworth, there a man here to see you," she said. Her disapproval of someone calling this late at night was plain to hear in her voice.

"Thank you, Ophelia," Aylesworth said. "Show him in here."

"In *here*?" she repeated, as if the visitor wasn't fit to set foot in the room.

"That's right," Aylesworth snapped.

"Yes, suh. Whatever you say."

As Ophelia disappeared, Aylesworth recalled that a third person knew the truth about what had happened that night several months earlier . . . that bloody, terrible night. Ophelia had been there and had witnessed the whole thing.

But she was no fool. When the sheriff came, she had told the same story her master did, laying the blame for the shooting at the feet of Breckinridge Wallace.

Of course, it wouldn't have done her any good to call Aylesworth a liar. The law would have believed him without question, and he would have sold Ophelia as a troublemaker. No one would have thought twice about him doing it, either. She was smart enough to know that.

The door opened and a man followed Ophelia into the study. He was big, broad-shouldered, roughly dressed like a teamster or a tradesman. He held a battered hat in one large, knobby-knuckled hand, revealing a bald head. Bushy black eyebrows matched a thick mustache. The man's prominent nose had been broken more than once, and there were numerous other signs that life had not treated him gently.

He jerked his head in a nod and said to Aylesworth, "Guv'nor." His accent betrayed his English origin.

"You can go," Aylesworth told Ophelia. "And close the door behind you."

She went out. Aylesworth suspected that she would linger on the other side of the door, eavesdropping, but he didn't care. She couldn't do him any harm.

"Would you like a drink?" he went on.

"What've you got?" the man asked.

There was a bottle sitting on a tray on the desk, along with a pair of glasses. Aylesworth gestured toward it and said, "Port."

The bald man grunted.

"Rather have rum or beer, but if that's all you've got . . ."

He sounded a bit less English now. Aylesworth supposed he had been in the States for a while and was starting to lose his accent.

Such speculation was nothing but an attempt to distract himself, thought Aylesworth. He resolved to stick to the matter at hand, once he had poured a drink for the man.

He handed the glass to his visitor and said, "I'm afraid I don't know your name, Mister . . . ?"

"Sykes," the bald man said. "Harry Sykes."

"To your health, Mr. Sykes."

The visitor tossed back the drink, clearly not worried about savoring anything about it. He licked away a couple of drops that clung to his mustache, then said, "It ain't my health you're worried about, is it, Guv'nor?"

"Actually, no, it's not," Aylesworth admitted. "I put the word out among some of my, ah, associates that I was looking for a man who's good at finding things. A man who's also not too particular about the jobs he takes on."

"You must have some *associates* who ain't quite so fancy, elsewise they never would've known to get word to me," Sykes commented.

That was true. Since his father's illness, Aylesworth had taken over the running of the lucrative mercantile store, so as a successful and respected businessman, he couldn't afford to frequent any of the seedier establishments in Knoxville.

In his younger years, though, he had gambled, drank, and wenched his way through many of them, and he still knew people in those places. He had sent notes to several of the proprietors, and one had responded that he knew just the man and would send him to Aylesworth's home, late at night so the visit would be a discreet one, of course.

Aylesworth didn't care for Sykes's sneering tone, but he told himself to ignore it. Some things were more important than his pride. His need for revenge was one of them.

"I want you to find someone," he said. "He's not here in Knoxville. The last I heard, he was headed out west. There's really no way of knowing where he might be by now."

Sykes grunted and said, "You don't ask for much, do you? 'Out west' takes in some mighty big ground."

"Hire as many men as you need to help you," Aylesworth said flatly. "Take as long as you need in order to do the job. Money is no object."

"What *is* the object?" Sykes asked with a sly smile.

"I want you to find a man named Breckinridge Wallace, and when you do, I want him to die." Aylesworth paused, then added, "As painfully as possible."

Chapter Six

The fight with the Blackfeet had made Breckinridge and his friends wary enough that they took turns standing guard that night, even though the likelihood of any more Indians showing up so soon was small.

Indeed, the night passed quietly, and the next morning, after a quick breakfast, the four men paired off to check the traplines. Breckinridge and Morgan Baxter went one way, Akins and Fulbright the other.

Before they parted, Breckinridge told Akins and Fulbright, "If you run into trouble, fire a shot. Morgan and me will do the same. We got to look out for each other, 'cause we're all we got."

That was true, as far as Breckinridge knew. He wasn't aware of any other white men for miles around. They certainly hadn't seen any other trappers since they'd arrived in this valley.

Several weeks earlier, though, while they were still scouting around for a good place, they had run into another group that had welcomed them with a mixture of hospitality and wariness.

That reaction was understandable in these days when making any money in the fur trade was more of a challenge than it had ever been. Nobody wanted strangers bulling their way into an area where beaver might be found.

Breckinridge and his companions had made it clear that they intended to move on, though, and so for a pleasant night they had shared a campfire with the other trappers, who were six in number. They were all experienced frontiersmen, and they had brought up something that Akins had already mentioned on the way out here.

"Yeah, there's gonna be a rendezvous 'fore too much longer," one of the trappers had said. "Fellas'll come from all over these here mountains to have their-selves a good ol'-fashioned hooraw for a few days. Be lots of drinkin' and dancin', and some of the fur company men will be there to buy pelts. Best thing about the whole season, if you ask me."

"I've been to a few of those fandangos," Akins had said. "You won't ever see the like back East."

That had led to snorts of agreement from the other men.

"Where will they hold this rendezvous?" Breckin-ridge had asked.

"Don't rightly know just yet. But don't worry. When the time comes, word'll get around. Just keep an ear to the ground, boys."

Since then, they hadn't heard anything else about the gathering, but Breckinridge was looking forward to it and hoped he and his friends wouldn't miss it. He loved the solitude of the wilderness and always had, ever since he was a boy, but he enjoyed being around people, too.

And the talk of whiskey had given him a thirst that night. He and his friends didn't have even a single jug among them. That was probably a good thing—a man didn't need to get his mind all muddled up by liquor when there were dangers all around, every hour of the day and night—but it would be nice to cut loose for a spell and lubricate his tonsils.

He wasn't thinking about that as he and Morgan Baxter made their way along the creeks, checking their traps. They tramped several miles up and down the streams that day and found two beaver. When they came across the second, Breckinridge tied the carcass to the first one and carried both. The varmints were heavy, especially since they were wet and dead, but he was strong enough that the load didn't bother him. He could have carried more if he needed to.

The valley had been quiet all day, with no shots from Akins and Fulbright. Breckinridge hoped that the party of Blackfoot warriors finding their camp had been just a fluke and that no more of the savages would come along.

Somewhere, though, there was a village where those men belonged, and when they never returned, the rest of their band would grow curious and start to worry. It was likely they would send out a search party.

Breckinridge hoped he and his friends would have enough pelts and be gone before that happened.

One thing he had learned was that if he hung around anywhere long enough, something bad was bound to crop up.

* * *

The wagon rolled out of the livery barn in St. Louis not long after dawn. It was a sturdy vehicle, pulled by a team of six equally sturdy mules, and the back was filled with crates and sacks of supplies that were covered with canvas tied down at the corners.

Two men sat on the driver's seat. The one handling the reins was roughly dressed and stick-thin, with a black hat shading his gaunt face.

The man beside him was heavy enough to have made two of the driver, but he didn't give the impression of being fat. Instead he looked powerful, filled with the sort of driving energy that made a man rich. The well-cut suit he wore, along with the wide straw hat, added to that appearance.

Balanced across his knees was the finest shotgun money could buy, its polished wood and brass gleaming in the early morning sunlight. Fingers like sausages closed around the stock.

Under the brim of the straw hat was a wide, moon face, flushed with good living and habitual anger. Coarse, graying, rust-colored hair stuck out from under the hat. The man's pale gray eyes were set deep in pits of gristle. They watched as more than a dozen men on horseback moved up to the wagon and reined in.

One of them, who had white hair and a rugged, deeply tanned face, said, "We're ready to go whenever you are, Mr. Ducharme."

Otto Ducharme nodded. He asked in a slightly guttural voice, "You are all well-armed?"

"Yes, sir. You made it pretty clear that we need to be ready for trouble. You've got plenty of powder and shot in the back of that wagon, I expect."

"Of course," Ducharme snapped. "And everything else we will need for our journey."

"You know," the white-haired man ventured in a cautious tone, "it's still not too late for you to leave this to us. There's really no need for you to go traipsin' all the way out there to the mountains or wherever it is we wind up."

"No need?" Ducharme repeated. His beefy face slowly turned an even deeper shade of red. "There is every need. It was *my* son that man murdered. *My* boy who lies cold and dead in the ground because of that . . . that . . ."

In his rage, his words dissolved into a sputtering series of curses in his native German.

He had come to this country to make a life for himself and his wife. His father had been a Hessian, a mercenary soldier who had fought for the British during the war in which the Americans had won their freedom.

Otto had grown up hearing stories about those Americans and their homeland. Even though his father had fought for the British, he had admired the enemy, the way a fighting man will do. In America, he had said, a man could make of himself whatever he was capable of.

That idea appealed to Otto, so as a young man with a new bride he had answered the summons and dared to make the long voyage across the Atlantic. They had landed almost penniless, unable to speak more than a few words of English . . .

And ten years later, Otto Ducharme had owned a successful freighting company and been the proud father of a new son.

Unfortunately, Rory's birth had been hard on his
mother, and eventually her weakened state had caused
her to sicken and die. Bitter and grieving, Otto Ducharme had thrown himself into his business, and as
a result he had become more and more successful.
Eventually his wagons rolled from one end of the new
country to the other, and he and his young son had
settled in St. Louis, at the western terminus of the
freight lines, on the edge of the vast wilderness that to
Ducharme's way of thinking provided fertile ground
for even more expansion.

With all of that to occupy his mind, it was understandable that Rory had grown up without much of a
firm hand to guide him. Otto knew that his boy was a
bit of a wastrel . . . but that was the nature of boys, was
it not? Sooner or later he would grow out of it, and
until he did, Otto had plenty of money to buy him out
of whatever predicament he found himself in.

Unfortunately, no amount of money in the world
could buy a rifle ball out of his son's chest.

When enough time had passed and the sharp edge of
his grief was dulled, Otto Ducharme knew what he had
to do. He began hiring men, hard, dangerous men with
few scruples. There were plenty of those in St. Louis.
He bought supplies the same way he bought men,
paying whatever was necessary to get what he wanted.

He had bought the shotgun that now rested across
his knees, the shotgun he planned to use personally
once he found what he was looking for. As his hands
tightened on the weapon, he brought his angry reaction
under control and said to the white-haired man, "I am
coming along, Powell, just as we planned. There will
be no more discussion."

"Whatever you say, Mr. Ducharme," Powell agreed with a shrug.

Ducharme went on as if he hadn't even heard the man, saying, "Your job is only to find Breckinridge Wallace and bring him to me." He lifted the shotgun and ran his right hand along the smooth wood of the stock. "And then I will blow his *Gott*-damned head off."

Chapter Seven

Two weeks had passed since the fight with the Blackfeet. During that time, Breckinridge and his companions hadn't seen any more hostiles. Breck could usually sense when somebody was watching him, and he didn't experience that, either. As far as he could tell, he and the other three trappers were the only human beings in this valley.

That was the way they wanted it, at least for now.

They had taken three dozen more pelts and now had a pretty good stack of them. Breckinridge wasn't sure how many they needed in order to make the trip profitable. He was willing to keep working as long as the other men were. There was a limit to how many pelts they could carry in their canoes, though.

One morning, he and Morgan were out checking the traps on one of the creeks when something caused him to pause and lift his head as a frown creased his forehead.

Morgan saw the reaction and asked, "What's wrong, Breck?"

Breckinridge sniffed the air a couple of times and then said, "You smell that?"

Morgan took a deep breath, as well, causing his chest to expand. His eyes widened in surprise as he looked at Breckinridge and said, "Maybe I'm crazy, but that smells like . . . coffee!"

"Yep," Breckinridge agreed. "It surely does."

"Maybe one of the other fellas went back to camp and started a fresh pot brewing."

Breckinridge shook his head.

"We're too far from camp to be smellin' it like that, and anyway, the wind's comin' from the wrong direction."

"Yeah, that's true," Morgan agreed, slowly nodding. "But who else could it be?"

"More trappers, I reckon. Injuns don't drink coffee, do they?"

"I never heard tell of it if they do."

"I don't know about you," Breckinridge said, "but I'm a mite too curious not to find out who's doin' that. Chances are, they don't mean us any harm . . ."

"But there's no guarantee of that," Morgan finished. "We know there are murderers and thieves out here. We ran into enough of them on the way upriver!"

Both young men wore grim expressions now. They remembered what had happened to the rest of their original party, including Morgan's father. If there was danger lurking in the area, they needed to know about it.

"Come on," Breckinridge said. "Let's follow our noses."

Since they hadn't come across any beaver carcasses in their traps so far this morning, they were able to move pretty quickly as they trotted alongside the creek.

Breckinridge knew that up ahead the stream twisted around several sharp bends that formed a big S-curve.

At the first of those bends, the creek pooled up to form a swimming hole. Breckinridge and his friends had splashed around in that pool a few times since coming to the valley. The snowmelt that helped feed the stream meant that the water was pretty chilly, but Breck found it invigorating.

There was also a big, slanted slab of rock at the edge of the pool where a fella could stand and dive off. Breckinridge enjoyed that, too.

As they drew closer, the aroma of coffee got stronger. Somebody definitely had a camp somewhere up here, Breckinridge thought. The creek's curving course left a good-sized piece of ground sticking out with water on three sides, complete with trees for firewood and plenty of grass for horses or mules to graze on, if somebody had draft animals like that with them. He and the others had actually considered making their camp there, before deciding on the spot on the bluff about a mile north of here.

Breckinridge slowed down and held out a hand to signal for Morgan to do likewise. As they came to a stop, Morgan asked quietly, "Do we just waltz in?"

"Seems like a good way to get ourselves shot," Breckinridge replied.

"That's what I was thinking. Maybe we'd better scout out the lay of the land first."

Breckinridge nodded in agreement. It was difficult for somebody as big as him to make himself smaller, but he tried to crouch as he warily moved forward through the cottonwoods, aspens, and willows along the creek bank.

As they came in sight of the first bend where the

swimming hole was located, Breckinridge suddenly froze. Beside him, Morgan did likewise.

Both young men had spotted movement on that big rock looming over the pool. As they watched from about fifty yards away, a figure climbed to the top of the slanting stone slab and stood at its edge, poised there to dive into the water.

The sight that greeted their eyes was just about the last thing Breckinridge and Morgan would have expected to see out here in the middle of the wilderness.

The person standing at the edge of the rock was a young woman.

And she wore not a stitch of clothing on this fine morning.

Morgan muttered something under his breath. Breckinridge didn't know what it was, nor did he care. He was too entranced by the unexpected beauty of this discovery to think about anything else.

The girl had fair hair so pale it was almost white. It was loose and hung around her bare shoulders and far down her back. Her skin had a golden tinge to it, and there was plenty of it on view. She was finely shaped, fine enough to take a young man's breath away like a punch in the gut.

She raised her arms, bent her knees slightly, and sprang off the rock, cleaving the air in a dive that demonstrated she had an abundance of grace to go along with her beauty. She struck the surface of the pool cleanly and vanished underneath it. There was barely a splash, and hardly any ripples.

After a few heartbeats, Breckinridge realized he was holding his breath, waiting for her to come back up again.

When she did, it was with an explosion of water

droplets that seemed to hang suspended in the air around her. Her skin shimmered with moisture. The water had turned her hair slightly darker, but it was still pale as she slicked it back on her head, away from her face.

She treaded water for a moment, then stroked easily over to where the pool wasn't as deep. She was able to stand up there as she began washing.

"We . . . we shouldn't be watching this," Morgan said, his voice husky.

"No, I reckon not," Breckinridge agreed. He had trouble tearing his eyes away from the young woman, though, and he noticed that Morgan wasn't looking down at the ground or turning away, either.

They were both so captivated by what they were seeing that neither would have noticed if an entire herd of buffalo had stampeded up behind them.

But there was no ignoring the harsh voice that suddenly rasped, "Turn around and stop starin' at my gal, you scurvy varmints, or I'll blow your damned heads off!"

Chapter Eight

Breckinridge knew a threat like that almost had to be backed up by a gun. His first impulse was to whirl around, bring up his rifle, and fire.

With an effort, he controlled that urge. From the sound of it, the girl in the pool was the stranger's daughter, so Breckinridge figured the man had a right to be upset when he found a couple of two-legged varmints staring at her unadorned charms.

"Take it easy," he told Morgan, who had jumped a little at the threat. As a rule, Breckinridge had never been the voice of reason in any group—he was more the impulsive type—but in this case he thought deliberation might be a good idea. "Let's do what the fella says."

"And put them guns down," the man added. "I see 'em comin' my way, I'm gonna shoot."

Breckinridge bent over and placed his rifle on the ground. Morgan sighed and did likewise, with obvious reluctance. Breck held his hands at elbow height and a little away from his body so they were in plain sight, then slowly turned around so that his back was to the pool.

He felt a pang of loss and disappointment when he couldn't see the young woman anymore. She'd been running her fingers through her hair, completely unself-conscious and obviously unaware that she was being watched, and the sight was a spectacular one.

The man facing them about ten feet away wasn't an impressive specimen. He was a bandy-legged little runt, in fact, wearing an old set of buckskins that appeared to be stiff with accumulated grease and filth. A coonskin cap perched on a tangled bird's nest of gray hair. A tuft of beard hanging down from his weak chin made him look like a billy goat. His nose was crooked and his mouth had only stubs of teeth left in it.

If a gorgeous young woman like the one bathing in the pool had indeed sprung from this disreputable geezer's loins, it was a plumb miracle, thought Breckinridge.

"Who are you," the old-timer whined, "and what're you doin' here 'sides spyin' on a innocent gal?"

"We could ask you the same thing, mister," Morgan snapped.

"Don't you mouth off at me, boy," the old man growled as he lifted the gun in his gnarled hands. "My patience is wearin' mighty thin."

He might not be impressive, but the weapon he held was. It was an old-fashioned blunderbuss with such a wide barrel that looking down it was like staring into the mouth of a cannon. A gun like that could blow a huge hole through a man, especially at short range like this.

"Hold your horses, mister," Breckinridge said. "We're not lookin' for trouble. My name is Breckinridge Wallace, and this here is my friend Morgan Baxter. We're fur trappers."

"Didn't figure you was whalers," the old man said with a sneer. "We's a long ways from the ocean."

"What the hell does that even mean?" Morgan asked.

Breckinridge went on hastily, "We didn't intend to spy on your daughter, mister. Truly we didn't. It's just that when we walked up, she was standin' up there on that rock, and then she dived into the pool, and . . . well, it was sort of hard to look away, if you know what I mean."

The old man's tongue came out and licked over his dry lips, reminding Breckinridge a little of a lizard.

"She is a right toothsome morsel o' gal flesh, ain't she?" he asked with a leer.

Breckinridge frowned. The comment struck him as an improper thing for a father to be saying about his own daughter, but he supposed there were all types in the world and not everybody shared his notions of what was fitting.

The old man suddenly leaned to the side, while still keeping the blunderbuss pointed at Breckinridge and Morgan, and shouted, "Annie! Annie Belle! Get on outta there and get back to the wagons! You done wasted enough time with that bathin' nonsense."

Breckinridge tried not to, but he turned his head to look toward the pool again. It was like a giant hand had hold of his chin and was twisting his neck around. The girl waded to shore, water rolling off her skin in sparkling trails, and called, "All right, Nicodemus!" She paused on the bank to wring some of the water from her long, pale hair and added, "What're you doing over there in the woods?"

"Never you mind about that," he told her. "Get that saucy behind o' yours movin'."

Definitely not the way a father would talk, thought Breckinridge. And the girl had called the old-timer Nicodemus, not Pa.

She shrugged and disappeared around the big rock slab.

"You're lookin' at her again," the old man accused. "I seen you. I got a good mind to charge you."

"Charge us?" Morgan said. "You charge men to look at your daughter while she's naked?"

Nicodemus frowned and asked, "What're you talkin' about? I said she was my gal, not my daughter."

"Good Lord!" Breckinridge exclaimed as the dawn broke inside his brain. "She's a whore!"

"I reckon I'd rather call her a good-time gal," the old-timer said. He sucked on a tooth stub for a second, then went on, "That don't sound bad. Nicodemus Finch's Good-Time Gals. Maybe I'll have one of 'em paint that on the wagons, if any of 'em can write."

Breckinridge was starting to grasp what was going on here. He asked, "How many, uh, good-time gals do you have with you, Mr. Finch?"

"Half a dozen, and they're all too good for the likes o' you, if that's what you're thinkin'."

"It wasn't," Breckinridge said, although to tell the truth the thought had sort of snuck into the back of his mind.

Finch motioned with the blunderbuss and said, "You never did tell me how come you're sneakin' around here."

"We smelled your coffee," Morgan said. "We knew somebody had to be camped nearby, and we just wanted to find out who you were."

Breckinridge added, "We've been trappin' in this valley for a while."

"Ain't tryin' to claim it belongs to you, are you?" Finch asked sharply.

"No. I don't reckon it belongs to anybody, except maybe the government, since all this territory was part of the Louisiana Purchase, wasn't it?"

"I don't know nothin' about that," Finch snapped. "All I know is my bunch is settin' up for the rendezvous, and ain't nobody hornin' in on it, especially not that damned Mahone." His already beady eyes narrowed even more. "Say, you two varmints ain't Mahone men, are you?"

"Never heard of the fella," Breckinridge said honestly.

"If I find out you're lyin' to me, you'll be sorry. I can't abide that damn Mahone or anybody who'd be low-down enough to work for him."

"Well, that's not us," Morgan said. "Like Breck told you, we don't know anything about anybody named Mahone."

"We did hear that there was gonna be a rendezvous somewhere around here, though," Breckinridge added.

The old-timer snorted and said, "Damn right. Biggest and best rendezvous since Green River. And it's gonna be right up there 'round the bend on Finch's Point." He looked pleased with himself. "That's what I'm gonna call it. Finch's Point."

"Sounds like a fine idea." Breckinridge started edging back toward his rifle. "Now, if you'll let us get our guns, we'll be movin' on. Need to get back to our traplines—"

Finch took a quick step forward and jabbed the blunderbuss's huge barrel at them.

"You just hold on, the both o' you!" he said. "I ain't sure I trust you yet. You could still be lyin' to me about workin' for Black Tom Mahone. You reckon I want you runnin' back to him and tellin' him all about my plans? No, sir, you're comin' with me into camp until I'm satisfied you're tellin' me the truth."

"But we got traps to check—" Breckinridge began.

"Now, hold on, Breck, like the man says," Morgan spoke up, taking him by surprise. "Mr. Finch has got a point. We need to go with him and talk to him some more so we can convince him we're not working for his enemies."

Breckinridge's eyes narrowed. He said, "You mean go with him to the camp where the rest of those, uh, good-time gals are?"

"I suppose that's right," Morgan said, as if he hadn't thought about that very thing.

For a second, Breckinridge considered arguing with both of them. Then he thought about the blunderbuss Nicodemus Finch kept waving at them. As old at the thing was, it might not fire at all—or it might have a hair-trigger.

He thought about the young woman they had seen dive off the rock into the pool, too. Annie Belle, Finch had called her. If they went with the old man, they might get an even better look at her, Breckinridge realized.

Well, a closer look, anyway. Breckinridge doubted if it could get any better.

Finally he nodded and said, "All right, Mr. Finch, we'll come with you. I don't want to lose these rifles, though."

"I'll send somebody to fetch 'em in," Finch promised. "Now, rattle your hocks and head on up the creek!"

Chapter Nine

Breckinridge and Morgan followed the creek bank with Nicodemus Finch trailing along behind them. Breck glanced over his shoulder and saw that Finch had let the blunderbuss sag until its barrel was pointed at the ground. The old man was close enough that Breck figured he could whirl around, swat the gun aside, and then wrench it out of Finch's hands before the old-timer could do anything to stop him.

On the other hand, Finch wasn't trying to shoot them. He just wanted more assurances that they weren't part of Black Tom Mahone's bunch—whoever Black Tom Mahone was.

Also, Morgan wanted a chance to meet the other girls Finch had with him, and if Breckinridge was being honest, he was more than a tad curious about them himself.

So it seemed like the sensible thing to do was play along. If it looked like the situation was about to take a turn for the worse, he and Morgan could make a move then.

Morgan heaved a sigh as they passed the pool and

the big rock. Breckinridge figured his friend was thinking about Annie Belle. Breck still had her image pretty clear in his mind, too. He suspected it would linger there for a while.

They went around the next bend, and as they emerged from some trees that screened off the view, they saw the promontory formed by the creek's S-curve, the place the old man had dubbed Finch's Point.

It was a big piece of land, half a mile wide at its base, tapering to a quarter of a mile at its end where the stream bent back on itself. There were several groves of trees, as well as some large, grassy open areas dotted with wildflowers. All in all, it was a very pleasant place, especially in a valley situated between two ranges of picturesque, snowcapped mountains.

Four wagons were parked in one of the open areas. They were large, heavy vehicles with tall, arching canvas covers over their beds.

Breckinridge had seen wagons like that back in St. Louis. Immigrants used them to travel west, loading all their worldly possessions under those covers. Breck had heard somebody refer to them as prairie schooners, and there was talk that one day soon, long trains of them would be setting out across the plains from Missouri, bound for the Oregon country and the Pacific Ocean.

Nicodemus Finch and the members of his party weren't what anybody would call immigrants, though. They weren't interested in settling anywhere. Folks like these would always be on the move, thought Breckinridge, chasing vice and the money that went along with it.

Not that he had any room to talk, he reminded himself. His reputation wasn't exactly a good one. In his young life, he had been accused of two murders—one of those killings had been accidental, and both had occurred while Breckinridge was acting in defense of his own life—and as far as the law was concerned, he was also guilty of shooting Maureen Grantham.

Maureen Aylesworth, she had been then, because she had already married Richard. Had, in fact, been carrying Aylesworth's child. Breckinridge had never been much for praying, but after the incident he had sent plenty of pleas heavenward that both mother and child would be all right.

Fact of the matter was, though, he didn't know if either of them had survived that tragic night.

Richard Aylesworth was really the man who had pulled the trigger, and one of these days, if Breckinridge lived long enough, he was going back to Knoxville and find out what had happened. If Aylesworth had killed Maureen and the baby . . .

Well, Breckinridge would settle the score for them. He owed Maureen that much.

Thinking about his own checkered past had distracted him momentarily from his surroundings. His attention was jerked back to the present by the six women who came out to meet them.

All the women were young and pretty. Breckinridge figured the oldest, who had long, flowing chestnut hair, was in her early twenties. The others, including Annie Belle, were several years younger than that.

They were quite an assortment. One was short and lushly built, with honey-gold tresses. The chestnut-haired gal was tall and lanky, like an eager colt. Another appeared to be an octoroon, with light brown skin and dark hair. The fourth girl was a brunette, as well, and the fifth had a wild mass of strawberry-blond hair.

The sixth was Annie Belle, and she was the loveliest of the whole bunch, in Breckinridge's opinion. But every one of them was pretty enough to make a man look twice and take his breath away, especially in the low-bodiced dresses they wore that clung to the curves of their bodies.

Breckinridge didn't figure any of them had been soiled doves for very long. From what he had seen of it, that was a mighty hard life that aged a gal in a hurry. He had no idea how any of them had wound up out here in the middle of the wilderness with a disreputable outfit such as Nicodemus Finch's, but he supposed each had her own story. Most folks did.

The group wasn't composed only of Finch and the six whores. There were three men with the wagons, as well, all of them big and rugged-looking. As little and scrawny as Finch was, he would need help around to handle any trouble he encountered. He'd probably hired these fellas to provide that help.

All the women looked at Breckinridge and Morgan with intense curiosity. More than likely it had been a while since they had seen anybody except Finch and his three helpers. The tall, slender chestnut-haired gal asked, "Who are these men, Nicodemus?"

"They told me their names," Finch answered, "but I done plumb forgot 'em."

"Morgan Baxter," Morgan said smoothly, smiling as he took off his hat and ran his other hand over his sandy hair. According to the bragging he had done during the early days of the journey up the Missouri

River, he had quite a reputation as a ladies' man. He seemed eager to prove that now.

"I'm Breckinridge Wallace from the Great Smoky Mountains," Breck introduced himself. He didn't have a hat to doff, but he smiled pleasantly and nodded to the women.

Finch said, "I'm a-feared Black Tom might've sent 'em to spy on us. I caught 'em sneakin' around up the creek where Annie Belle was takin' her doggone bath."

"What!" the fair-haired girl exclaimed.

"I told you it weren't a good idea to wash so much," Finch groused at her. "Plumb unnatural, that's what it is."

"You were spying on me?" Annie Belle said angrily to Breckinridge and Morgan.

"No, ma'am," Morgan answered instantly. "It was an accident, pure and simple. We smelled your coffee brewing and came to see who was camped here. We just happened to get to that bend in the creek where the pool is when you, ah, when you climbed up on that big rock to dive off into the water."

"So you *were* looking at me," she said, glaring.

The short, chubby honey-blonde said, "Oh, don't get your drawers in an uproar, Annie. It's not like these fellas are the first ones to see you in the altogether, now, is it?"

"You just shut up, Martha," Annie snapped. "That's different."

"That's right," the tall one said dryly. "You didn't get paid for the privilege this time."

"You stay out of it, too, Francesca. It wasn't you they were leering at."

"Beggin' your pardon, ma'am," Breckinridge said,

"we weren't really leerin' at you. I'll admit, it was a mite hard to look away—"

"You *didn't* look away, did you?" Annie asked sharply.

"Well, no. But I give you my word, we didn't mean any disrespect."

"No disrespect at all," Morgan added. "But it was like . . . stumbling on a beautiful painting in the middle of the wilderness. It was just so unexpected—and so lovely—that we couldn't tear our eyes away."

"There's more to look at here," Martha said with a coy smile.

"That's enough," Finch said. "You gals go on back around t'other side o' the wagons. I got to talk to these fellas, to make sure they ain't lyin' to me about not workin' for Mahone, and I don't need y'all standin' around makin' calf eyes at 'em and distractin' 'em. Shoo! Gilbert, Moffit, Jackson, the three o' you get these gals outta here."

The three burly men, who probably worked as drivers for Finch, too, herded the young women around the wagons. Several of them complained, but the stoic trio ignored that and followed Finch's orders.

The old-timer surprised Breckinridge and Morgan by saying, "There might still be a little coffee in the pot, if you fellas want any."

"That sounds good," Breckinridge responded.

"Tin cups hangin' on the tailgate o' that wagon," Finch said, pointing. "Help yourselves."

With the blunderbuss tucked under his arm, he followed them over to the campfire, where Breckinridge used a thick piece of leather to pick up the coffeepot and pour for himself and Morgan. The brew was thick and black and not very good, but it had a bracing effect.

"Now, tell me again that you don't work for Black Tom Mahone," Finch said to them. "And if I don't believe you, I'm liable to up and shoot you both."

"You can believe us," Morgan said. "We just here trapping furs. We never even heard of this fellow Mahone."

"Who is he, anyway?" Breckinridge asked.

"My cousin, damn his soul," Finch replied with a scowl on his grizzled face, "and the man who's swore an oath to see me dead!"

Chapter Ten

"Black Tom and me grew up together back in Ohio," Finch began the story. "O' course, he was just Tom then, not Black Tom, 'cause in those days nobody knowed what a disreputable scalawag he really was. His ma was my pa's sister, and the farms were next to each other. Me an' Tom, though, we never cared for all the chores that go with livin' on a farm. Once we growed up some an' got some size on us, we went to work on the keelboats that travel up and down the Ohio River."

"Looks to me like you still don't have much size on you," Morgan put in with a grin.

"You just hush your mouth, boy, less'n you're willin' to 'fess up to bein' one o' Mahone's henchmen!"

"We're not anybody's henchmen," Breckinridge said, "as we've been tryin' to tell you ever since you marched us in here at gunpoint. Speakin' of that . . . you said you'd have somebody fetch in our rifles . . . ?"

"Oh yeah." Finch turned his head and bellowed,

"Moffit!" For a scrawny little fella, he could summon up considerable lung power when he wanted to.

One of the helpers came over, and Finch told the man, "Go back up the creek a ways and find the rifles these varmints left up there. Bring 'em back when you do."

Moffit grunted and indicated Breckinridge and Morgan with a nod of his square, rock-like jaw.

"Want me to give the guns back to these two?" he asked.

"Not until I tell you," Finch snapped. "Now get on with it."

After Moffit had walked off, Morgan said, "You're just naturally sharp-tongued with everybody, aren't you, old-timer?"

"I don't believe in wastin' words."

"Sounded to me like you were winding up to get pretty long-winded in that story of yours."

Finch glared and demanded, "You want to hear about Mahone and me, or not?"

"Go ahead," Breckinridge said. "We're listenin'."

"Well . . . anyway, Mahone and me worked on the boats when we was young. We decided to save up our money, and after a while we had enough to buy a boat of our own."

"So you went into business for yourselves," Morgan said.

"That's what I just said, ain't it? Good Lord, you two are thick in the head! I ain't sure even Mahone'd be desperate enough to hire such a pair o' numble-brained musharoos."

Breckinridge frowned and said, "Now you've gone to makin' up words, I think."

"No such thing! Them's perfectly good words. Now quit interruptin' me, dadblast it!"

Breckinridge held up his hands in surrender and waited for Finch to go on.

After a moment, the old man said, "Things went along all right for a while, but then you can guess what happened." He jabbed a grimy finger at them. "And no, I ain't askin' you to guess! I'm just sayin', it was the sort o' thing that's happened too many times to fellas who are goin' along thinkin' ever'thing's just fine."

Morgan couldn't resist. He said, "A woman came between you."

"Son of a—" Finch snatched his coonskin cap off his head and slammed it to the ground. "You frazzle-tongued peckerwood! Won't shut up and let a man tell a story!"

"You met a woman," Breckinridge said, trying to prod Finch into continuing.

Finch drew in such a deep breath that his nostrils flared. He said, "Not just any woman. Eula Mae Culli-gan. Prettiest li'l gal up and down hunnerds o' miles o' river. You never saw the like. First time I ever laid eyes on her, I knowed I was gonna marry her. Trouble is, that damned ol' cousin o' mine thought the same thing. He went to courtin' her right off, and so did I. It got to where ever' time our boat pulled up to the wharf at that little riverfront town where she lived, it was a dadgum race to see which of us'd get off the boat first an' make it to Eula Mae's house." Finch smirked. "I was faster a-foot than Mahone, so most o' the time it was me."

"Probably because you're so little," Morgan said. "That's why you could move faster."

Breckinridge thought Finch was going to explode

again, but somehow the old-timer kept his rage under control this time. He said, "Eula Mae and me was fixin' to get married, but then one week before the weddin' . . . one gol-dang, fripperty-footed week! . . . I come across the two of 'em in her pa's barn. They was . . . Well, I don't have to draw you a picture, do I?"

"Rather you didn't," Breckinridge said.

Finch sighed and went on, "It was a sight like to seared my eyeballs plumb outta their sockets. After that, I couldn't marry her, o' course, and I couldn't keep workin' on the river with that damn traitor Mahone, so I left." Finch flung both hands in the air. "Took off for the tall and uncut, just like that." A sly smile appeared on his face. "But not before I went back to the boat and set it on fire."

"Your own boat?" Breckinridge exclaimed.

"Not mine anymore. I took the money me and Mahone had made on that trip—we was on our way back home after settlin' up for our cargo—and figured we was even. He had the boat, and I had the gold." Finch cackled. "And then he didn't have the boat no more, 'cause I burned it down to the water, boys! Damn woman-stealin' son of a gun had it comin'!"

"But you stole his part of the money," Breckinridge said.

"No, I just explained that, you muddy-eared galoot. I took the money, and Mahone got the boat. And then I burned the boat! It makes perfect sense!"

Breckinridge and Morgan looked at each other, and then Breck said, "So that's how come Mahone swore to be your mortal enemy from then on?"

"Yep!" Finch punched his right fist into his left palm for emphasis.

"So how did you wind up out here?" Morgan asked.

"Oh hell, lots o' things happened after that. I ain't got time to talk about 'em all. None of it really matters, anyhow. I'm here, you're here, them gals are here, those fellas workin' for me are here, and a dozen barrels o' the finest moonshine to ever come outta the Kentucky hills are here. I got ever'thing I need! Question is, do I shoot you for Mahone men, or do I let you go?"

Breckinridge said, "Don't you think if we were workin' for Mahone, he would've told us that same story before now?"

"Prob'ly. He likes to complain about how I done him wrong, when the truth o' the matter is, it was him and Eula Mae who wounded me so deep I still ain't got over it."

Finch put his right fist against his heart and draped his left hand over it. He sighed again.

"Did we look like we'd ever heard that story before?" Breckinridge asked.

"For a fact, you did not. Maybe you was tellin' the truth after all."

"Finally!" Morgan said.

Finch glared at them and asked, "You really ain't workin' for Mahone?"

"You've got our word on it," Breckinridge assured him.

"All right, then. I won't shoot you." The old man cocked his head to the side. "You boys lookin' for jobs? I might could use you. 'Specially you, the big ugly one." He frowned at Morgan. "Not you. You'd be pesterin' my gals the whole damn time, wantin' to take a tumble with 'em and not pay for it. I can tell just by lookin' at you."

"We don't need jobs," Breckinridge said. "We're fur trappers, remember?"

"Oh yeah. Got any pelts?"

"Some," Breckinridge allowed. He wasn't going to tell Finch how many pelts they had taken.

"You can use 'em for trade at the rendezvous, you know. Spend 'em just like money for whiskey and a turn with whichever o' the gals suits your fancy."

"We'll think on it," Breckinridge promised. It seemed to him, though, that Finch might be getting the best of the deal. It might be better to sell the furs to one of the company men who were supposed to attend the rendezvous, then use actual coins for any transactions with the old-timer.

"Suit your own selves," Finch said. "Here comes Moffit with your rifles."

When the man came up carrying the two long-barreled flintlocks, Finch motioned for him to hand the weapons to Breckinridge and Morgan. It felt good to hold the rifle again, Breck thought. He and it were old friends.

"We'll be on our way now," he told Finch. "We're obliged to you for the coffee."

"No charge," Finch said. "But that's the only thing you'll get for free 'round here! You best remember that!"

"I don't think we're likely to forget," Breckinridge said.

"And watch out for Black Tom Mahone!" Finch called after the two of them as they started to walk away. "He'll cut your heart out soon as look at you!"

Breckinridge turned and frowned.

"Are you saying Mahone is somewhere out here now?" he asked.

"Why, damn it, o' course he is! Wasn't you listenin'? You got potatoes in your ears? Mahone's on his way out here for the rendezvous! He's got hisself a whole wagon train full o' whiskey and whores just like I do, and he's plannin' to horn in on the deal. But I tell you right now . . . if he tries, it's gonna be war, pure and simple! That there creek will run red with blood!"

Chapter Eleven

"That old man is crazy!" Morgan said a short time later as he and Breckinridge headed back to the area where they had been checking their traps when they first smelled coffee brewing. They were well out of earshot of the so-called Finch's Point by now.

"He was a mite colorful," Breckinridge said.

"Colorful! Crazy as a loon is more like it."

"He's got barrels of whiskey and half a dozen really pretty gals around him all the time," Breckinridge pointed out. "We've got the four of us smelly, unshaved trappers and a pile of pelts that are startin' to stink a little, too."

"Yeah, well . . . well . . . I still say he's crazy. He burned that fella Mahone's boat, didn't he? He even bragged about it."

"Mahone stole his girl just as Finch was fixin' to marry her. Some folks would say that was a good enough reason."

"Did Mahone really do that?" Morgan asked. "All we've got to go by is what Finch told us. For all we know, that girl Eula Mae might not have ever wanted anything to do with him. She could've been planning to marry Mahone all along. The rest of that yarn about her picking Finch over Mahone could be just in that old man's addled brain!"

Breckinridge had to admit Morgan might be right about that. They had to ask themselves just how reliable Finch's story was. It might've all been a pack of lies.

"I don't reckon it really matters," Breckinridge said after a moment. "It's none of our business."

"We're going to the rendezvous, aren't we?"

"I figured we would."

"Then it'll be our business if those two old codgers start shooting at each other and ruin the rendezvous for everybody else."

Breckinridge frowned and said, "Maybe it won't come to that."

He hoped it wouldn't. For the trappers in these parts, the big gathering would be the high point of the season. Nobody would want it disrupted by Finch and Mahone going to war against each other, the way Finch had promised.

After they had gone a little farther, Morgan said, "Are we going to tell Roscoe and Amos about what happened today?"

The question took Breckinridge a little by surprise.

"Well, it's a pretty good story, don't you think?" he asked.

"Yeah, sure, but if they know those girls are down there, they're liable to want to go get a look at 'em for themselves."

"What would be wrong with that?"

"Why, they'd be neglecting their work," Morgan said as if it were the most logical thing in the world. "They'd ought to be checking their traps, and instead they'd be hanging around the point trying to catch a glimpse of something."

"Like we did," Breckinridge said.

"Exactly! Not only that, but it could be dangerous for them. You saw how touchy Finch is. If he catches any more strangers lurking around the place between now and the rendezvous, he's liable to shoot that old blunderbuss of his and find out who they are later."

Breckinridge suspected that Morgan just wanted to keep the knowledge of what had happened to themselves for now because he enjoyed having a secret, especially one that involved pretty girls.

But at the same time, Morgan was right about the possible danger the newcomers to the valley represented. After all they had been through together, Breckinridge didn't want anything to happen to Akins or Fulbright.

"All right," he said. "We won't say anything. They can find out when it comes time for the rendezvous. But until then, we'd better steer clear of the point ourselves. Finch is convinced that we're harmless, but he could change his mind."

"Deal," Morgan said. He grinned. "After what we saw today, that rendezvous can't get here soon enough to suit me!"

Over the next few days of working their traplines, Breckinridge thought quite a bit about not only what had happened but what Morgan had said, as well. Like his friend, Breck was eager for the rendezvous time to arrive. He wasn't sure how they would know when the time came.

When it did, he wondered what he would do. He

didn't have any money, but he had a share in the pelts they had taken. He could sell them to one of the fur company men, or he could trade them directly with Nicodemus Finch for . . . What was it going to be? Whiskey? Women?

Both?

Breckinridge enjoyed an occasional drink as much as the next man, and he was mighty partial to the company of the ladies, especially when they were as comely as the ones traveling with Finch's outfit. What would it cost to spend an hour with Annie Belle? Would it be worth it?

There was only one way to find out, as far as Breckinridge knew.

At the same time, he felt a smidgen of guilt about Maureen. She had been his first real love, even though he had never done anything more than kiss her a few times. He didn't even know for sure if she was alive or dead, and yet he was thinking about Annie Belle with a heart full of passion.

It was quite a dilemma for a young man, all right. Breckinridge tried to tell himself that Maureen would understand, wherever she was, but he couldn't be certain of that.

Of course, she had gone and married Richard Aylesworth, he reminded himself. It wasn't like she had remained faithful and pined away for him. She had never promised to remain faithful to him, nor had he to her.

More than once he found himself sighing. Figuring out such affairs of the heart could be mighty vexing. Fighting Indians and running away from angry mama bears was a lot simpler.

Breckinridge and Morgan were down near the lower end of the valley one afternoon, not far from the pass where a trail of sorts entered the valley. Nicodemus Finch and his wagons would have had to come in this way. Breck and his companions had followed one of the creeks in, paddling upstream through a narrow canyon where wagons wouldn't be able to make it. They planned to leave the same way when it came time to depart.

Today they had just removed the soaking carcass of a beaver from a trap when Breckinridge lifted his head and frowned.

"I know that look," Morgan said. "Did you just smell something again, like coffee brewing?"

"No," Breckinridge said. "I thought I *heard* something. Sounded like . . . men yellin' at each other."

"There shouldn't be anybody else around," Morgan said. "Roscoe and Amos went the other direction from us when we left camp, and we're a long way from where Finch's outfit is camped." A look of alarm appeared on his face. "You don't think it's another Blackfoot war party, come to search for those others, do you?"

"I'm not really an expert on such things, but it don't seem likely to me a bunch of Blackfeet would be hollerin' at each other. They only yell when they attack, I think."

"Then who else could it be?"

Breckinridge pointed and said, "Sounded to me like the voices were comin' from up in the pass. Let's go see."

The last time they had gone to investigate something mysterious, they had wound up staring at the beautiful, very bare Annie Belle. Breckinridge didn't expect anything like that to happen this time.

But you couldn't ever tell.

Breckinridge had no choice but to carry the dead beaver with him. If they left the carcass behind, scavengers would drag it off and the pelt would be lost. He slung a cord around the beaver and carried it in his left hand while he carried the rifle in his right.

After a few minutes the two young men reached the primitive trail leading to the pass. It wasn't much more than a pair of tracks where the wheels of Finch's wagons had worn down the grass. It was entirely possible the wagons were the first wheeled vehicles that had ever visited this valley.

But they wouldn't be the last, Breckinridge figured. As he and Morgan climbed toward the pass, he heard the men's voices shouting again. Another group had arrived in the valley, and Breck had a pretty good idea who they were.

Couldn't be anybody else but Tom Mahone and his bunch, he thought.

The vegetation thinned out on the rocky slopes to either side of the trail. They could see the pass now, and sure enough, there was a wagon just this side of it. A team of mules had been unhitched from the vehicle and led off to the side. A thick rope tied to the back of the wagon had been passed around a rock spire, and now it was being paid out slowly by the half-dozen men who had hold of it. They were inching the wagon down the steep trail, which was the safest way of getting it to more level ground.

Off to one side stood a broad-shouldered man with a black mustache that curled up on the ends. His hat was shoved back on his head, revealing a mostly bald dome. He leaned on a heavy wooden walking stick.

Something was off about the man, and after a second Breckinridge realized what it was. The man's upper body appeared muscular and powerful, but from the waist down his legs were slender and seemed barely capable of supporting his weight. Breck wondered if he'd been born that way, or if he'd been stricken with some disease that had caused his legs to wither away.

There was nothing wrong with the man's voice. He bellowed, "Easy now, boys, easy! Let 'er down slow! Humphries! Lay off that brake. We don't need it, and you'll just burn it up."

A man sitting on the wagon seat nervously eyed the brake lever. Breckinridge supposed he was there in case the rope slipped or something. If the wagon ran away with itself, he could try to slow it down. That would be a dangerous job. On this rough trail, an out-of-control wagon was likely to crash.

The men holding the rope continued letting it out as Breckinridge and Morgan approached. The mustachioed man had both hands on the walking stick, but he took the right one off and moved it closer to the butt of a pistol stuck behind his belt as he saw them coming.

"Mornin'," Breckinridge said with a nod to the man on the wagon seat as he and Morgan passed.

"Not a very good one," the man replied. He was pale and clearly frightened. Breckinridge suspected that if the wagon started rolling free, he would leap off and abandon it as quickly as he could.

"Who in blazes are you two?" the mustachioed man demanded as Breckinridge and Morgan came up to him. He glanced down at the beaver carcass Breck was carrying. "Trappers, by the looks of you, I'd say."

"And you'd be right," Breckinridge said. "I'm Breckinridge Wallace, and this here is Morgan Baxter."

The man grunted and said, "Tom Mahone."

That introduction came as no surprise to Breckinridge, and he could tell that Morgan expected it, as well. He started to say something about Black Tom, then caught himself. That would be a giveaway that they were acquainted with Nicodemus Finch, and if Mahone felt the same way his former partner did and took them for Finch's friends, he might be tempted to shoot, too.

"You're here for the big rendezvous, I'll bet," Morgan said.

"I ain't here for my health," Mahone said sourly.

Breckinridge could see now that several more wagons were in the pass, with at least one still on the other side. It looked like Mahone had a bigger outfit than Finch.

He was looking at the wagons, thinking—maybe even hoping—that he might catch a glimpse of a woman or two, when one of the men on the rope suddenly yelled, "Look out! The rope's frayin'!"

"It's liable to snap!" another man exclaimed.

That was true, Breckinridge realized as he turned to look at the nearby rope. It was coming apart in one place, strands twisting away from each other.

And if it broke, the wagon it was attached to would hurtle down the steep trail, on its way to no telling what violent end.

Chapter Twelve

Breckinridge didn't stop to think about what he was doing. He just dropped his rifle and the dead beaver and leaped over to grab the rope with both hands. He planted his feet and threw his prodigious strength against it.

He had caught hold of the rope ahead of the spot where it was trying to break. Even with the power in his brawny frame, he couldn't hold that heavy wagon and its cargo by himself.

But he took enough of the weight to ease the strain on the weakened part. He grunted with the effort as he hauled back on the rope.

"Humphries, set the brake!" Mahone yelled. "You other boys, get over there and help the big fella!"

Both of those orders seemed like good ideas. Unfortunately, they didn't work out as well in execution as they sounded in theory.

The other men let go of the rope at the same time to leap to Breckinridge's aid, but when they did, that threw the whole weight of the wagon on Breck. That made the vehicle lurch forward suddenly as Breck's feet began to slip.

Humphries grabbed the brake lever and shoved it just as that happened, and the jolt made it give out with an audible *crack*.

There was nothing holding the wagon back except Breckinridge's strength—and that just wasn't nearly enough. It picked up speed in a hurry as it rolled down the trail. With a frightened yell, Humphries leaped off the seat, throwing himself far to the side so the wagon wheels would miss him.

Stubbornly, Breckinridge still clung to the rope. He ran after the wagon, hoping that if nothing else, his weight might act as an anchor and slow it down a little. But his long legs could move only so fast, especially on the rough ground, and after a few yards he tripped. His momentum pitched him forward.

Still, he wouldn't let go of the rope. He landed hard on his belly but managed to keep his hands clamped around the rough strand. The wagon dragged him along, bouncing him roughly.

The smart thing to do would be to just let go and let the wagon take its chances. It would probably wreck when it reached the bottom of the slope, but Breckinridge couldn't help that. He had done what he could to stop it.

Then, over the rumble of the wheels and the pounding of his own heart, he heard something that seemed to freeze the blood in his veins.

Somebody was screaming, and it sounded like a woman.

Breckinridge struggled to lift his head. Canvas flaps had been closed over the back of the wagon, but they were open now and a woman's face peered out between them.

A young, pretty, and absolutely terrified face.

From the sound of it, she wasn't alone in there, either. Breckinridge heard other screams.

That ended his thoughts of letting go of the rope.

Breckinridge gritted his teeth and started pulling himself hand over hand along the rope, closer to the wagon. He didn't know what he could do if he made it to the vehicle, but he was going to try anyway.

Several times he slammed against the ground hard enough to almost knock his grip loose, but he managed to hang on until he was just behind the wagon. Holding on to the rope with his left hand, he reached up with his right arm and tried to grab the top of the tailgate. His hand fell well short of it.

He continued trying, though, and as he lunged upward something grabbed his wrist. He looked up and saw that one of the women had leaned far over the tailgate and reached down to clamp both of her hands around his wrist. Two more women were behind her, holding on to her to keep her from falling out the back of the wagon.

"Come on!" the young woman cried. "We'll help you! But you'll have to let go of the rope!"

The rope was the only thing connecting Breckinridge to the wagon—except for the woman's grip on his wrist. Could he trust her not to let go?

He looked up at her, saw strands of dark hair flying around her face from the wind, saw fierce determination burning in blue eyes. That answered the question for him, at least as far as his instincts were concerned, and Breckinridge trusted his instincts.

"Pull up as hard as you can!" he shouted to the young woman, and at the same time he let go of the rope with his other hand and lunged up.

She exclaimed from the effort she put forth as she hauled up on Breckinridge's great weight. An instant later his other hand found the top of the tailgate and clung to it with desperate strength. That allowed the woman to pull him a little higher. More female hands reached down from the wagon, grabbed hold of his buckskin shirt, and lifted.

With their help, Breckinridge rose until he was able to get a foot braced against the bottom of the tailgate. That allowed him to throw his weight forward. The women were pulling so hard on him that they toppled over backward as he practically dove through the gap in the canvas cover.

He landed inside the wagon, sprawled on top of several of the women, including the brunette who had grabbed his wrist in the first place.

Breckinridge knew he had to get to the front of the wagon. He might still be able to stop the runaway somehow. Muttering, "Sorry, ladies," he put down hands and knees and found purchase on yielding female flesh.

One of them went "Ooof!" as he clambered over them.

He thrust his head and shoulders through the opening in the canvas cover at the front of the wagon and spilled over the seat. Rolling over, he landed in the floorboard and almost slid out. Catching himself, he looked around for the brake.

The top of the lever had broken off, but the bottom part with its attached wooden blocks was still intact. Breckinridge reached over, took hold of it, and pulled it back. The blocks scraped against the wheel. Smoke began to rise from them as they heated up.

The wagon was starting to slow down, though, Breckinridge thought. He hauled back even harder on the bottom part of the lever, partially hanging off the edge of the seat as he did so.

Somehow the wagon had stayed upright so far. That was almost a miracle in itself. Now as it slowed and the slope became less steep, Breckinridge began to hope that the vehicle would roll to a halt without any further mishaps.

That probably jinxed it, he thought a second later as the wagon hit a particularly bad bump and started to tip to the side.

"Hang on back there!" he shouted to the women. He hoped the wagon would settle back down, but it leaned even more and he knew it wasn't going to recover. He let go of the brake, twisted around, and scrambled for the other side of the floorboard. Maybe his weight would make a difference, he hoped.

It didn't. The wagon was going over and there wasn't a blasted thing he could do about it.

He jumped clear.

Breckinridge seemed to sail through the air for a long time before he crashed back to the earth. At least he hadn't slammed into a tree or a rock. He rolled over and over and finally came to a stop on his belly. The impact had knocked the air out of his lungs, so for a long moment all he could do was lie there and gasp for breath.

When he was able to raise his head and push himself up on his hands, he saw the wagon lying on its side about ten yards away. It didn't appear to have busted apart, although it had gouged a short path in the dirt before coming to a stop. He heard frightened shouts from inside it.

More yelling came from up the slope. Breckinridge looked and saw Morgan, Tom Mahone, and the other men hurrying down the trail. On his spindly legs and using the walking stick, Mahone was having a hard time of it.

"Breck, you crazy fool!" Morgan shouted as he reached Breckinridge's side. "What did you think you were doing? Are you all right?"

"I . . . I think so," Breckinridge said, still a little breathless. "You better check on . . . the gals in that wagon."

"Gals?" Morgan repeated as his eyebrows went up in surprise. "There are women—"

The other men were already at the overturned wagon. Mahone brought up the rear, limping along and yelling, "Dulcy! Emma! Sally! Poppy!"

One of the men pulled the canvas at the rear of the wagon aside and leaned down to ask, "Are you girls all right?"

"Give us a hand, Danny," a female voice said from inside the vehicle.

The man reached into the wagon and helped one of the women climb out. She was the one who had reached down to grab his wrist, Breckinridge realized. He was relieved when he saw that she appeared to be all right. A little unsteady when she got to her feet, maybe, but she had a right to be shaken up.

The next woman to crawl out of the wagon seemed to be unhurt, too. She had long blond hair and wasn't as pretty as the brunette, but she still had an earthy attractiveness about her.

Breckinridge had already figured out that these women were probably some of the soiled doves who worked for Mahone. He was bringing in whores for the rendezvous just like Finch.

Breckinridge heard whimpering from inside the wagon and knew that at least one of the other women hadn't been as lucky as the first two. The brunette said, "I think Poppy's arm is broken."

"I'll go in and get her," the man called Danny said.

"Be careful," the brunette told him. "If you jostle her around, you might make it worse."

"I'm not gonna jostle her," Danny snapped. "I'll take it easy."

He disappeared inside the wagon, and a minute later he crawled out with a sobbing figure cradled against his broad chest. This young woman had light brown, almost blond, hair falling in wings around her tear-streaked face. Her right arm lay at a funny angle across her body. It was likely broken all right, Breckinridge thought.

"Gimme a hand," he told Morgan. The smaller man clasped Breckinridge's wrist and helped him to his feet.

The fourth woman clambered out of the wagon. She appeared to be all right, too. She was petite, with very short black hair. In a shirt and trousers, she might have passed for a boy.

Puffing and blowing, Mahone leaned on his cane and tried to recover from his exertion. The brunette who had helped Breckinridge into the wagon walked over to him with her face set in angry lines.

"Damn it, Tom!" she said. "You almost got us killed!"

Her hand flashed up and cracked across Mahone's face.

Chapter Thirteen

Breckinridge was shocked by the unexpected blow. From the look on Mahone's face, so was he.

Mahone got over his surprise quickly, though. One hand shot out and grabbed the brunette's wrist, twisting it sharply. She grimaced in pain.

"Damn your hide, Dulcy!" he yelled. "You ever lay a hand on me again and I'll make you sorry you were ever born!"

"Too late," she told him through clenched teeth. "I've felt that way ever since I met you."

Breckinridge and Morgan glanced at each other. It wasn't their place to interfere here, but neither of them liked seeing a woman being manhandled like that. Breck was about to step forward and say something when Mahone snarled and let go of Dulcy's wrist.

"Just remember what I told you," Mahone muttered.

"I'm not likely to forget," Dulcy said. She turned and stalked away, heading for the grassy spot next to the trail where Danny had placed the injured Poppy. Dulcy knelt next to her and started carefully examining her arm.

Mahone limped over to Breckinridge and Morgan, looked up at Breck, and said, "Thank you for trying to help, young fella."

"I just couldn't hold the wagon," Breckinridge said. "It was too much for me."

Mahone snorted and said, "It would've been too much for anybody to hold by themselves. And that was a mighty crazy stunt you pulled, hanging on to the rope like that and pulling yourself into the wagon."

"Crazy is the word for it, all right," Morgan agreed. "You could've been killed, Breck."

"Well, that goes for those women who were inside the wagon, too," Breckinridge said. He frowned at Mahone. "You should've made 'em get out before your men started lettin' the wagon down the trail on that rope."

"I know, I know. Just didn't occur to me. I like to keep 'em out of sight as much as I can. Don't want the sight of such fine specimens of womanhood inflaming the passions of any men around here until the time is right."

"You mean at the rendezvous," Breckinridge said.

"What else would I mean?"

Dulcy came over to join them again. She reported, "Poppy's arm is broken, all right. I've got Danny looking for some branches that'll do to splint it with. She's going to be in considerable pain, though. I want to fill a jug from one of the whiskey barrels. She'll need it."

"That whiskey's to sell to the trappers," Mahone objected with a frown. "Is Poppy gonna be able to work?"

"Have you lost your mind?" Dulcy asked him. "I told you, she's hurting really bad. You can forget about her entertaining any customers for a while. And she needs that whiskey now, Tom."

Mahone rubbed his chin, scowled, and said, "I dunno. Drinking up the profits while she can't even earn anything . . ."

Dulcy folded her arms across her chest, gave him a determined glare, and said, "Unless you want all of us to go on strike here and now, Tom, you'd better do whatever is necessary to take care of that girl and make her as comfortable as you can."

Mahone drew in a sharp breath and demanded, "Are you threatening me?"

"No, I'm just telling you the way things are," Dulcy replied coolly.

Breckinridge couldn't help but admire her. He liked the way she stood up to Mahone, and there was no denying how attractive she was.

She was older than he had taken her for at first, probably in her late twenties. Her dark hair was fairly short and pulled back behind her head except for some strands that had escaped and fell around her face. She had a tiny scar just above her upper lip at the right corner of her mouth, but rather than detracting from her looks, it gave her character, Breckinridge thought.

Dulcy and Mahone traded dueling stares for a couple of seconds, then Mahone said with grudging agreement, "All right, you can give her some of the whiskey. But only as much as she needs to dull the pain. I don't want to catch any of you other gals nipping at the jug, either!"

"If working for you hasn't already driven us all to drink, I doubt if this will," Dulcy said in a dry tone of voice that made Mahone flush angrily. He didn't say anything else, though, until she had turned and walked back over to Poppy again.

Then Mahone muttered to Breckinridge and Morgan,

"That woman and her stubborn, highfalutin ways are gonna be the death of me yet." He frowned at them and went on, "Now, what was it you boys wanted?"

"Just to see what was goin' on up there at the pass," Breckinridge said. "We heard the hollerin' and wanted to check on it."

"Well, now you know, so you can be on your way."

Breckinridge ignored that and asked, "How are you gonna get the rest of your wagons down? You can't trust that rope."

"Speaking of that rope," Mahone said, "I want to take a look at it."

Leaning heavily on the walking stick, he went over to the wrecked wagon. The frayed rope was still tied to the back of the vehicle. Mahone bent down awkwardly and picked it up so he could examine the place where it had started to come apart.

"That's just what I thought!" he exclaimed. He thrust the rope toward Breckinridge and Morgan. "Look there! Somebody cut that rope part of the way through and weakened it. They were trying to wreck that wagon and kill my girls!"

"Let me see," Breckinridge said. He took the rope from Mahone and studied it for a long moment. "I don't know. Looks like it might've been sawed on, but the way so many of the strands have come apart, it's hard to be sure."

"Well, damn it, *I'm* sure," Mahone said. "I've got a damn spy working for me! Somebody's trying to ruin me, and I know who's responsible for it—that sorry, no-good Nicodemus Finch!"

That theory seemed a mite far-fetched to Breckinridge, but he supposed there could be something to it. He asked, "Do you have any new men along on this trip?"

Mahone frowned and shook his head.

"No, they've all been with me for a while. Couple of years, at the least. But every man's got his price, and there ain't any other explanation!"

"Unless the rope just wore out," Morgan said.

"Well, I've got another rope," Mahone said, getting back to Breckinridge's original question, "and you can damn well bet that I'll take a good look at it before we use it to let any of the other wagons down the slope!"

"How many wagons do you have?" Breckinridge asked.

"Five more, filled mostly with whiskey barrels, but I've got some trade goods, too. Sometimes Injuns show up at a rendezvous, and if they're friendly, I'll trade with 'em. A pelt brought in by a redskin is worth just as much as one I get from a white man."

"Wait a minute," Morgan said. "You only brought four women with you?"

"Four's enough. I need the wagon space for whiskey. I make more money off of it." Mahone scowled. "But damn it, with Poppy laid up because of that busted arm, now I only got three whores to keep all you trappers happy. That's not gonna be easy. Wonder if I could find any squaws around here who might want to earn some beads or cloth?"

"The only Indians we've seen in this valley were Blackfeet," Breckinridge told the man. "And I'd advise against tryin' to get any of their women to work for you, Mr. Mahone. I don't think they'd take kindly to that."

Mahone blew out a disgusted-sounding breath.

"I'm not afraid of any damn Blackfeet. They're an

ornery bunch, no doubt about that, but I've got plenty
of rifles, powder, and shot and good men to use 'em."
He paused, then added, "Except for the blasted traitor
who sawed through that rope, whichever one he is."

Breckinridge still wasn't convinced that Mahone's
suspicions were correct, but that was really none of his
or Morgan's business. As long as the rivalry between
Mahone and Finch didn't spill over into open warfare,
they could hate each other all they wanted.

Mahone suddenly frowned at them and said, "What
are you two still doin' here? I told you, you can be on
your way."

"When's the rendezvous start?" Breckinridge asked.

"Let me think . . . It'll take the rest of the day to get
those other wagons down, maybe even part of the day
tomorrow . . . then part of a day to set up . . . Ought to
be ready to go day after tomorrow. The day after that at
the latest. We've been spreading the word along the
way, and the men we talked to will spread it more, so
there ought to be a couple hundred trappers headed this
way already."

"That many?" Breckinridge exclaimed. The valley
was going to get crowded, he thought. It was good that
he and his friends had already taken as many pelts as
they had.

"That's right. Now skedaddle. Come back when
you're ready to do business."

Mahone turned away dismissively and hobbled over
to the wrecked wagon. He shook his head as he looked
at it, probably wondering if they could get it upright
again and continue to use it.

Breckinridge and Morgan had turned to leave when
a voice said from behind them, "Wait a minute, please."

Breckinridge looked over his shoulder and saw

Dulcy standing there. He stopped and swung around, as did Morgan.

"What can we do for you, ma'am?" Breckinridge asked.

"You've already done it," Dulcy said. "You slowed down that wagon as much as you could, and you risked your life doing it, too. If it had been going full speed when it crashed, there's a good chance more of us would have been hurt. Maybe even killed."

"Yeah, you could break your neck in a mishap like that," Breckinridge agreed. "I was glad to do what I could."

"Well, we appreciate it." She held out a hand. "I'm Dulcy Harris."

Breckinridge wasn't accustomed to having women offer to shake hands with him, but he didn't hesitate. He gripped Dulcy's hand in his, liking the smooth, warm, strong feel of it.

"Breckinridge Wallace," he told her. "My friend here is Morgan Baxter."

"Breckinridge," she said after she'd shaken hands with Morgan, too. "That's a distinguished name."

"I don't know where my ma and pa came up with it, but they always said it seemed to suit me," he said with a smile.

"I think it does, too." She reached out and rested her hand lightly on his arm. "Once the rendezvous is set up, you'll come by and see us, won't you, Breckinridge?"

"Yes, ma'am. I reckon you can count on that."

"Good. I'll be looking forward to it."

As Dulcy walked away, Morgan nudged Breckinridge with an elbow and said, "I think she's a mite taken with you, Breck."

"Naw, that's just the way gals like her are. They're in the habit of makin' a fella feel good about himself."

"Whores, you mean."

"Sure."

But actually, Breckinridge wasn't sure. Dulcy's gratitude and friendliness had seemed genuine. And she was mighty pretty, too. Maybe not as breathtakingly lovely as Annie Belle, but as he pictured both of them in his mind, he realized that if a man had to choose between them, it would be quite a dilemma.

This might make that rendezvous a little more interesting than it already promised to be . . .

Chapter Fourteen

Because of the encounter with Black Tom Mahone's group, it took Breckinridge and Morgan longer to check the traplines than it normally would have. It was late in the afternoon before they started back to camp with four beaver carcasses. The animals were yoked together so that Breck could drag them behind him.

It was going to be dark before they reached camp. Along the way, they debated what to tell Akins and Fulbright about what had happened.

"They're our partners," Breckinridge said. "I don't much like the idea of keepin' secrets from 'em. Anyway, they're bound to hear about that rendezvous in the next couple of days, if Mahone was right about a lot of other men headin' for this valley."

"I'm sure he was," Morgan said. "News spreads surprisingly fast out here, considering how isolated and sparsely populated this part of the country is. But what harm will it do to keep the news to ourselves, just for the time being?"

"Are you thinkin' about slippin' off to the rendezvous first, so that you can get first choice on those gals?"

"Well, what would be the harm in that?" Morgan asked.

"It ain't like any of 'em are what you'd call innocent," Breckinridge pointed out.

"I suppose you're right." Morgan sighed. "And we're already running the risk of Roscoe and Amos being offended because we didn't say anything to them about Finch and his bunch. If we do that again, they're liable to be really insulted."

"So we go ahead and tell 'em about it?"

"I guess that would be the best thing to do."

The whole thing turned out to be moot, however. As the two of them approached the camp a half hour or so after nightfall, they heard horses stamping and blowing and saw several figures moving against the glow of the flames from the fire pit.

"Somebody's here," Breckinridge said as his right hand tightened on the rifle he carried.

"Can't be Blackfeet," Morgan said worriedly. "We'd have heard shooting."

"Unless they caught the fellas by surprise and took 'em prisoner . . . or already killed them." Breckinridge's voice was grim as he spoke.

"Maybe we'd better be careful and not walk right in," Morgan suggested.

"Yeah, I was thinkin' the same thing. Let's circle around and come in from the other side."

If they were going to be faced with a fight, Breckinridge didn't want to be burdened with those beaver carcasses. He took the rope he had been using to pull them, tossed it over a tree branch, and hoisted them up high enough to be out of the reach of most predators. He could come back and get the beaver later if everything turned out all right.

With that done, he and Morgan slipped through the shadows as they skirted around the bluff where the camp was located.

Even though they weren't experienced frontiersmen yet, they had been out here long enough to pick up the knack of moving through the brush without making much noise. Breckinridge was already pretty good at that from his time spent in the woods back home in Tennessee. He led the way with Morgan following close behind him, emulating his every move.

When they were close, Breckinridge stopped and motioned for both of them to get down on the ground. They crawled forward until they could hear men talking. Even before he could make out the words, Breck recognized the sound of Akins's and Fulbright's voices.

The two men were alive, at least, and neither of them sounded alarmed. It was beginning to seem like Breckinridge and Morgan had gotten spooked unnecessarily.

When Breckinridge was close enough, he came up on a knee and parted some brush to peer through the gap. From where he was he could see both Akins and Fulbright. The two trappers were sitting next to the fire, drinking coffee, and talking in friendly fashion to four men Breck had never seen before.

One of the strangers was dressed in buckskins, while the others wore wool trousers and rough, homespun shirts. They were all good-sized, competent-looking men with powder horns and shot pouches slung over their shoulders. Breckinridge spotted four rifles stacked not far from the fire pit, and the butts of flintlock pistols stuck up from the waistbands of a couple of the men.

Four saddled horses were picketed on the far side of the camp, grazing and shifting around. That was what

Breckinridge had heard as he and Morgan approached the camp.

The strangers looked like trappers, and that made perfect sense. They had heard about the rendezvous and come to the valley to attend. They must have run into Akins and Fulbright, who had invited the men back here to share the fire.

Breckinridge eased the branches together again and backed off. He whispered to Morgan, "Nothin' to worry about. Just some fellas who've come for the rendezvous. Let's backtrack, pick up those carcasses, and go on in like nothin' happened."

He didn't particularly want to admit that he'd been spooked by something so innocuous.

A few minutes later, making plenty of noise as they approached, Breckinridge and Morgan tramped up the bluff to the camp. The six men who had been sitting around the fire were on their feet now. Out here in the wilderness, it made sense to be wary any time someone was moving around at night.

Akins and Fulbright relaxed as Breckinridge sang out, "Hello, the camp!"

"That's one of our partners," Fulbright explained to the strangers. A moment later, Breckinridge and Morgan stepped into the glow cast by the flames in the fire pit.

"I see we've got company," Breckinridge said. "Howdy, boys."

"Howdy," the man in buckskins said in return. "You've got some good-lookin' animals there."

Breckinridge nodded and said, "Thanks. We've had pretty good luck. You fellas trappers?"

"They're here for a rendezvous," Akins said. "You know anything about that, Breck?"

Breckinridge and Morgan glanced at each other. Breck said, "As a matter of fact, we heard somethin' about it today. We ran into a bunch that's bringin' in wagonloads of whiskey . . . and some women."

"Women!" Fulbright exclaimed as his eyes widened. "All the way out here in the middle o' nowhere?"

"That's right," Morgan said. "Good-looking women, too."

"Lord have mercy!" A big grin split Fulbright's whiskery face. "Now I'm lookin' forward to that rendezvous even more!"

"My name's Sterling," the buckskin-clad man said. "My pards are Hamilton, Wellman, and Price."

Akins gestured at Breckinridge and said, "That big redheaded galoot is Breck Wallace, and the other fella is Morgan Baxter."

Morgan said, "That's all I'll ever be as long as I'm hanging around you, Breck—the other fella."

"Well, at least you're a smaller target any time there's trouble," Breckinridge said with a grin. He shook hands with the four visitors, as did Morgan.

"There's still some stew in the pot," Akins said. "Why don't you and Morgan help yourselves while Amos and me skin out them beaver?"

"That sounds good to me," Breckinridge agreed.

"And while you're at it," Fulbright said, "tell us more about them women you saw!"

For the next half hour, the men talked and laughed while Breckinridge and Morgan had supper and Akins and Fulbright worked on the pelts. Breck felt a little uncomfortable telling about his adventure with the runaway wagon, so Morgan took over and spun that yarn.

"Actually, he looked a little like Hercules, standing there and holding that wagon up by himself," Morgan said.

"You're leavin' out the part about how it started rollin' and jerked me flat on my face," Breckinridge put in.

"Yeah, but you kept things from being a lot worse. That woman Dulcy said as much while she was standing there feeling your big, manly arm."

"Sounds like you've already made a conquest, Wallace," one of the visitors said. Breckinridge couldn't remember which one was which.

"All it takes to make a conquest with gals like that is a coin in your pocket," one of the other men said, slapping his thigh in amusement at his own joke.

Unaccountably, that gibe got under Breckinridge's skin a little. He knew perfectly well what sort of woman Dulcy was, but at the same time, he had sensed something different about her. He wasn't sure what that difference was yet, but he knew he wouldn't mind having the chance to find out.

Morgan saw his friend scowling and went on hurriedly with the story, concluding with, "So one of the women wound up with a broken arm, but it could have been a lot worse if Breck hadn't slowed down that wagon."

"That makes you a hero," Sterling said. Breckinridge could remember him because he was the one in buckskins.

"I'm no hero," Breckinridge insisted. "Just a fella who tried to help."

"Sounds pretty gallant to me. Of course, you were

tryin' to help out a bunch of pretty girls, and what man in his right mind wouldn't do that?"

They talked some more about the upcoming rendezvous. Breckinridge and Morgan didn't say anything about meeting Nicodemus Finch and his group. With any luck, that wouldn't even come up during the big gathering, at least not while Akins and Fulbright were around.

Finally the four visitors stood up and Sterling said, "I reckon we'd better be gettin' back to our own camp north of here. We've already got everything set up, and we don't want to intrude on you fellas."

"Wouldn't be any intrusion," Akins said, "but I understand about wantin' your own place. Just be careful on your way back. Haven't seen any Indians prowlin' around, but you never know."

"That's for sure." Sterling lifted a hand in farewell. "So long, boys."

They waved and said their good-byes, and the four men mounted up and rode off into the night. As the sound of hoofbeats faded, Akins said quietly, "We'd better keep a good lookout tonight."

"Why do you say that?" Breckinridge asked.

"Because while those fellas seemed friendly enough, they might decide it'd be easier to slit our throats and take our pelts than to work at trappin' their own."

"They didn't strike me as the sort to do that," Morgan objected.

"Maybe not, but that could've been an act."

"Roscoe's right," Breckinridge said. "It never hurts to be careful. Maybe we'll get to know 'em better at the rendezvous."

* * *

Several miles north of the camp on the bluff, the four men rode into another, larger camp, this one with a good-sized fire sheltered under an overhang of rock. Close to a dozen men and horses were gathered there.

The man who strode out to greet Sterling and the others was tall, broad-shouldered, and had a battered face and a thick black mustache. His voice displayed a trace of a British accent as he asked, "Well? Was that his bunch? Did you see him?"

Sterling swung down from the saddle and grinned.

"We did more than lay eyes on him, Sykes," he said. "We talked to him. That's the son of a bitch we're supposed to kill, all right. That's Breckinridge Wallace."

Chapter Fifteen

When Breckinridge and Morgan set out from camp the next morning, Breck was tempted to head south again, toward the pass. He was curious whether Mahone and his men had been able to get the rest of their wagons down the slope.

And if he was being honest, he had to admit that he wouldn't mind seeing Dulcy again.

But there were other traplines to check, and just because a rendezvous was coming up soon, that didn't mean they could neglect their work. They went west today, across the valley, while Akins and Fulbright started off to the north to check the traps in that direction.

Breckinridge's dreams had been visited by both Dulcy and Annie Belle, and that made his conflicting emotions even stronger. He'd been smitten with any number of gals over the years, going all the way back to Charity McFee, the neighbor's daughter who had taught him about the joys of the flesh in the hayloft of her pa's barn.

He had never found himself attracted to two women at the same time, though. He'd always been a one-woman man. But there was no denying that was the way he felt now.

"Looks like Roscoe was wrong about those other fellas," Morgan commented as they walked along one of the streams. "They didn't come back and try to murder and rob us."

"Roscoe didn't say he thought they were goin' to," Breckinridge pointed out. "He just said there was a chance of it."

Indeed, the rest of the night had passed quietly and peacefully as the four trappers took turns standing guard. Breckinridge hadn't seen or heard anything unusual during his stint on duty.

Today the first two traps were empty. Breckinridge and Morgan were approaching the third one, which was near a hill topped by a thick stand of pines, when Breck spotted something unusual among the trees. A ray of morning sunlight had reflected off something shiny up there. It was nothing more than a split-second wink, but he was sure he hadn't imagined it.

Another split second later, he realized the implications of what he had just seen, and his hand shot out to snag Morgan's collar.

"Get down!" Breckinridge exclaimed as he dived toward the ground and hauled his friend along with him.

He heard a distant *boom* and at the same time a low, menacing hum. The boom was a rifle shot, Breckinridge knew, and the hum was the sound of a heavy lead ball passing through the air not far above their heads.

He was pretty sure that ball would have smashed right through him if he'd still been walking along the creek bank.

A puff of powder smoke drifted out of the trees. When Breckinridge saw it, his first instinct was to aim his rifle at it and return the fire.

There might be more than one man up there, though, so he couldn't count on a momentary lull while the would-be killer reloaded. He and Morgan could still be in danger, so he called to his friend, "Roll to your right!"

While Morgan did that, Breckinridge rolled left. It was a good thing he did, because an instant after he moved, another rifle ball smacked into the ground where he'd just been. The shot kicked up dirt and grass.

"Hunt cover!" Breckinridge yelled as he surged to his feet. He knew he had to keep moving so it would be harder to draw a bead on him. From what he had seen so far, it seemed like the men in the trees wanted him dead and didn't care as much about Morgan. Both shots had been directed at Breck.

There were no trees nearby, but he spotted a little grassy hummock. It wouldn't offer much protection, but it was better than nothing. A couple of lunging strides and a leap landed Breckinridge behind it. As he sprawled there, he heard another shot hum through the air nearby.

He twisted his head and saw Morgan crawling rapidly toward the creek where they had been checking traps. As Breckinridge watched, Morgan rolled off the edge of the bank and disappeared with a splash.

Breckinridge knew that water was mighty cold, even in the summer like this. The creek bank gave Morgan some good cover, though, so Breck was glad his friend had reached the stream. He called, "Morgan! Are you all right?"

"Yeah, just wet!" Morgan sounded angry, and he had every right to be. "Who the hell is shooting at us?"

"I don't know, but I think they're shootin' at me, not you. All the shots have come closer to me."

"Well, you s-said you were a b-bigger target!"

Breckinridge could tell by his friend's voice that Morgan's teeth were starting to chatter from the chill of being immersed in the frigid water. He said, "If you can, crawl along under the bank until you get to a spot where you can get out of the creek and still have some good cover. You don't want to freeze to death in the middle of summer!"

"What about you?"

"I'm sort of stuck here," Breckinridge admitted. "However many varmints are up there on that hill, they've probably all got their rifles lined up on this little hump. If I stand up or try to crawl one way or the other, they'll see me."

"You say they're up in the trees on that hill?"

"Yeah. I saw the sun reflectin' off a rifle barrel. That's why I hit the dirt in the first place. And I've seen powder smoke coming from up there, too."

"Maybe I can w-work my way around and c-come up behind them," Morgan suggested.

"Too dangerous," Breckinridge said. "You'd be out-numbered. There are at least two of 'em up there. Good chance there's even more."

"So what are you going to do? Lay there the rest of the day and try to sneak off when it gets dark?"

Breckinridge didn't like the idea of sneaking off any time. He wasn't the sort to skulk away from danger. He was more likely to bull straight forward and tackle any trouble head-on.

In this case, though, doing that probably wouldn't

get him anything except a .50-caliber ball in the face
or guts.

"You let me worry about my own hide," he told
Morgan. "If you can get away from here without them
seein' you, head back to camp. Roscoe and Amos
might've heard those shots and be comin' to see what's
goin' on. Maybe the three of you can come back and
give me a hand then."

"Damn it, Breck! If I do that, it'll feel like I'm running
on you."

"No such thing," Breckinridge insisted. "That's
what I'm tellin' you to do. It's the best way you can
help me."

"I don't like it . . ."

"Do it anyway. I'll see you later, Morgan."

"Damn right you will."

He heard some splashing as Morgan moved along
the creek to the east. When the sounds faded, a sense
of relief came over Breckinridge. No matter what happened to him, he was glad that his friend might be out
of harm's way.

He slid the barrel of his rifle up over the hummock's
crest, moving slowly so as not to cause the grass to
wave around too much and draw attention. He'd never
been one to wear a hat, but he sort of wished he had
one now. If he did, he could stick it up a little and try
to draw the fire of the men on the hill. That might give
him a chance to peg a shot back at them.

But he didn't have a hat, so all he could do was wait.
He lifted his head just enough to peer through the
grass.

The dirt exploded about eight inches from his left
ear. Yelling curses, Breckinridge ducked lower. One of
them had spotted that red hair of his. If he couldn't risk

looking over the top of the little hump, he really and truly was as good as blind.

All he could do was lie there and wait for them to kill him.

Then another thought entered his mind. Morgan had suggested circling around to jump the men on the hill from behind.

There was nothing stopping them from doing the same thing to him. Some of them might have flanked him already. They could be out there in the grass somewhere, unseen, getting ready to blow his brains out . . .

The hell with it, Breckinridge thought.

If he was going to die, it would be while he was on his feet.

With an angry roar, he sprang up and charged toward the hill.

Chapter Sixteen

Breckinridge's sudden action must have surprised the men who wanted to kill him. A pair of shots blasted from the hilltop, but the shots went wide, whipping through the grass on either side of Breck.

At the same time, a rifle roared somewhere off to his right, followed instantly by yet another shot from the same general area. A man howled in pain.

Breckinridge didn't know what was going on over there, but he didn't allow himself to be distracted. He spotted movement in the trees atop the hill and paused long enough to fling his rifle to his shoulder and cock it. Aiming by instinct more than anything else, he pressed the trigger. The long-barreled flintlock kicked hard against his shoulder as it boomed.

A cloud of smoke from the exploding black powder wreathed Breckinridge's head for a second, blinding him. He charged through the stinging stuff. Knowing that he couldn't stop to reload in the open, he ran for the bottom of the hill as fast as his long legs would carry him.

Another shot sounded somewhere behind him. He

didn't know whether the rifleman was aiming at him, but he didn't hear the ball come anywhere close.

Morgan! he thought suddenly.

His friend hadn't headed back for camp after all. Instead he had lingered and was now taking part in this fight.

Another shot roared from the top of the hill. Breckinridge felt the hot breath of the ball as it passed close beside his cheek. That spurred him to run even faster. He saw some brush up ahead, growing along the base of the slope, and dived into it.

He lay still, hidden now from the riflemen. One of them fired anyway. The ball clipped branches several feet away from Breckinridge. He forced himself to remain motionless for a minute or two, then began crawling to his left. He moved slowly and carefully in order to disturb the vegetation as little as possible.

A shot came from over by the creek. Morgan had found some cover and was harassing the ambushers, Breckinridge thought. If Morgan could make them keep their heads down part of the time, Breck would have a better chance of reaching them.

He paused to reload his rifle, then began creeping up the hill, using every bit of cover he could find along the way. Morgan continued his covering fire, blasting regularly spaced shots at the hilltop.

Breckinridge began to think there was only one man still shooting up there. The return fire was spaced out, too, as if one man had to reload between each shot. Some of the rifle balls whipped through the trees and brush on the hillside, others searched along the creek. Breck hoped that Morgan was keeping his head down.

He had to suppress the impulse to stand up and rush

the rifleman. That reckless charge had worked to get him to the bottom of the hill, but now he had to depend on stealth. That didn't come naturally to him, but he had stalked enough game back in the Tennessee hills to be able to move quietly when he had to.

The sound of the shots from the crest gave Breckinridge something to steer by. He didn't head directly for them but angled to the left instead in an attempt to flank the ambusher. After what seemed like an hour but was really much less than that, he reached the top and lay there in some tall, thick grass for a few moments to get his bearings.

Warily, Breckinridge raised his head and peered along the hill. He saw powder smoke rising from a deadfall where several trees had toppled sometime in the past and landed so that they lay atop each other, forming a bulwark of sorts. Over by the creek, a hundred yards away, more smoke rose as Morgan fired again. Breck heard the ball thud into one of the logs. The hidden rifleman had pretty good cover behind them.

Breckinridge set his rifle aside and pulled both pistols from his belt. He checked to make sure they were loaded, then primed them and eased the hammers back down. Holding a pistol in each hand, he began crawling toward the deadfall.

After several minutes, he was close enough to see the ambusher, or at least part of the man's head and one shoulder as he crouched behind the fallen trees. Breckinridge studied the deadfall more closely and saw something else that caught his interest.

A booted foot stuck out from behind one of the logs. It wasn't moving, and Breckinridge could only figure that one of the shots he and Morgan had thrown up here had found its mark, by chance as much as anything.

But a lucky shot could kill a man just as dead as a perfectly aimed one.

The surviving attacker knelt and started reloading his rifle. Breckinridge couldn't see the man anymore, but he knew what was going on because he could see the rifle barrel moving around, going in and out of sight. As the echoes of the last shot died away, Breck heard the man muttering to himself. The fella didn't sound happy at all.

That was understandable. This ambush hadn't gone the way he and his companions had planned it.

The man stood up again, and this time Breckinridge could see more of him. Something about him seemed familiar, as if Breck would recognize his face if he could see it. The man's back was to him, though.

There was one way to change that.

Breckinridge stood up and yelled, "Hey!"

The man jumped and whirled around and tried to bring his rifle to bear. Breckinridge was about fifteen feet away, so he got a good look at the man's face. He couldn't put a name with it, but he knew the man was one of the visitors he and his partners had entertained in their camp the night before.

Then the pistols in Breckinridge's out-thrust hands roared as smoke and flame gushed from their barrels. Both balls smashed into the rifleman's chest and drove him back against the stack of logs behind him. The unfired rifle flew from his hands.

He leaned against the deadfall for a moment as blood welled from the two holes in his chest. His eyes were wide with shock and pain. He opened his mouth, but no words came out. The only thing that did was a trickle of blood from the corner of his lips.

Then his knees buckled and he pitched forward on his face.

Probably should have fired only one of the guns, just in case the other fella wasn't dead after all, thought Breckinridge as he advanced slowly.

But that wasn't the case, he saw when he reached a spot where he could look around the logs. The second man, who was also one of the bunch from the night before, was definitely dead. His eyes stared wide and unseeing at the blue sky. The front of his homespun shirt was dark and wet with blood.

Faintly, Breckinridge heard hoofbeats drumming somewhere in the distance. By the sound of them, a rider was getting out of there in a hurry.

"Breckinridge!" The shout came from below. "Breck, are you alive up there?"

"I'm here!" he told Morgan. "Are you all right?"

"Yeah. How about you?"

"Fine! What about the other two?"

"One of them is down here with a hole in his head! I think the other son of a bitch lit out!"

Breckinridge agreed with that. He reloaded his pistols, recovered his rifle, and then started down the hill to join up with Morgan.

He left the two dead men where they were. The varmints didn't deserve to be put under the ground proper-like. Share a man's fire and then try to kill him the next day . . . that was just about the lowest of the low, Breckinridge thought.

"Looks like Roscoe was right," he said as he walked up to Morgan, who had come out of the brush to reload his rifle. "Those fellas decided to pick us off, then kill Roscoe and Amos and take our pelts."

"Yeah, but one of them is still alive and got away," Morgan pointed out.

"I don't reckon there's much chance he'll come back and try again on his own." Breckinridge frowned. "You didn't go back to camp like I told you to."

"And it's a good thing," Morgan said. "Two of them were sneaking up on you, and they were just about ready to start taking potshots at you. I downed one of them, and the other got spooked and took off."

Breckinridge nodded and said, "I'm obliged to you, all right. I just hope you don't catch your death from bein' soaked in that cold creek."

"My clothes are already drying in the sun. Don't worry about me." Morgan shouldered his rifle. "Come on. We've got more traps to check."

"You don't want to bury those fellas?"

"Not hardly. Do you?"

"Not hardly," Breckinridge agreed with a grin. "Their friend can come back and do it if he wants."

"I think we've seen the last of him," Morgan said.

Sterling showed up leading three riderless horses. Fury boiled up inside Harry Sykes's broad chest at the sight.

"What the bloody hell happened?" Sykes demanded.

"The others are dead," Sterling reported.

"I figured that much, you fool! What about Wallace? Is *he* dead, too?"

Sterling grimaced and shook his head.

"That big redheaded bastard must be the luckiest man alive," he said. "I know damn well several of our shots came within inches of him. But somehow he and his friend didn't get hit. They managed to kill Wellman, Hamilton, and Price, though."

Sykes blew out a disgusted breath and said, "I knew good an' well I shouldn't have trusted just the four of you to get the job done. You found Wallace, and you said you'd take care of him. More the fool I am for believin' it."

"Harry, I tell you we should have had him," Sterling insisted. "Give me another chance—"

"You had your chance," Sykes interrupted. "I want Wallace dead before that blasted rendezvous starts and complicates everything." He nodded decisively. "Next time we'll all go after him—and then Breckinridge Wallace will die."

Chapter Seventeen

Other than the four men trying to kill them, it was a good day for Breckinridge and Morgan. They collected five beaver from their traps, so they had an impressive load as they headed back to camp.

Akins and Fulbright were already there. The bushy-bearded Amos Fulbright greeted them by saying, "We thought we heard some shots 'way off in the distance this mornin'. You fellas know anything about that?"

"A little," Morgan answered dryly. "We were fighting for our lives."

"What?" Akins exclaimed.

"Those four fellas from last night jumped us," Breckinridge said.

Akins cursed and said, "I knew it! I knew somethin' was off about that bunch. They acted mighty friendly, but I could tell they were up to something. They saw what a fine bunch of pelts we've got, and they wanted 'em for themselves."

"That's the only explanation that makes any sense," Breckinridge agreed with a nod.

He wished he didn't have a nagging feeling that

there might be even more to the ambush than that. The hunch had grown stronger during the day while he and Morgan were checking the traps, although he had nothing to back it up.

"What happened to the varmints?" Fulbright asked. "They get away?"

"One of them did," Morgan said. The grim look on his face made it clear that the other three hadn't.

After Breckinridge and Morgan had told their friends more about what had happened, Fulbright said, "You reckon there's any chance that other fella will come back and cause any more trouble?"

"You can't ever rule anything out," Akins said, "but the chances of it seem mighty slim to me. He's on his own now. More than likely he'll want to get out of this part of the country while his hide's still in one piece."

"He might come to the rendezvous," Breckinridge suggested.

Akins snorted and said, "If he does, we'll recognize him. Out here, justice is pretty swift and final-like for anybody who tries to steal another man's pelts."

Breckinridge didn't doubt that. He already knew that these mountain men, of whom he was now one, lived by a rough code of honor that suited him just fine.

Akins and Fulbright had had good luck, too, bringing in four beaver. That made nine pelts to add to their catch for the season. They worked until late skinning out the animals, scraping the pelts, and staking them out to dry. Morgan and Fulbright hauled off the skinned carcasses to keep scavengers away from the camp.

As usual, the men took turns standing guard during the rest of the night. Nothing happened, and they were up before dawn the next morning, also as usual.

Fulbright, who'd had the last shift on guard duty, was at the fire pit, about to get the coffee on to boil, when a rifle shot sounded somewhere on the other side of the creek. With a wicked whine, the ball bounced off one of the flat rocks that formed the pit. The shot came so close to Fulbright that he yelled and jumped, and the coffeepot in his hands went flying.

Akins was close by. He yelled, "Get down, you fool!" and dived behind the fire pit. Fulbright followed his example.

Breckinridge and Morgan had wandered off to different areas in the trees to take care of their morning necessities. Breck had just pulled up his buckskin trousers when he heard the shots and Akins's shout. Heedless of danger, he plunged out of the pines and into the camp at the edge of the bluff.

More rifles blasted on the other side of the creek. Breckinridge heard one of the balls whip past his head. He grabbed his rifle from the stack and dived to the ground, rolling over a couple of times before he came to a stop behind their stack of dried pelts, which was tall enough and thick enough to provide some cover.

Morgan came running out of the woods, too, but yelped in pain as soon as he emerged. He stumbled and put a hand to his suddenly bloody cheek.

"Morgan, get back!" Breckinridge bellowed at him.

Morgan reversed course and threw himself back into the pines. He pressed against one of the thick trunks.

"How bad are you hit?" Breckinridge called to him. Breck was worried about his friend because he'd seen the splash of blood on Morgan's face, but the spryness with which Morgan had sought cover was encouraging.

"I'm all right," Morgan said. "A ball just nicked me. It hurts like blazes, though—and the scar's going to ruin my good looks!"

Despite the danger in which they found themselves, Breckinridge had to chuckle at Morgan's response. He said, "Naw, it'll just make you more dashin' lookin'!"

From where he sprawled behind the fire pit with Fulbright, Akins asked, "Who the hell is that over there shootin' at us? Sounds like half a dozen or more men. I thought you said only one of those bastards got away yesterday!"

"Only one of them did," Morgan said. "I'm sure of it."

"Then the varmint had some other friends," Fulbright said, "because there sure as hell is more than one man shootin' at us!"

Breckinridge agreed with that. He'd been taking some quick glances at the stretch of woods across the creek and located three different places where powder smoke was visible. He focused his attention on one of them and after a moment caught a glimpse of a man leaning out slightly from behind a tree with a rifle. Breck even saw the muzzle flash as the man fired, then ducked back.

Breckinridge slid the barrel of his rifle over the pile of beaver pelts and drew a bead just to the side of that tree. He eared back the hammer and waited. Fifteen or twenty seconds went by, just about long enough for a man to reload if he wasn't hurrying too much.

Another flash of movement.

Breckinridge stroked his flintlock's trigger.

The long rifle boomed and kicked, and as the smoke cleared the sight of a man flopping around on the ground over there rewarded Breckinridge's gaze.

Then he had to duck as several rounds from across the creek slammed into the stack of beaver pelts. Breckinridge hoped the balls weren't doing too much damage to the furs. Trying to kill him and his friends was bad enough, but ruining the pelts they'd worked so hard for would really get his dander up!

"I'm pretty sure I got one of 'em," he called to the others, "but there's no tellin' how many more are over there."

"With all this lead flyin' around, I don't see how Amos and me can get to our rifles, either," Akins complained.

From behind the tree where he had taken cover, Morgan said, "I might be able to get to them and toss them over to you fellas."

"You're liable to get your head shot off if you try that," Breckinridge said sharply as he reloaded his rifle.

"I don't see any other way we're gonna be able to put up a fight. You have your pistols, Breck?"

"Sure I do."

"Roscoe, how about you and Amos?"

"We've got pistols," Akins said, "but those bastards across the creek are out of range of them."

"Doesn't matter," Morgan insisted. "When I tell you to, all three of you let off as many rounds as you can. Just the sound of a volley like that ought to make those men duck their heads, and that'll give me time to reach our rifles."

Breckinridge wasn't sure about that, but it seemed like the plan stood at least a slight chance of working. And a slight chance was better than any others he could see at the moment.

"All right," he said. "I reckon we can give it a try. Wait a minute and let me get my pistols ready."

The barrage from across the creek continued as Breckinridge, Akins, and Fulbright prepared their weapons. When they were all ready, Breck turned his head, looked at Morgan, and gave him a tense nod.

"All right, boys!" Morgan called as he crouched, poised to leap out from behind the tree. "Give 'em hell!"

Chapter Eighteen

Breckinridge had two pistols, Akins and Fulbright one each. Breck had his rifle, as well, which he fired first as his two friends leaned out from behind the fire pit and triggered their weapons. Instantly, Breck dropped the rifle, snatched up the pistols he had laid out so they would be handy, and they boomed and bucked against his palms.

The five rounds coming so close together made a thunderous barrage. A cloud of powder smoke rolled from the top of the bluff. As the blasts filled the air, Morgan darted out from behind the tree and raced toward the three rifles. When he was close enough, he dived for them.

Breckinridge turned his head to look, saw Morgan go down abruptly, and for a second thought his friend had been hit.

But then Morgan grabbed one of the rifles and tossed it toward the fire pit. He followed it with a second rifle, then grabbed the third one and hugged the ground as closely as possible.

He summoned up a weak grin and called to

Breckinridge, "They don't have a good angle on me from over here. As long as I keep my head down, they can't hit me. Sounds like a swarm of bugs flying right over my head, though."

"We'll see if we can't give 'em something else to worry about," Breckinridge promised as he finished reloading his rifle.

Over behind the fire pit, Akins reached for one of the rifles, only to jerk his hand back as a shot kicked up dirt near it. He uttered a curse, then said, "Should've got these flintlocks a little closer, Morgan."

"I didn't have much time to see where I was tossing them," Morgan pointed out. "Just be glad they're as close as they are."

"Yeah, I reckon," Akins groused. He lunged again for the rifle and this time closed his fingers around its barrel. He rolled back behind the fire pit and drew the rifle with him.

Fulbright repeated the maneuver. One of the rifle balls from the ambushers came so close it clipped a little hair from his bushy beard.

"Dadgum it!" he yelped as he grabbed the rifle and scrambled back to safety. "If I'd'a wanted to shave, I'd'a done it myself!"

Now Breckinridge, Akins, and Fulbright were all armed with weapons that could reach their enemies on the other side of the creek. All three men were crack shots, too.

That meant they could put up a fight, anyway, and men such as them never asked for a guarantee, only a fighting chance.

As the sun rose higher, the battle settled down to a duel of rifles. Shots zipped back and forth across the creek. Breckinridge thought he scored again on one of the ambushers, but he wasn't sure.

After a while, Morgan called, "I'm gonna see if I can crawl backward and get in the trees again. I want to get in on this fracas."

"Just be careful," Breckinridge told him. "Better keep your head down and eat dirt the whole way."

"I intend to, I assure you."

Morgan began inching backward. It was a long, tedious process, but at last he reached the pines and was able to roll behind one of the thick trunks. He stood up and leaned against the rough bark, his face pale from the strain except where the bloody streak ran across his cheek.

It seemed to Breckinridge like the battle had been going on for hours, but he knew that wasn't right. The position of the sun told him it had been less than an hour since the first shot was fired. He had enough powder and shot to keep going at this pace for quite a while yet, and he hoped the others did, too.

Because this seemed like a standoff, and he didn't really see any way of breaking it.

A new concern began to gnaw at his mind. When he and Morgan had been pinned down the day before, their enemies had tried to flank them and then get behind them. Would these ambushers do the same?

It was certainly possible that some of them could go upstream or down, cross the creek, and then work their way through the woods until they had Breckinridge and his friends trapped in a crossfire.

"Morgan!" Breckinridge called into the trees when both of them were reloading. "Keep an eye out behind you. Some of 'em could be comin' up that way."

"I already thought of that," Morgan replied as he

used the ramrod to tamp a patch-wrapped ball down on a fresh charge of powder. "I'm the only one who can risk moving around much, so I thought I'd fade back and do a little scouting."

"Be careful. If you do run into any of 'em, they're liable to outnumber you."

"You'll likely know it if I do."

Breckinridge knew what Morgan meant. He would hear the shooting.

Breckinridge eased his rifle over the pile of pelts, waited until he saw a spurt of powder smoke on the other side of the creek, and fired at it. As usual, he couldn't tell if he had hit one of the attackers or not, but he was confident that he had come close.

Of course, close might not be enough to do any good.

When he glanced toward the trees again, Morgan was gone. Breckinridge's jaw tightened. He wasn't really the praying sort, but he sent up a short plea that his friend would be all right.

Then it was back to the grim work of loading, firing, and reloading. Acrid gray smoke hung so thick in the air it stung his eyes and nose, and the almost continual roar of gunfire made his ears ache.

Back in Knoxville, there'd been a Revolutionary War cannon on the square, a monument to the men who had won the nation its freedom from the British. Breckinridge didn't understand how men who were around artillery like that all the time could ever hear anything again. Maybe they couldn't. Maybe that was part of the price they paid to defeat the enemy.

Fulbright yelled and cursed. Breckinridge asked, "Are you hit, Amos?"

"Not to amount to anything," Fulbright replied. "Rifle ball just knocked a little hunk of meat off my arm."

"Little hunk of meat, hell," Akins said. "You're drilled, Amos, and you're bleedin' like a stuck pig. Let me see that arm."

Fulbright snapped, "You just tend to your own rat-killin'. I'll be fine. Go back to shootin' at those varmints over there."

"And let you bleed to death? I don't think so. Now, let me see that arm, blast your ornery hide!"

Grumbling and complaining, Fulbright allowed Akins to examine his wounded arm. Akins drew his knife and cut away some of the buckskin sleeve. From where Breckinridge was, he couldn't really see the wound, but the blood was plain enough as it dripped down Fulbright's arm.

Akins was wearing a homespun shirt. He cut several pieces off the bottom of it, wadded up two of them and shoved them into the entrance and exit wounds, then used the other strip to tie them in place. That had to hurt like hell for Fulbright, but he didn't make a sound and his face was impassive except for a faint scowl.

"That ought to slow the bleedin' down enough to keep you alive," Akins said. "But that hole will need to be cleaned out good, and then some real bandagin' ought to be done on it."

"We'll do that," Fulbright said, "assumin' we all get outta this mess alive."

Breckinridge was practical enough to know they were in a bad spot, but he certainly hadn't given up hope. His natural optimism told him they would come out of this alive. If they didn't . . . well, he supposed that meant it was their day to die, and a man couldn't really argue with that. There was no point in worrying about it, either. All they could do was just fight on, as hard as they could, for as long as they could.

That thought was going through his mind when a sudden flurry of gunfire somewhere behind them made him jerk his head around. Breckinridge's jaw tightened, and he muttered, "Morgan."

Somewhere back there, his friend had run into trouble, just as Breckinridge had feared would happen.

Chapter Nineteen

Morgan Baxter's cheek still burned like fire where the rifle ball had grazed him, but he tried to ignore the pain as he hurried through the trees, moving in a low, crouching run. His searching gaze flicked from side to side as he watched for any sign that the enemy was about to steal on them from behind.

It wasn't far to where a steep slope rose to form the first of the foothills that led to the mountains on this side of the valley. Morgan reached it without encountering anyone, and he began to hope that his and Breckinridge's suspicions had been wrong.

He could still hear the shots ringing out steadily from the camp, and he hoped Breck and the others were all right. There had been a time in Morgan's life, not so long ago, really, when he hadn't cared what happened to anybody else. The lessons he had learned since then had been hard but valuable ones.

He just wished his father hadn't died without seeing that his son had become a decent man.

Those thoughts distracted Morgan. He almost didn't

see the man who leaped at him from the top of a boulder until it was too late.

Morgan tried to twist out of the way, but the man slammed into him anyway, just not with full force. The impact was still enough to spin Morgan halfway around and make him lose his balance. He stumbled and fell to his knees.

Two more men burst out of some nearby brush and brandished pistols. Morgan lifted his rifle and fired first. One of the men went over backward, knocked off his feet by the rifle ball that shattered his shoulder.

The other fired his pistol, but Morgan was already diving aside. The ball cut through the air where he had been a second earlier.

Morgan rolled and came up swinging the rifle by the barrel like a club. The attacker who was still on his feet flung up an arm to block the blow. Morgan heard bone snap as the rifle caught the man on the forearm. The man howled in pain.

Brush crackled behind Morgan. He dived to the side again as two more shots blasted. The unlucky man whose arm he had just broken crumpled as one of the shots struck him instead.

Feet pounded against the pine needle–littered ground as more men rushed in. One of them yelled, "Stop shootin', you fools! Take him alive! He's Wallace's friend."

Morgan knew what that meant. They wanted to capture him and use him as a hostage so they could force Breck to do what they wanted. Surrender, more than likely.

And if that happened, the men would then just kill all of them. Morgan wasn't going to let that happen.

He gripped the rifle's long barrel and whirled it around and around his head as the men closed in around him. He walloped a couple of them and knocked them off their feet, but there were too many.

A rifle butt drove into his back and made him cry out as he staggered forward. Another caught him on the right shoulder and made his arm go numb. The rifle slipped out of his hands.

But his left arm still worked. He used that hand to pluck the knife from the sheath at his waist and slashed back and forth with the blade, feeling it rip through clothing and flesh. A man cried out again.

Morgan wasn't going to surrender. He would keep fighting until he forced them to kill him.

That would be better than being captured and letting them use him as a weapon against Breckinridge . . .

In addition to the gunshots, Breckinridge heard yelling from the direction Morgan had gone. It sounded like a desperate battle was going on back there, and he knew that Morgan had to be badly outnumbered.

It was all he could do not to leap to his feet and turn to race to the aid of his friend. Breckinridge knew that as soon as he did, though, he would be riddled with rifle balls from the men across the creek.

With fear for Morgan's safety gnawing at him, Breckinridge thrust his rifle over the pelts and fired again. Then, as he ducked down and started to reload, he heard more shots from across the creek than ever before.

That wasn't all. He thought his half-deafened ears

heard men shouting in alarm, and then the pounding of hoofbeats.

What in blazes was going on over there? he wondered.

He wasn't the only one who was puzzled. Akins risked a look over the top of the fire pit and then said, "Hey, I don't think they're shootin' at us anymore!"

"Sounds like somebody else might've shown up and taken a hand," Breckinridge said. "I would've sworn I heard horses!"

"Me, too," Fulbright agreed. "But who'd come along and help us?"

"I don't know," Breckinridge said, "but Morgan's in trouble and I'm gonna go give him a hand. You fellas stay here and keep your heads down until you're sure what's goin' on."

"Breck, wait—" Akins began, but it was too late. Breckinridge didn't hear any shots hitting the fire pit or the pelts or whipping through the brush, so he was going to assume it was safe for him to stand up again.

He surged to his feet and charged toward the trees where Morgan had disappeared. No rifle balls found him. None even seemed to come his way. Clearly, the attackers on the other side of the creek had their hands full right now. Someone had come along and turned the tables on them.

Breckinridge charged through the pines with his rifle held at a slant across his chest. He weaved around tree trunks, hurdled logs, crashed through brush. He followed the sound of shouting and within minutes burst onto the scene of battle.

Morgan was on his feet, slashing around him with a knife. A roughly dressed man had gotten behind him, though, and was about to brain him with a rifle butt.

Breckinridge threw his gun to his shoulder and fired. The man flew backward with blood spurting from his throat where the ball had struck him.

Breckinridge waded into the other men. He held his rifle parallel to the ground and plowed into two of them with it, driving them off their feet. A swift butt stroke shattered another man's jaw.

While Breckinridge was doing that, Morgan took advantage of the distraction to plunge his knife into the chest of another attacker. He ripped it free and whirled to look for another opponent, but Breckinridge already had all the others on the ground. Breck's booted foot lashed out and crashed into the head of one man who tried to get up again. A sharp *crack* sounded as the man's neck broke.

"Is this all of 'em?" Breckinridge asked.

"I don't know," Morgan said. "I thought there was another one, but I don't see him now. Lord! Are all these varmints dead?"

"They appear to be," Breckinridge said. He hadn't held back, and bones were no match for his massive strength when he had a weapon in his hands. Crushed skulls and splintered ribs had done for the men he had bowled over.

"What about Roscoe and Fulbright?"

"They were all right when I came after you. As best we could tell, somebody else came along and jumped those men who ambushed us."

"Who would do that?" Morgan asked with a frown.

"I don't know. I don't hear any more shootin', though. We'd best get back and find out what's goin' on."

"Sounds good to me," Morgan said as he bent down to retrieve his rifle.

* * *

Fifty yards away, Harry Sykes paused and bent over, resting his hands on his thighs as he tried to catch his breath. His pulse hammered inside his head, and he felt a little sick at his stomach. He was a big man, and plenty tough, but he had never seen anything like Breckinridge Wallace. The man was like a cross between a whirlwind and an avalanche. He had killed at least three men in a matter of heartbeats.

It didn't matter, Sykes told himself. He would still do the job Richard Aylesworth had paid him for. Right now, though, he was the only survivor from the group of men he had taken with him to get behind Wallace and the others. That hadn't worked out too well. Sykes needed to get back to his other men and regroup, come up with another plan for killing Wallace.

Too bad there was no way to just drop a mountain on the son of a bitch. That might be what it was going to take . . .

When Breckinridge and Morgan got back to camp, they found strangers there again. A couple of men stood holding the reins of horses as they talked to Akins and Fulbright. One of them, who had a thatch of white hair under his broad-brimmed hat, turned a weathered face toward Breckinridge and grinned.

"You're the one Roscoe and Amos here have been tellin' me about," he said in a gravelly voice. "You're Breck Wallace." He stuck out a hand. "My name's Powell."

Chapter Twenty

"We're on our way to the rendezvous," Powell explained a short time later as he and his companion, a man he introduced as Harding, sat and shared coffee with Breckinridge, Morgan, Akins, and Fulbright. "Heard all the shootin' and came to see what was goin' on." His lined face creased even more in a grin. "It sounded like the British had invaded and we were fightin' the War of 1812 all over again."

"Just a bunch of thievin' ambushers," Akins said. "As best we can figure, they were after our pelts. This is the second try the bunch has made against us."

Breckinridge frowned slightly and asked Powell, "If you didn't know what was goin' on, how'd you know whose side to take in the fightin'?"

Powell sipped from his tin cup of coffee and said, "Well, we could tell you fellas were outnumbered, so we just jumped in on the side of the underdog. Seemed like as good a plan as any."

"And it sure saved our bacon," Fulbright said.

By now Akins had passed a ramrod with a clean rag wrapped around it through the wound in Fulbright's arm, packed both holes with a poultice made from moss, and bound up the arm as tightly as he could without cutting off the circulation. Fulbright had endured the whole process in stoic silence.

"What happened to the men who ambushed us?" Morgan asked.

He had washed the bullet graze on his cheek with creek water, but other than that it hadn't required any medical attention. The wound was going to leave a scar, but in all likelihood it wouldn't be a large, ugly one. As Breckinridge had said, it would just give Morgan some character and make him look dashing.

"They put up a little fight when we hit them from behind," Powell said, "but mostly they just ran like hell. We killed a couple, and there were already two men lyin' dead over there, but the others got away. Half a dozen or so, I'd say."

"Maybe after this they really will leave us alone," Morgan said.

"You said you're headin' for the rendezvous," Breckinridge put in. "Are you fellas trappers?"

"Not really, although some of us have done some trapping before," Powell answered. "Actually, we were thinkin' about getting into the fur tradin' business. Might even build a tradin' post. There aren't many of them this far west, from what I hear."

Akins nodded and said, "That's true. Men have tried, but the Indians usually drive 'em out after a while."

"We've got a big enough party we don't have to worry too much about redskins," Powell said. "And the man we work for has enough money to provide plenty of supplies and trade goods and ammunition."

"You're not the boss of your bunch?"

Powell shook his head.

"No, we all work for another fella." He hesitated. "Call him the Colonel."

"This Colonel, where is he?" Breckinridge asked. "Back in St. Louis?"

"Nope. He came with us. We left a couple of men with him and the wagon, aways back, when we came to find out what all the shootin' was about. I sent a rider to let them know that everything was all right."

"I guess we'll see you all at the rendezvous, then," Morgan said.

Powell drank the last of his coffee and nodded.

"More than likely. We'll be around, that's for sure. You think you fellas will be all right now?"

"We'll be fine," Akins said. "After all the damage that gang of thieves has suffered, this time they really will pull out, I'm bettin'."

Breckinridge thought that was likely, too . . . but he reminded himself that when they got up this morning, they had all believed they were in no real danger, too.

That was one thing about life . . . trouble had a way of coming at you when you didn't expect it.

After leaving the camp on the bluff, Powell and Harding rode back across the creek to gather up the men who had come with them.

"The Colonel," Harding said with a grin. "That was pretty fast thinking, calling him that instead of his real name. Wallace might have remembered that."

Powell grunted and said, "Remember the name of the kid he gunned down back in St. Louis? Yeah, there's a good chance of that."

"Rory Ducharme was an arrogant, trouble-makin'

little bastard," Harding said. "You've likely heard the same stories about him that I have. There's a good chance Wallace had every right to shoot him. He might have been stopping Rory from killin' him or somebody else."

"Doesn't matter. His pa loved him and is willing to pay to avenge his death. That's all that matters to us."

"Well, sure. But how come we didn't just go ahead and grab Wallace and take him back to Ducharme?"

"You really think his friends would've let us take him without a fight?"

"There are enough of us we could've done it. We've got 'em outnumbered."

"Yeah. And some of us would've gotten killed, too, more than likely. I had another idea as soon as I heard about that rendezvous. There'll be a whole mess of people around then. We'll find a way to cut Wallace out of the bunch, get him away from his friends, and turn him over to Ducharme before anybody else even knows what's happenin'. If we're smart about it, we might be able to earn our money without anybody having to get shot for it . . . except Breckinridge Wallace."

Harding grinned and said, "There's a good reason you're in charge of this bunch, Powell. You're better at thinkin' than the rest of us."

"It's kept me alive this long," Powell said.

When they had heard the shooting and gone to investigate, they'd had no idea they were going to run into the man they were looking for so soon after reaching the valley. They had been on Wallace's trail for weeks, ever since leaving St. Louis.

Luckily folks tended to remember a giant young man with flaming red hair.

The trail had led here, and now Powell and his companions even knew where Wallace's camp was. That was the payoff for picking a side and plunging into the battle. Powell's instincts had been reliable once again.

Now all he had to do was convince Otto Ducharme that the smart thing was to wait and use the rendezvous as a cover for their activities, rather than go after Wallace right away.

He and Harding gathered up the other men, who reacted much as Harding had when they found out that their quarry was right there on the other side of the creek, several hundred yards away. Powell explained his plan again and none of them argued with him, but he could tell that some of the men weren't too happy about the decision.

They were cunning, but in a way they were simple-minded, as well. They thought the best option was always to smash straight ahead and grab what you wanted, killing anybody who got in your way.

Ducharme was liable to feel the same—but there was only one way to find out.

They had left the German merchant about half a mile away with a couple of guards. It didn't take long to get back to where Ducharme waited, sitting on the wagon parked under some trees.

"Well?" Ducharme asked sharply when Powell and the others had ridden up and reined in. "What did you find? What was all that shooting about?"

Ducharme's always beefy face turned an even darker, mottled shade of red as Powell explained. The gunman knew that his employer was about to explode with rage as he heard that his son's killer was so close by—

and not only had Powell failed to capture him, he had actually helped save Breckinridge Wallace's life.

When Powell finished, though, and Ducharme finally spoke, it wasn't in a roar. Instead, in a quiet, carefully controlled voice, Ducharme asked, "Why did you not bring my son's killer to me, Herr Powell?"

"Because there's a better way," Powell answered without hesitation.

"It was my son who was murdered by this man. It is *my* right to choose how he should die. I thought you understood that."

"I do understand," Powell said. "But if we'd tried to grab him, Wallace would have put up a fight, and so would his friends. If we wait until that rendezvous we heard about, we can grab him and get him away from there without anybody bein' the wiser about what happened to him. Think about it, Mr. Ducharme . . . you can take Wallace out miles from anybody else, where nobody can hear him yellin', and you can do whatever you want to him. You can make your revenge last as long as you want." Powell paused and let an evil grin spread over his rugged face. "How does *that* sound to you, boss?"

Ducharme's face was still flushed and he was breathing hard, but maybe not from anger now, thought Powell. Maybe it was because he was thinking about what Powell had just said.

"Yes," Ducharme finally said. "You are smarter than I gave you credit for, Herr Powell. That is exactly the way Breckinridge Wallace should die: slowly, agonizingly, and all alone."

Chapter Twenty-one

Dulcy Harris held her hands clasped in her lap and rocked back and forth a little on the seat beside Jed Humphries as the man drove the lead wagon in the little caravan.

The vehicle that had overturned the day before had been the lead wagon, but now it was relegated to the back of the line because its axle was bent slightly and caused it to jerk and wobble because one of the wheels wasn't straight. Mahone had promised they would repair it when they reached the rendezvous site, but he didn't want to take the time to do the work now.

"If we delay too long, that bastard Finch might beat us to the spot," Mahone had said while the group was camped the previous night. "I'm not gonna let him steal a march on me again, damn it."

Not many maps of this region even existed, but Mahone had gotten hold of one that he claimed was accurate. On it he had picked out a site on a big S-curve of a creek that he said would be perfect for them to set up during the rendezvous. That was the spot he wanted to beat Nicodemus Finch to.

And that desire to get the best of Finch was why he had driven them all so hard to get here, risking life and limb in the process. Finch was Tom Mahone's archenemy and always would be, until one or both of them was dead.

One time, Dulcy had asked Mahone about that. They'd both had a little too much brandy that night, she supposed, and she had felt a mellow affection for the man who wasn't there at other times.

Most of the time she had regarded him simply as her employer, and not a particularly friendly or pleasant one, at that. This had been at a trading post Mahone owned at the time back in Missouri, when Nicodemus Finch had owned a rival post a mile away.

"Ah, hell, all that damn mess goes back too far," Mahone had said. "Finch and me are blood kin. We've knowed each other nearly all our blamed lives."

"I'll bet the trouble between you started over a woman, didn't it?" Dulcy had asked.

The hour was late and they were sitting at a rough-hewn table in the tavern attached to the trading post after the place had closed down for the night. Dulcy had only been working for him a few months, after the fever that had taken both her husband and their daughter.

The only way to live with pain like that, she had discovered, was to wall yourself off from it. The squalid existence she had chosen for herself did a good job of dulling everything until the grief didn't bite so hard anymore.

"I reckon that was part of it," Mahone had said in answer to her question. "There was a gal . . . Eula Mae was her name . . . and she told me she loved me. But then, out of the blue, she said she was gonna marry that damn runt Finch. I might've been able to live with that, even though it would'a been hellacious hard, if Finch hadn't gone and burned the boat we was partners in."

"Burned your boat?" Dulcy had exclaimed in surprise. "Why in the world would he do that?"

"Because he's the craziest son of a bitch the Good Lord ever put on this green earth!" Mahone had leaned forward with an intense look on his face. "Sometimes these fits'll come on him, and he'll hop around and cackle like a chicken. Other times he'll start spoutin' nonsense, just a bunch of crazy words I swear he makes up. There's never any tellin' what he might do next." Mahone threw back the rest of the drink he had in his hand. "I should've put a pistol ball through his brain when I had the chance. It'd have been a mercy killin'. I'd have been puttin' the rest of the world out of its misery at havin' him around!"

"And the two of you have been competing with each other ever since?"

"Yeah. Every time I try some new business, here comes Finch, showin' up to ruin everything. I haven't had the best luck, and he's been the worst of it!" Mahone had gotten to his feet then and jerked his head toward the sleeping quarters in the back. "Come on. I'm tired of talkin' about the little varmint."

Dulcy had gone with him, of course. None of the girls who worked for him dared turn him down when he demanded their company, but in truth Dulcy hadn't really minded all that much. Mahone was quite a bit older than her, but at the time he'd still been a vital, energetic man, able to make her forget her sorrow for a while. That was before the sickness had struck him down and left him with weak, withered legs.

The sickness hadn't done anything to blunt his

anger and greed and hatred of Nicodemus Finch, though. Those things were as strong as ever.

Dulcy had stayed with him because there was really nothing else she wanted to do with her life, other than get to the end of it. Back in the early days of her mourning, she had thought about hurrying that end along so she could be reunited with the ones she'd lost. She knew they wouldn't want that, though, and gradually that desire had left her.

Now, from time to time, she felt some unexpected stirrings inside her. A sense of longing, maybe, for a real life again, something in which to find some joy.

It was too late for that, though. The morass of her existence these past few years had seen to that.

Beside her on the wagon seat, Humphries said, "Those tracks worry me. Somebody else brought wagons in here not long ago. You reckon it was Finch?"

"Not necessarily," Dulcy said. "I don't know much about these rendezvouses, but don't a bunch of fur traders usually show up for them? The wagons could belong to some of them."

"I hope so," Humphries said with a worried frown. "If Finch beat him here, the boss is liable to have a fit."

That was true, thought Dulcy. And it was certainly possible that Finch had beaten them to the valley. Mahone had heard that his old enemy was putting together an outfit to come here, and that was what had prompted him to do the same thing.

Mahone always made it sound like Finch followed his lead and showed up to compete with and ruin whatever business venture he'd attempted. Dulcy would have been willing to bet that plenty of times it had been the other way around.

Humphries spat tobacco to the side and said, "Sure is pretty country."

Dulcy agreed with that, as well. The broad, green valley with its fast-flowing creeks and stands of towering pines was indeed beautiful between the flanking ranges of snowcapped peaks. This was the farthest west she had ever been, and the farthest from civilization, too. It frightened her, in a way, being so far from anywhere, but at least there were people around.

Interesting people, too, she thought, briefly remembering that big, redheaded young man who had helped them the day before. Breckinridge Wallace was good-looking in a rugged way, but there had been something else about him that intrigued Dulcy . . .

"Oh Lord," Humphries said, hauling back on the team's reins and breaking into what might have been a pleasant reverie for Dulcy if it had been allowed to continue. "Look over yonder, across the creek. Is that . . . ?"

A number of wagons were parked on the other side of the creek, on a broad point of land formed by the stream's curving course. Tents had been set up, as well, and people were moving around, including some women. Dulcy saw sunlight flash on fair hair.

She also saw a short, scrawny, billy goat–bearded man in filthy buckskins standing at the edge of the creek. As she watched, he grabbed his own hat off his head, flung it to the ground, and started stomping on it, leaping up and down and waving his arms as he spewed forth a torrent of unintelligible but obviously outraged gibberish.

"Yes," Dulcy said, dreading what was bound to happen now. "That's Nicodemus Finch."

Chapter Twenty-two

Annabelle Walters heard Nicodemus yelling and jabbering and knew something had happened. Only one thing could get him that worked up, Annie knew.

Black Tom Mahone had arrived.

All the members of Finch's group had expected that to happen. For two men who hated each other so vehemently, each kept track of what the other was doing with the unwavering intensity of jealous lovers.

If Finch moved his base of operations from one place to another, Mahone knew it. If Mahone started some new business venture, Finch was aware of it.

They were never apart for long. Something always drew them back together. Hate was just as strong a passion as love.

Annie had been just about to go inside one of the tents when Nicodemus started acting crazy. She paused, and while she was standing there watching his display out at the head of the point, Francesca emerged from the tent and said, "What in the world is he carrying on about now?"

Annie pointed at the group of wagons approaching on the other side of the creek.

"What do you think?" she asked. "Black Tom is here, unless I miss my guess."

Francesca sighed disgustedly.

"Why can't that man and his harlots leave us alone?" she said.

That was pretty rich, Francesca referring to Mahone's girls as harlots, Annie thought wryly. They were all in the same line of work, after all. None of them had been at it for very long, but that didn't change what they were. Sisters under the skin, so to speak.

A year ago, Annie never would have dreamed she would wind up being a whore, let alone one that was brought out here into the middle of the wilderness to service a bunch of dirty, smelly mountain men who reeked of beaver carcasses.

A year ago she had been Annabelle Walters, the pampered daughter of a plantation owner from Alabama. That was before her father had lost everything gambling, including the family's ancestral home, and had taken the easy way out by pressing a pistol to his head and putting a ball through his brain.

Annabelle's mother had died six weeks later, too stunned by her sudden change in circumstances to carry on. That had left Annabelle, barely nineteen years old and with absolutely no skills other than flirting and looking pretty, to care for four younger brothers and sisters.

What the hell else was she *supposed* to do other than sell herself? she had asked herself many times.

She had saved her money until she was able to take

her brothers and sisters to Mobile, where she shamed an aunt and uncle into taking them in and promising to raise them. The money that Annabelle had given them had helped persuade them to do the right thing.

Annabelle herself couldn't stay, though. She was already too tainted. Her aunt had put her foot down about that.

Annabelle hadn't put up much of an argument. In truth, she didn't *want* to stay with her relatives. If a new life had been forced upon her—and it had—then it only made sense to turn her back on her old life and get on as best she could.

That was how she'd come to be in New Orleans, and after that on a riverboat plying the stately waters of the Mississippi, and then in a house in St. Louis, where Nicodemus Finch had found her and bought her from the madam, adding her to the group of girls he was putting together for a journey he planned to make to the mountains.

"What's your name, gal?" he had asked her, and when she told him Annabelle—because she had never given up her true name, unlike so many of the women in her profession—he had grinned and said, "Annie Belle. That's a mighty pretty name to go with a mighty pretty gal."

So he had introduced her to the others as Annie Belle and she hadn't corrected him, so the name had stuck and was soon shortened to Annie. That was fine with her. Maybe it was even a good idea, she decided. Maybe stubbornly calling herself Annabelle had been clinging to the last vestige of who she had been before.

For all intents and purposes, Annabelle Walters, the

plantation owner's daughter, was as dead as her poor father.

Annie the whore was alive and in the middle of the wilderness, with trouble about to break out.

Finch finally bent and picked up his muddy, battered hat from the ground where he had been dancing on it in rage. He turned and rushed toward the wagons.

"Get your guns! Get your guns!" he yelled to the men who worked for him. "We got to shoot us some snakes!"

Caleb Moffit, who was Finch's unofficial second-in-command, came up to him and said, "Boss, we can't start shooting at Mahone's bunch. They'll shoot back at us."

"What of it?" Finch demanded with a wild-eyed stare. "That's what a war is, ain't it?"

"Some of the girls are liable to get hurt."

"It's a war! They knowed the job might get dangerous when they signed on with me!"

Annie didn't recall anybody actually "signing on" with Finch. She and the other girls had just been told that they were working for him now, and they were going to the mountains for some sort of fur trappers' get-together. They hadn't been given any choice in the matter, and they sure hadn't been warned that it might be dangerous.

But the life of a soiled dove was never without its dangers, so what was the point of worrying about it?

"Are you sure those wagons belong to Mahone?" Moffit asked. "Did you see him?"

"No, but who else could they belong to? They're his, I tell you! It's gotta be that sassafrassin' bunglebender!"

"They're stoppin' over there. Let's walk out to the point and make sure," Moffit suggested.

"I can't start shootin' at 'em?"

"Not yet," Moffit said, trying as usual to be the voice of reason.

"All right," Finch said with a sigh. "But mark my words, it's that burr-butted musharoo!"

"Where are you going?" Francesca asked Annie as the blonde started to follow Finch and Moffit.

"I want to see what's going to happen," Annie said.

"You'll get shot once all hell breaks loose, that's what's going to happen."

"I'll take my chances," Annie said.

She wasn't the only one who followed Finch out onto the point. Gilbert and Jackson went along, too, and so did several other of the girls. Francesca hung back with a look of derision on her face.

The Irish girl Siobhan came up beside Annie and asked, "What do you think's going to happen?" Her voice was a mixture of fear and excitement.

"I think Nicodemus and Mahone are going to stand there threatening and yelling at each other across the creek for a while, and then they'll go on about their business," Annie said with a smile. "They're both too greedy to do anything else."

"I hope you're right. I'm counting on making some money at this rendezvous."

That was her mistake, thought Annie. None of the girls would make much money from their efforts, not as long as Finch collected it and kept the lion's share for himself.

Finch and Moffit stopped at the very tip of the point, not much more than a stone's throw from the wagons parked on the other side of the creek. Annie had seen Black Tom Mahone a few times and would recognize him if she saw him again, but so far he wasn't in sight. On the seat of the lead wagon were a fox-faced, middle-aged man who had hold of the reins and beside him a dark-haired woman who was probably one of Mahone's doves. She regarded Annie with a cool stare, and Annie returned the look.

That one was trouble, Annie thought.

Before she could ponder any more, Mahone came limping into sight from one of the other wagons, leaning on the heavy walking stick he used.

As soon as Finch laid eyes on his old enemy, he threw back his head, howled like a wolf, and bellowed, "I'm gonna choke the life outta him with my bare hands!"

He lunged toward the creek, clearly bent on crossing it and attacking Mahone.

Chapter Twenty-three

Dulcy had seen Nicodemus Finch enough times to recognize him easily. It would have been hard to mistake that bedraggled little banty rooster of a man.

She didn't know the name of the big, dark-haired man who grabbed Finch just as he was about to plunge into the creek. The man held on to Finch and kept him from trying to attack Mahone. That didn't stop Finch from flailing around in front of him with his fists.

"Lemme go!" Finch howled. "I'll murder the swamp-guzzled hoptoad!"

"Take it easy, boss," the dark-haired man advised. "You're not gonna make things any better by actin' this way."

Mahone rested both hands on the head of his walking stick and leaned forward. He called, "Finch! Nicodemus Finch! You're squattin' in my rightful place! You're gonna have to move that ragtag camp of yours!"

Finch stopped waving his arms around and stared at Mahone in apparent astonishment.

"*Your* place?" he repeated. "This here is Finch's Point! It says so right on the map!"

"The hell you say!" Mahone responded. "If it really does say that on a map, it's because you wrote it on there, you boat-burnin' old scalawag!"

Dulcy didn't see how Mahone could justify claiming that the point was his by right. None of this land out here belonged to anybody, except in the most general sense that it was part of the Louisiana Territory and as such part of the United States.

That behavior was typical, though. Anything Finch had, Mahone wanted, and vice versa.

Finch shook his finger at Mahone and said, "You better just turn around and go back where you come from, Black Tom! You ain't welcome here!"

"It's a free country," Mahone responded. "We're here for the rendezvous, and we intend to stay." He swept his right hand toward the wagons. "I've got the finest whiskey and women west of the Mississippi!"

"You got alligator piss and disease-ridden harridans! Any man who drinks your whiskey will get the blind staggers, and any man who consorts with your females will be scratchin' hisself for the rest of his borned days!"

Dulcy frowned. Finch could insult Mahone all day as far as she was concerned, but she didn't care for the accusation the man had just made. She and Sally, Emma, and Poppy were all in good health, other than Poppy's broken arm.

"You're wrong, Mr. Finch!" she called in a clear, ringing voice. "No man has to fear our company."

One of Finch's girls sauntered forward. Her long hair was so pale it was almost white. Dulcy had seen the sun shining on it a few minutes earlier. Tresses that fair were quite visible.

The girl was lovely, too, in a low-cut woolen dress

that hugged her curves. With a smirk on her face, she said, "No man would *want* your company, I'm thinking."

Dulcy's eyes narrowed as she felt an instinctive dislike for this young woman. She snapped, "You'd be wrong about that. Very wrong."

"We'll see, I suppose," the blonde said with that self-satisfied smile still on her face. Dulcy felt an undeniable urge to go over there and slap it off of her.

Mahone said, "Are you gonna get off that land, Finch?"

"Hell, no!" Finch shouted back. "And you can't make me, you dingle-plated foofaraw!"

"You're as big a lunatic as you ever were," Mahone muttered under his breath. Then he raised his voice again and said, "We'll just set up over there on this side of the creek, then."

"You do that! See if it means a diddle-butted damn to me!"

"What you'll see is all the trappers at the rendezvous comin' over here to visit my tents," Mahone said with a sneer.

"That'll be the day," Finch snorted.

Mahone ignored that and turned to face his people. Leaning on the cane with one hand, he waved the other in the air and called, "Unhitch those teams! Get to work settin' up the tents! This'll be our spot, right here."

To tell the truth, it didn't appear to Dulcy to be a bad place to set up. Just like the land on the other side of the creek, there was plenty of graze for the animals and water for all their needs and level ground on which to set up the tents. Anything Finch's company could do over there, Mahone's group could do just as well over here. It was just the sheer stubborn hatred the two men felt for each other that made the location an issue.

Dulcy climbed down from the wagon and went back along the line of vehicles to check on Poppy. The injured girl was riding in the third wagon with Sally to look after her. Dulcy lowered the tailgate and asked, "How are you doing in there?"

"Have we gotten where we're going?" Poppy asked.

Dulcy had rigged a sling to support the broken limb. Poppy was propped up with pillows all around her to cushion her splinted and bandaged arm from the jolts of the trail. Her face was pale and drawn anyway from the discomfort.

"Yes, we're here," Dulcy told her. "We won't be going anywhere else for a while."

"Good. Maybe my arm will be better by the time we move on."

"I hope so."

Dulcy started to turn away, but Poppy stopped her by saying, "You girls are going to need my help. You can't handle all the business you'll have, just the three of you."

Sally said, "We'll be fine. Tom always says it's more important to sell whiskey, anyway."

"Well, if there's anything I can do . . ."

"For now, just rest and try to get better," Dulcy said. "We'll worry about everything else later."

Danny, Humphries, and the other men were unhitching the teams of mules from the wagons. When that chore was finished, they would set up the big tent first, the one that would serve as a tavern. Some of the whiskey barrels would have to be trundled into it. The bar would be planks placed across the tops of those barrels. It was a crude but effective operation.

The trappers who would show up for the rendezvous would only care about the whiskey, not the surroundings in which they drank it.

The soiled doves would live and work in smaller tents near the big one. Those quarters would be spartan in their simplicity. A candle, a small table, a cot . . . that was all they needed.

And all they deserved, Dulcy sometimes thought. At other times, she wished there could be something more, some small touches of home . . .

None of them had homes anymore, though. She knew the other girls' sad stories, although she had never shared hers with them. Since she was somewhat older than them, she supposed they saw her as a mother figure.

That was as close as she would ever come to being a mother again, so she supposed it was better than nothing.

She walked toward the creek again, and on the other side she saw the blonde with whom she had traded words earlier. The young woman stood there regarding her coolly for a moment, then turned and walked away with her back stiff and hostile.

Dulcy wasn't sure why the blonde had taken an immediate dislike to her . . . but whatever the reason, the feeling was mutual.

"Careful, there! Careful!"

Mahone's shout drew her attention. She turned and saw that several of the men had laid wide planks from the ground to the lowered tailgate of one of the wagons. Now they were trundling out a small cannon, one of Mahone's proudest possessions. They rolled it down the planks onto the ground.

"Load her up," Mahone ordered.

The cannon was capable of firing a three-pound ball, but Danny loaded it only with a charge of powder and some wadding. He primed the artillery piece, then looked to Mahone.

"This'll let everybody in the valley know that the rendezvous is on," Mahone said with a satisfied nod. "Fire away!"

Danny gave the lanyard attached to the cannon a sharp jerk. Flint and steel struck sparks and set off the priming charge, which was followed instantly by a huge *boom* as the main charge went off. The sound rolled across the valley and echoed back from the hills and mountains, loud enough to be heard for several miles. The trappers might not know for sure what the signal meant, but they could make a pretty good guess.

Now it was just a matter of time before they began to show up.

Chapter Twenty-four

Breckinridge and Morgan were checking traps when they heard the loud boom in the distance. Both young men lifted their heads at the sound.

"What in the world?" Morgan exclaimed.

"That sounded like a cannon," Breckinridge said. "But who in blazes would be settin' off a cannon out here?"

"You know what I bet it was?" Morgan asked with a grin. "I'll bet that was a signal letting everybody in the valley know that the rendezvous has started."

Breckinridge thought about it and nodded.

"You're probably right," he told his friend. "I sure can't figure out what else it could have been."

"Well, are we going to finish checking these traps, or are we going to the festivities?"

"We're gonna finish checkin' the trapline," Breckinridge answered without hesitation. "There'll be time enough to go to the rendezvous tomorrow."

"Or tonight," Morgan suggested. "I'll bet everything goes on around the clock."

He was probably right about that, thought Breckin-ridge. Morgan was anxious to see those gals again, as soon as possible, and Breck couldn't really blame him for feeling that way.

It might be interesting, too, to see what went on be-tween Nicodemus Finch and Black Tom Mahone.

"Let's get movin'," Breckinridge said. "The sooner we finish checkin' these traps, the sooner we can go see what's happenin' down at Finch's Point."

It was an abbreviated day's work anyway because of the ambush and the battle that morning, so Breckin-ridge decided not to worry too much about how diligent he and Morgan were. They checked several more traps, found only one beaver, and Breck announced, "Hell, let's head back to camp."

Morgan didn't argue.

Since Fulbright had the wound in his arm, Akins had decided that the two of them would remain in camp and work on getting the pelts they had already taken baled up and ready to transport. By the time Breckinridge and Morgan got there, the two older men had the bundles of pelts loaded in the canoes. The creek that ran beside the camp was the same one on which Finch's Point was located, so it wouldn't be difficult to paddle down to the rendezvous site.

"I reckon you fellas heard that cannon go off," Ful-bright greeted them. "Either the rendezvous's fixin' to start, or else we're goin' to war."

"That fellow Powell said this morning sounded like the War of 1812 all over again," Morgan said with a smile. "But I sure hope it's the rendezvous."

"Ready to see those gals you didn't want to tell us about, are you?" Akins asked.

"I won't lie to you, Roscoe . . . they've been on my mind, sure enough."

Breckinridge said, "Let me get this carcass skinned and the pelt staked out, and then we can head on."

That didn't take long. By now Breckinridge was an old hand at removing the pelt from a dead beaver. The sun was still up when the four men climbed into the canoes and pushed off from the bank. The current caught the lightweight craft and carried them downstream, aided by the paddles the men wielded.

When they came in sight of the point, they saw wagons parked on both sides of the creek. Tents had been erected, and lanterns hung from poles, giving the place a festive look. Breckinridge and his friends had the closest camp, so Breck wasn't surprised to see that they appeared to be the first ones to arrive.

"Is that all the same bunch?" Akins called over from the other canoe. "Or are there different outfits on different sides of the creek?"

"Let's find out," Morgan said, although he and Breckinridge already knew the answer to that, having encountered Nicodemus Finch and his party first.

Morgan was sitting in the front of the canoe with Breckinridge, and he angled the craft to the left, toward the point where Finch was set up. If it had been up to Breck, he might have gone to Mahone's group first. He wanted to see Dulcy again.

On the other hand, that fair-haired Annie Belle worked for Finch, and she was certainly worth a man's attention, too.

When you looked at it like that, thought Breckinridge, he couldn't lose either way.

Nicodemus Finch was waiting on the creek bank in the gathering dusk. He waved his arms in the air and called, "Welcome, boys, welcome! Come right on in for the biggest, dang-tootin'est rendezvous there e're was!"

The men got out and splashed ashore, dragging the canoes and their loads of pelts onto the bank with them.

"Any fur traders here yet?" Breckinridge asked.

"Naw, but I reckon they're bound to show up tomorrow. You boys are the first ones here, so you get the best deal! Trade your furs to me and you'll have all the whiskey and women you want for the next three or four days, you can bet your hide on that!"

Finch seemed to be a little more coherent than usual this evening. That didn't last long, however, because Black Tom Mahone came up to the edge of the creek on the other side, cupped a hand around his mouth, and called, "Over here, boys! Better whiskey, better women, better deals for your furs!"

"You hush your tarnal mouth, Tom Mahone!" Finch screeched at him. "These fellas are doin' business with me, and you ain't gonna steal 'em away!"

"Man's got a right to trade with whoever he wants to!" Mahone shouted back.

Akins looked back and forth between the two men and muttered, "These varmints don't like each other very much, do they?"

Morgan asked Breckinridge, "What are we going to do? Should we go ahead and trade our furs with Mr. Finch?"

Quietly, Breckinridge replied, "I think I'd rather wait until the fur company men get here. They're liable to give us a better price than either of these bunches."

Akins said, "You're right. We ought to at least wait and find out what they're offerin'."

"Somebody's gonna have to stand guard over the pelts," Fulbright rumbled. "Why don't I do that, whilst you boys go on and have you some fun?"

"That don't hardly seem fair," Akins objected.

"Yeah, well, with this sore arm of mine, I ain't sure I'm up to too much sportin' just yet. Give me a day or two of recuperatin', and then I'll be rarin' to go. If one of you was to offer to bring me a jug of whiskey, though, I wouldn't argue."

"We can do that," Akins said. "Just don't get so drunk you can't keep an eye on those furs."

"You know me, Roscoe. Whiskey don't muddle me overmuch."

"Just keep it in mind," Akins warned. He turned to Breckinridge and Morgan and went on, "I'll get Amos his jug. You boys go on and suit yourself."

"You don't have to tell me twice," Morgan said with a grin almost big enough to swallow his face. "C'mon, Breck!"

They started toward the tents. Breckinridge cast a glance across the creek, toward the lantern-lit encampment over there, and thought about Dulcy again.

Then he heard a low-voiced exclamation from Morgan, and as he turned his head a sight greeted Breckinridge's eyes that drove any thoughts of other women out of his mind, at least for the time being.

Blond Annie Belle, standing there with the soft light flowing through the thin shift that clung to her body, was enough to make a man forget that any other woman in the world even existed.

Chapter Twenty-five

Breckinridge couldn't seem to make his mouth work. He stood there with his jaw hanging open as he looked at Annie. Morgan was equally dumbfounded.

She seemed amused by their stunned reaction. She smiled as she sauntered toward them and said, "Hello, boys. Remember me?"

There was no way in hell any man could ever forget her, Breckinridge thought. Especially considering the way they had first seen her, poised in all her splendor on that rock, about to dive into the pool . . .

Annie hadn't forgotten that incident, either.

Her smile disappeared as she said, "You know, that time you spied on me."

"We . . . we didn't . . ." Morgan stumbled.

"Don't try to make excuses," Annie snapped. "You know good and well what you did. You can just find somebody else to cuddle up with. I don't want anything to do with either of you."

Morgan looked a little like he was about to cry.

Tall, lanky Francesca came out of one of the tents in time to hear Annie's sharp voice. She was in the same half-dressed state as the blonde. She moved around Annie and linked her right arm with Morgan's left.

"Never you mind, honey," she said. "You just come with me. There's nothing she can do for you that I can't do just as well." She gave Annie a sidelong glance as she led Morgan past her. "Or better."

For a second Breckinridge thought Annie was going to go after the brunette, but she settled for sneering and turning her back.

Francesca looked over her shoulder at Breckinridge and said, "You can wait for me, big fella, or one of the other girls will be glad to see you."

"I'll, uh, think on it," Breckinridge said.

"Tonight's not a night for thinking."

She was right about that, Breckinridge told himself as he watched Francesca take Morgan into the tent she had come out of a couple of minutes earlier.

Unfortunately, he couldn't concentrate on the pleasures that might await him while something else was nagging at his mind. He was a little aggravated, and it wasn't like him to hold his anger inside. He turned away from the tents and looked for Annie.

It wasn't difficult to find her, even in the shadows of night that were gathering. She had walked over to the parked wagons and now stood there with her left hand resting on a wheel as she looked toward the encampment across the creek.

Breckinridge came up behind her and said, "I want to talk to you."

She jumped a little and turned around quickly.

"I told you I don't want anything to do with you," she said.

"Maybe you don't, but you're gonna listen to what I have to say, anyway."

"The hell I will." She started to step around him.

Breckinridge reached out and closed his hand around her upper arm. The flesh was soft and warm in his grip, although there was a hint of strength underneath as she tried to pull away. She wasn't able to do so, of course.

"Damn you," she said. "Let go of me or I'll scream."

"Why should I be worried about that?"

"Because Nicodemus's men will give you a beating and throw you in the creek to cool off—or drown!"

"You really reckon they'll have an easy time of that?" Breckinridge asked her. "I'm not hurtin' you, and I'm not *gonna* hurt you . . . but if you go to yellin' and cause a ruckus, somebody *will* get hurt, and it won't be just me."

She glared up at him for a long moment, then blew out an obviously exasperated breath and told him, "Fine. Say whatever it is you want to say, and then leave me alone."

"All right. What I want to say is . . . I'm not sorry."

Her forehead creased in a surprised frown as she asked, "What are you talking about?"

"Before, Morgan and me apologized to you for lookin' at you down that at the swimmin' hole. But now I'm takin' it back. I ain't sorry I looked at you."

"You've got a funny way of mending fences."

"I'm not tryin' to mend fences. I'm tryin' to tell you the truth as straight out as I can. I'm not sorry I looked at you because you're one of the prettiest gals I've ever seen in my whole life, and if anybody in this world deserves to be looked at and admired, it's you."

Annie was still frowning, but now she was starting to look confused in the faint lantern light.

"You think I'm . . . that pretty?"

"Well, of course I do! You're bound to have seen yourself in a lookin' glass, and I can tell by the way you talk that you ain't a fool. You know you're down-right beautiful, and I reckon there's a good chance men have been starin' at you the way me and Morgan did for a long time."

"Yes," Annie said quietly. "They have."

"So it ain't nothin' new to you, and it ain't anything that should've upset you that much."

Some of the old fire reappeared in her as she said, "You don't have any right to tell me what makes me upset and what doesn't."

"I reckon you're right about that. I think what's really botherin' you is that you wanted that swim to be just you by yourself. You didn't want anybody else around, so maybe you could forget all about where you were and the things you've done. You wanted to feel like there was nobody else in the world except you, even if it was just for a few minutes."

As Breckinridge spoke, a look of amazement began to appear on Annie's face. By the time he finished, she was staring at him.

"How . . . how did you know . . . ?" she whispered.

"I've felt the same way sometimes," he said. "So I'm takin' back my apology for starin' at you when you were up there naked as a jaybird. Any man drawin' breath would've done the same thing. It's just natural. But I *will* say I'm sorry for bustin' up that private time o' yours. We didn't do it on purpose, but I'd just as soon it hadn't happened the way it did."

Another moment of silence stretched out between them. Finally, Annie said, "You know you're still hold-ing my arm, don't you?"

"Oh," Breckinridge said. "I reckon I am."

"You can let go of it now. I promise I won't scream for help."

"All right."

Breckinridge released her arm. He was sort of sad to do so. Holding her like that had felt pretty good.

"What was your name again?" she asked.

"Wallace," he told her. "Breckinridge Wallace."

"Well, you seem to be smarter than I gave you credit for, Breckinridge Wallace. I thought you were just a big, dumb trapper."

Breckinridge grinned as his brawny shoulders rose and fell in a shrug. He said, "I reckon most of the time, that's a pretty good description of me."

"And yet you understood why I was angry probably even better than I did."

"It just seemed to make sense you'd feel that way."

She took a deep breath and asked, "Do you want to come back to my tent with me, Breckinridge?"

Now he really was on the horns of a dilemma. No fella in his right mind would say no to an invitation like that.

But at the same time, he knew that Morgan was smitten with Annie, too. Of course, given her line of work, it didn't really make sense for one fella to be jealous of another, but since he and Morgan were such good friends, he figured that was a possibility.

On the other hand, Morgan had gone off with Francesca . . . but only because Annie had told him she didn't want anything to do with him.

All those thoughts were spinning around and around in Breckinridge's head, and the harder he tried to sort them out, the dizzier they made him. But Annie was looking up expectantly at him, and he knew he was going to have to give her an answer.

In all his life, he had never been so glad to hear a sudden outburst of angry shouting and the ugly sound of fists slamming against flesh and bone.

Chapter Twenty-six

Annie gasped when the commotion broke out, and Breckinridge swung around sharply toward the sounds of battle. It made sense that the trouble was between Finch's men and Mahone's bunch, but Akins was around somewhere and Fulbright was supposed to be watching over the pelts in the canoes, so for all Breck knew, his friends could be in the thick of it.

Annie clutched his arm and asked, "What is that?"

"I aim to find out," Breckinridge said. He shook free of her and broke into a run toward the creek.

As he turned to follow the bank, he spotted several knots of struggling men up ahead. Some whaled away at each other with fists while others wrestled, kicked, and bit. Angry curses filled the air.

Over to one side, Nicodemus Finch hopped up and down and bawled, "Get 'em, boys, get 'em! Frazzled-out thieves skulkin' around tryin' to steal our whiskey!"

Breckinridge didn't understand that. Mahone had brought along plenty of whiskey of his own; several of his wagons were full of it. He didn't have any need to steal Finch's liquor.

On the other hand, Finch couldn't sell whiskey he didn't have, and that would ruin his profits. Considering how Finch had burned the keelboat he and Mahone had owned jointly, stealing Finch's whiskey didn't seem like too underhanded a tactic.

There was just one problem with that, Breckinridge thought as he glanced across the creek.

The uproar had drawn the attention of Mahone and his men, as well as the women who worked for him, and they were all standing near the cannon, watching with interest as the fracas unfolded on the other side of the stream.

If Mahone's men were over there, Breckinridge asked himself, who was that fighting with Finch's men?

As he slowed to a trot, he got his answer. One of the battlers had his hat knocked off, and the light from the lanterns revealed a shock of white hair and a weathered face.

Breckinridge recognized the man called Powell from that morning. The others with him had to be the rest of the bunch that had run off the ambushers at the camp on the bluff.

That meant they were friends as far as Breckinridge was concerned, and he wasn't going to stand by and watch the fight. As he approached, the man trading punches with Powell landed a clean blow to the white-haired man's face and knocked him to the ground. The man drew back his leg in preparation for launching a kick at the fallen Powell.

Breckinridge lunged forward, grabbed the man's shoulder, and hauled him around. Breck recognized the startled countenance. The man was Caleb Moffit, who was almost as tall and brawny as he was.

Moffit was off balance, though, and had to take a stumbling step to the side to catch himself. That allowed Breckinridge to catch hold of the front of Moffit's shirt with his left hand and cock the right to throw a punch.

"Back off," Breckinridge said. "These fellas ain't thieves. They're friends of ours."

"Then maybe you're thieves, too!" Moffit yelled. He twisted, trying to get out of Breckinridge's grasp, and threw a wild, looping left.

Breckinridge ducked his head and let Moffit's fist shoot past him. Then he threw his right, straight and hard into the other man's jaw. The powerful blow rocked Moffit's head back and unhinged his knees. Breck let go of him and allowed him to fall.

There was no time for Breckinridge to feel any satisfaction. The next instant, somebody landed on his back and knocked him forward a couple of steps. An arm went around his neck and closed tight on his throat.

"I got him!" a man yelled triumphantly in his ear. "I got the big bastard!"

Getting Breckinridge Wallace wasn't exactly the same thing as keeping him, though. Breck reached behind his head and caught hold of the man's shirt. He bent forward and heaved, and suddenly the man who had leaped on Breck's back found himself heels over head flying through the air. He let out a frightened wail that was cut short by a huge splash as he landed in the creek.

With that annoyance disposed of, Breckinridge wheeled around in search of another combatant only to receive a hard, knobby-knuckled fist in the face. The man who had hit him started to swing another blow, but Breck blocked it with his forearm. He recognized the man and exclaimed, "Powell, hold on! I'm on your side!"

Powell stopped with his fist drawn back for yet another punch. His eyes widened in surprise.

"Wallace!" he said. "Good Lord! I was just hittin' whoever was in front of me."

"No harm done," Breckinridge said, although he figured there was a good chance his jaw might be a little bruised and sore by the next morning. "Look out behind you!"

Powell twisted around as one of Finch's men lunged at him swinging a broken branch. Breckinridge stepped past Powell and caught the attacker's wrist with his left hand, stopping the makeshift club cold. He smashed a right to the man's face that knocked him down.

"Come on, Wallace!" Powell said. "Back to back!"

That was the way they situated themselves as several more of Finch's men came at them. With their backs protected that way, they were able to lash out freely at their assailants. Fists smacked into faces and dug deep into bellies. The attackers began to pile up around Breckinridge and Powell.

Pretty soon there was no one left to come at them. The two of them were the only ones left on their feet. Finch's men and Powell's companions were all sprawled around, moaning and struggling to get up.

Powell grunted and said, "Looks like that's the end of the fight."

"Unless Mr. Finch wants to get in on it himself," Breckinridge said, glaring at the goat-bearded man.

Finch had stopped yelling and jumping up and down as it became obvious that his men were going to lose this fight. Now he scowled at Breckinridge and said, "Lemme go get my blunderbuss, and I'll blow holes in the lot of you!"

"Take it easy, old-timer," Breckinridge advised him. "This ruckus is over."

"Over! Not as long as these whiskey thieves are tryin' to ruin me!" Finch pointed a shaking finger at Powell. "Mahone put you up to this, didn't he? You're workin' for Black Tom!"

"I don't know anybody named Mahone, and my friends and I ain't whiskey thieves, you crazy old coot," Powell snapped. "We just came for the damn rendezvous!"

Finch stared at him in apparent disbelief and said, "But I seen you sneakin' around my whiskey barrels—"

"We weren't sneaking, just leadin' our horses into your camp," Powell insisted. "Then you started yellin' like a crazy man and jumpin' up and down."

That explained what had started the fight, thought Breckinridge. The excitable Nicodemus Finch had allowed his suspicions of his old rival Mahone to run away with themselves, to the point that he saw enemies everywhere, even in the most innocent circumstances.

Breckinridge and Morgan had seen proof of that for themselves a few days earlier when Finch had threatened them and accused them of working for Black Tom Mahone as soon as he laid eyes on them for the first time.

Of course, those circumstances hadn't been entirely innocent, Breckinridge reminded himself, since the two of them had been staring at Annie's unclad beauty . . .

"Listen, Mr. Finch," Breckinridge said, "I can vouch for these fellas. They're not thieves or troublemakers. In fact, just this mornin' they helped me and my friends fight off some varmints who were tryin' to kill us and steal our pelts. They're lookin' to get into the fur tradin' business themselves." Breck looked over at Powell. "I thought there were more of you than this, though."

"There are," the white-haired man replied. "The Colonel sent me and a few of the boys on ahead to scout out the rendezvous. We didn't know exactly where it was bein' held." He grunted. "Now we know. I'm not sure we're welcome, though."

On the stream's other bank, Mahone was close enough to hear what Powell was saying. He called, "That's because you went to the wrong side of the creek, stranger! Come on over here, and you'll be more than welcome, by God! We got the best whiskey and the prettiest gals west of St. Louis, too."

Finch yelled, "That's a plain damn lie, you shingle-tongued dockwalloper! My whiskey's better, and there ain't no prettier gals than mine even *in* St. Looey! You and your pards just stay here, mister, and I'll sure set this misunderstandin' right. I'll make it up to you, I swear—"

"Settle down, old-timer," Powell said, sounding a little amused now. "I reckon there'll be enough business to go around, especially when the Colonel and the rest of the fellas get here tomorrow. I'll send a rider tomorrow to show them the way." He turned to Breckinridge. "Wallace, give me a hand gettin' these boys back on their feet?"

"Sure," Breckinridge said. He glanced around and didn't see Annie. He supposed she had given up on him after he ran off like that to plunge into the middle of the fracas.

That was all right. He could use more time to figure out just what he was going to do about her and Dulcy and the way he felt about both of them . . .

Chapter Twenty-seven

Once Breckinridge and Powell had finished helping Powell's groggy friends stand up, the white-haired man said, "Buy you a drink, Wallace? I reckon it's the least I can do after you pitched in to help like that."

Since Breckinridge had no money and really no assets other than his share of the pelts that hadn't been traded yet, he didn't think it would hurt to take Powell up on the offer. He said, "Sure. I'm much obliged."

"Over here, or on the other side of the creek?"

"Here's fine," Breckinridge said. He didn't figure there was actually much difference in the whiskey offered by Finch and Mahone. All the fiery stuff was pretty much alike.

They went over to Finch, and Powell said, "Get us a jug, old-timer."

"I'll sure do it!" Finch declared. "And to show you I meant what I said about makin' it up to you for that ruckus, you can have it for . . . let's say . . . half the reg'lar price."

"That's generous of you," Powell said dryly. Like Breckinridge, he probably knew that Finch would be overcharging the trappers during the rendezvous, so half of that was actually a pretty reasonable price.

Like Mahone's men on the other side of the creek, Finch's men had set up a large tent to serve as a makeshift tavern. Inside were rough-hewn tables and benches, and planks laid over whiskey barrels formed a crude bar. The strawberry-blond dove named Siobhan stood behind that bar talking to Akins, who seemed rather entranced by her.

He looked around when Finch led Breckinridge and Powell into the place. A surprised look appeared on his face as he recognized Powell.

"Howdy," Akins said. "Didn't expect to see you again so soon, friend."

"We keep runnin' into each other, all right," Powell said. He shook hands with Akins. "This frontier seems to be a smaller place than a fella might think."

Breckinridge had already noticed the same thing in the time he'd been out here. Despite the vast, empty spaces, news of what was going on traveled around fairly fast, and you might encounter the same man more often you'd expect.

"Girl, give these fellas a jug," Finch told Siobhan.

She frowned and asked, "You mean don't charge them for it, Nicodemus?"

"No, that ain't what I—" Finch began hotly. He brought his instinctive response under control and went on, "We're only chargin' 'em half-price for it."

"Oh. All right." She turned and picked up an earthenware jug from the ground where it sat with a number of its fellows. Powell slapped a gold piece on the bar, and Siobhan handed him the jug.

Powell inclined his head toward one of the tables and suggested, "Let's sit down."

Akins came with them. As the three men sat down, he asked, "Did you two just run into each other outside?"

Breckinridge frowned at him and asked, "Didn't you hear the commotion a little while ago?"

"Commotion?" Akins shook his head. "What commotion?"

"Finch took Powell and his friends for whiskey thieves and set his men on 'em," Breckinridge explained. "There was a big fight over by the creek."

Akins shook his head again and said, "No, I, uh, I was talkin' to Miss Siobhan, and I reckon I didn't notice."

Breckinridge looked at his friend for a moment and then laughed.

"So you're so smitten by that gal you weren't payin' attention to anything else that was goin' on," he said.

Akins looked annoyed and even a little embarrassed. He was older, stolid in his demeanor, and not the sort to have romantic feelings for a soiled dove. But sometimes things like that could sneak up on a man and take him by surprise.

"When I was in here earlier gettin' that jug for Amos, we got to talkin'," he said. "She seems mighty nice, and I, uh, I think she likes me a little, too."

Making men think that she was nice and that she liked them was sort of a whore's stock-in-trade, thought Breckinridge, but he didn't see any point in saying that to Akins.

Instead he said, "Well, I'm glad you're havin' a good time so far, Roscoe. We've worked mighty hard since we've been out here. We deserve to enjoy ourselves a mite."

"Speakin' of that . . . where's Morgan?"

"He went off with that tall girl, Francesca."

Akins grinned and said, "Sometimes those wiry ones can twist a man around so he don't know which way he's headed."

They sat there with Powell for a while, passing the jug around and making small talk. When Powell's friends came in, Finch greeted them effusively. He didn't make the same offer to let them have a jug for half-price, though, Breckinridge noted.

A while later, Morgan pushed aside the canvas flaps over the tent's entrance and walked in. He spotted Breckinridge and Akins at the table with Powell and came over to join them.

Morgan looked just as surprised to see Powell as Akins had. He gave the white-haired man a friendly nod as he sat down.

"I knew you were coming to the rendezvous," he said, "but I didn't expect to see you here tonight."

"A few of the boys and I came on ahead of the Colonel and the rest of the bunch," Powell explained again. "They'll be here tomorrow." He pushed the jug across the table. "Here, have a drink."

"Thanks. Don't mind if I do." Morgan picked up the jug and took a long swallow. As he lowered it, he went on, "Ah. I needed a restorative."

"That Francesca wore you out, did she?" Breckinridge asked with a grin.

"You'd be surprised how strong and, uh, active a slender girl like that can be," Morgan said with a bit of a sheepish look on his face. He took another pull on the jug. "What happened with you and Annie, Breck? The last time I saw the two of you, she didn't seem all that friendly."

"We sort of hashed things out between us," Breckinridge said.

"If that's what you want to call it," Morgan said, grinning.

"No, no, that's not what I mean," Breckinridge said, although it was true that he might have wound up going back to Annie's tent with her if things had worked out differently. "We were just talkin', and then there was this big fight that broke out . . ."

Morgan frowned and asked, "What big fight? I didn't hear anything."

"That's because you were too busy with Francesca," Akins said. He didn't mention the fact that he'd been unaware of the ruckus, too, because he'd been mooning over Siobhan.

With four of them sharing the jug now, it didn't take long for them to empty it. Powell offered to buy another, but Breckinridge shook his head.

"We'd best get back to our pelts," he said.

"You really think anybody would bother them?" Powell asked.

"Probably not. We left our pard Amos Fulbright there to keep an eye on 'em anyway. He's the fella who got drilled in the arm durin' the fight this mornin', so he didn't feel like doin' any sportin'."

Powell nodded and said, "I remember. You fellas plan to be around for the whole rendezvous?"

"I will be," Morgan declared. "This is my first one. I don't want to miss out on anything."

"I reckon we all will be," Breckinridge said.

"Then I'm sure I'll see you again."

"You can count on that."

As Breckinridge, Morgan, and Akins got up and headed for the tent's entrance, none of them looked back. So they didn't see the slow nod or the smile that spread across Powell's rugged face.

The white-haired man was counting on seeing them again, all right . . . especially Breckinridge Wallace.

Chapter Twenty-eight

Fulbright was mildly, pleasantly drunk when they got back to the pelts. He insisted that no one had bothered them, and a quick check on them showed that he was right.

Breckinridge and his friends had brought their bedrolls with them from their camp, so they were able to spread them on the grassy bank beside the spot where they had pulled the canoes out of the water.

With so many people around it seemed unnecessary to post a guard, but they had gotten into the habit of doing so and agreed to continue. Breckinridge, Morgan, and Akins split the rest of the night into shifts, since Fulbright had already spent some time watching over the furs. Breck took the first watch, declaring that he wasn't really very sleepy yet, anyway.

The other three men rolled up in their blankets and were soon snoring peacefully. Breckinridge sat down on a log with his rifle across his knees and tried not to think about Annie and Dulcy.

That effort was doomed to failure. It would have

been difficult for any man to banish two such lovely, intriguing women from his thoughts, under any circumstances.

It was downright impossible when Dulcy came strolling up out of the darkness and said quietly, "Hello, Breckinridge."

She wasn't exactly sneaky, just so graceful that she didn't make much noise when she moved around. Hastily, Breckinridge got to his feet when he realized she was there.

"Miss Dulcy," he said, trying to keep his normal bull's bellow of a voice toned down so he wouldn't disturb his sleeping companions. "What in the world are you doin' over here on this side of the creek?"

"You won't tell Nicodemus that I'm trespassing, will you?" she asked with a slight smile.

"No, and anyway, he don't have any right to tell people where they can and can't go. He can call this Finch's Point all he wants, but it don't really mean anything. This is still a free country, after all."

"You'd never know that if you spent much time around Tom and his old enemy. They seem to believe that the whole world is their own private battleground."

"No offense, but those two seem a mite touched in the head when it comes to each other."

Dulcy gave a soft laugh and said, "You're right about that. I don't think they'll ever make peace. They're just not capable of it. Those old grudges they're nursing are too strong."

Breckinridge swept a hand toward the log and invited, "Why don't you sit down? It's not very comfortable—"

"And it's also not the first log I've ever sat on," Dulcy said as she lowered herself onto the log and smoothed her long skirt down. Breckinridge sat beside her, not crowding her, just comfortably close.

"How'd you get across the creek?" he asked. "You didn't wade, did you? Your dress don't look wet."

"No, there are some rocks a little ways downstream that I was able to use as stepping-stones," she explained. "I noticed them earlier when I was looking around, before the sun went down, and when I saw you sitting over here by yourself, I decided I'd see if I could get across on them."

"You came over here just to talk to me?"

"There's nothing wrong with that, is there?"

"No, ma'am," Breckinridge told her. "Nothing wrong at all."

"You don't have to call me 'ma'am,' you know. I'm not old enough to be your mother. An older sister, maybe, or a young aunt."

The feelings Breckinridge was having toward her at the moment were nothing like what a fella would feel for a sister or an aunt, but Breck didn't see what purpose it would serve to mention that. Instead he said, "I suppose I should just call you Miss Dulcy, then."

"Just Dulcy," she said. "That'll be fine."

"All right . . . Dulcy. You won't get in any trouble with Mahone for bein' over here, will you?"

"Tom doesn't have any say in where I go or what I do when I'm not working for him. Since it appears that the rendezvous won't really get into full swing until tomorrow, it doesn't really matter where I am tonight."

Breckinridge would have just as soon she hadn't brought up the fact that she worked for Tom Mahone as a soiled dove. Just sitting here and talking like they were, it would have been easy to forget about that fact.

As if she sensed that maybe she shouldn't have mentioned it, Dulcy went on quickly, "Tell me about yourself, Breckinridge Wallace."

"Not much to tell," he said. "I'm just a big dumb galoot from the mountains of Tennessee."

"Big, no doubt about that, but you're hardly a dumb galoot."

"I ain't so sure about that. You've heard the way I talk. I never cared much for schoolin'. Our pa had me and my brothers out workin' as soon as we could stand up behind a plow, and when I wasn't doin' chores I was off roamin' around the woods." Breckinridge chuckled. "Sometimes when I was *supposed* to be doin' chores, I was off in the woods. My folks had their hands full with me, that's for sure."

"And none of that means you're dumb," Dulcy insisted. "Do you think I'm smart?"

"Well, you sure *sound* like a smart woman," Breckinridge said.

"But I'm sure you know a lot more about surviving in the wilderness than I do. And what's more important out here?"

"Well, I reckon you're right about that."

She laughed, and the sound had a slightly bitter edge to it.

"Besides, if I was all that smart, would I be doing what I'm doing?" she asked, then quickly added, "I'm sorry, I didn't mean to bring that up again—"

"It's all right," Breckinridge said. "Lots of things happen in folks' lives, and you can't help but wish that some of 'em had been different. But when you get right down to it, we are who we are because of all the things we've gone through, so you have to ask yourself . . . if there's anything good about your life, would it have been that way without all the trails you followed to get there?"

She looked at him without speaking for a long moment, then whispered, "You're definitely not a dumb galoot, Breckinridge Wallace."

With the way she was looking at him and the softness in her voice, it was just natural that he'd lean down and kiss her.

She responded without hesitation, reaching up to loop one arm around the back of his neck while she rested the other hand on his broad, buckskin-covered chest. Her mouth was warm and tasted sweet.

Breckinridge could have sat there kissing her like that for a long time . . . if they hadn't been interrupted.

"What the hell!"

Breckinridge's head jerked up and around at the startled exclamation. Between the moonlight and the glow from the lanterns still burning around the camp, he had no trouble seeing Annie standing several yards behind the log where he and Dulcy sat. He had been so wrapped up in kissing Dulcy that he hadn't even heard the blonde approaching.

Breckinridge stood up, and so did Dulcy. As they turned toward Annie, she strode forward and demanded harshly, "What are you doing on this side of the creek?"

"I go where I please," Dulcy replied coolly.

"Well, you're not supposed to be over here. Get back over there where you belong."

"I don't take orders from you."

"No, I guess not," Annie said with a sneer. "You belong to Black Tom Mahone, don't you?"

Dulcy's hands clenched into fists at her side. She said, "No more than you belong to Nicodemus Finch."

Annie ignored that. She snapped, "It didn't take you long to come over here and try to steal away our customers, did it?"

"Now, hold on," Breckinridge said. "Dulcy and me were just talkin'. There wasn't any stealin' away goin' on."

"Talking," Annie repeated scornfully. "From what I saw, neither of you were doing any talking. You were too busy doing other things with your mouths. I'm sure this slut can do plenty of other things with hers, too."

"That's enough," Dulcy said. She started to step forward.

Breckinridge put a hand on her shoulder to stop her.

"There's already been enough trouble tonight," he said. "No need for any more."

Dulcy turned her head to look up at him. She said, "Are you defending that . . . that blond harlot?"

"I'm not defendin' anybody," he told her. "I just don't want there to be another ruckus."

"Fine," Dulcy said with a definite chill in her voice now. "If I'm not wanted on this side of the creek, I'll just go back to the other side."

"Nobody said you're not wanted—"

"Tell us about that, Breckinridge," Annie cut in. "Do *you* want this woman over here?"

"I . . . I . . . hell!" Breckinridge didn't have the slightest idea what was the right thing to say or do in a situation such as this. Most of the problems he'd run into during his life, he could shoot or punch or wallop with a tomahawk. None of those things would do the least bit of good here.

Dulcy turned and started to stalk along the creek

bank. Her back was stiff and angry. She didn't even say good night.

"That's right," Annie taunted. "Scurry back to your hole like the vermin you are."

Dulcy stopped like she'd been slapped across the face.

"Damn it!" Breckinridge burst out, getting angry himself now no matter how pretty Annie was. "There's no call for talk like that—"

"It's all right, Breckinridge," Dulcy said. "I wouldn't expect anything else from a little tramp like her."

She started walking again. Annie glared murderously at her for a second, then suddenly lunged toward her. Breckinridge didn't realize what was about to happen until it was too late. He made a grab for Annie, but she was too fast, slipping past his outstretched fingers like a blond phantom.

The next second, she crashed into Dulcy, tackling her and driving her off the edge of the bank. Both women fell into the creek with a huge splash.

Chapter Twenty-nine

"Son of a *bitch*!" Breckinridge roared, no longer thinking about whether he was going to wake up his sleeping friends.

Dulcy and Annie had both gone under the surface, and he stood there on the bank waiting anxiously for them to come up again. He didn't think it was likely that either woman would drown since the creek was only two or three feet deep, but he supposed it was possible if they'd hit their heads and knocked themselves out . . .

Breckinridge was about to charge into the creek after them when they broke the surface, spitting and sputtering and choking.

That didn't stop them from fighting. They grabbed at each other's hair and tried to claw each other in the face. As they struggled, they lurched back and forth in the creek, spraying water all around them.

Breckinridge's shout had roused Morgan, Akins, and Fulbright from slumber. The three men threw their blankets aside and leaped to their feet. Morgan and Akins clutched their rifles, which they had snatched from the ground next to their bedrolls. They yelled questions and looked around frantically, trying to discover the source of the threat—if there was one.

The two battling women weren't any danger to anyone but themselves, however. Dulcy stopped trying to pull Annie's hair and scratch her eyes out. Instead, she doubled a fist and shot a short, straight, hard right to the blonde's jaw. That took Annie by surprise and knocked her back a step.

Dulcy lowered her head and tackled Annie around the waist, driving her backward off her feet. Once again both women sprawled in the water with a big splash. Dulcy came up a second later, but Annie didn't.

That was because Dulcy had her arms wrapped around Annie's neck and was holding her under the water.

By now the shouting had roused the camps on both sides of the creek. Nicodemus Finch, Tom Mahone, and the men who worked for them all started from opposite directions toward the site of the battle to see what was going on. Some of the soiled doves trailed them.

"Good Lord, Breck!" Morgan exclaimed. "She's trying to drown Annie!"

That was what it looked like, all right. Apparently Dulcy intended to hold Annie under the water until the blonde was dead.

Breckinridge didn't think Dulcy was really a killer. She was just caught up in the heat of the moment. So to save her from her own actions as much as anything, Breck plunged into the creek, kicking up water as he stomped toward the two women.

Before he could get there, Annie's hand shot up out of the water, closed around some of Dulcy's dripping hair, and pulled hard. Dulcy cried out and had to let go to keep Annie from ripping out a big chunk of dark hair.

Annie grabbed Dulcy's dress with her other hand and pulled her under, trading places with her. Annie gasped desperately for air once her head was above the surface again.

By now Breckinridge had reached the women. He got his hands under Annie's arms from behind and lifted her out of the water. She yelled and kicked, but she was no match for his great strength. Two long strides brought Breck to the bank, where he dumped Annie unceremoniously on the grass.

He turned back toward the middle of the stream. Dulcy came up coughing and gagging and spitting creek water. She floundered, obviously disoriented, and Breckinridge caught hold of the back of her collar to haul her out of the water.

She twisted in his grip and flailed at him. Her fists struck his chest and shoulders without much effect. Whether she thought Annie had hold of her and was striking out at her, or whether she meant to hit him, Breckinridge didn't know, and he figured it didn't matter. She could even be lashing out blindly, not knowing who was on the receiving end of those blows.

He let go of her collar, took hold of her upper arms, and lifted her. She tried to kick him. He said, "Dulcy! Dulcy, settle down! It's me, Breckinridge."

She stopped fighting and gaped at him. Her hair was plastered to her head except for several strands that hung limply over her face. She was still breathing hard. After a moment she said, "B-Breckinridge . . . ?"

He lowered her so that her feet were on the bottom of the creek bed again. He let go of her, but only for a second, just long enough for him to bend a little and scoop her up in his arms, one arm behind her knees, the other around her shoulders. Carrying her as if she weighed no more than a child, Breckinridge turned and waded toward the bank.

"Wait a minute!" Mahone yelled from the other side of the creek. "You bring her over here! This is where she belongs!"

Nicodemus Finch was waiting on the bank. He shook a fist at Breckinridge and bellowed, "Don't you bring that Mahone spy over here!"

Breckinridge ignored both of the feuding old-timers. With Dulcy cradled in his arms, he stepped up onto the bank. A few feet away, Annie had sat up and was coughing and shivering. At this elevation the nights were cool, even in the summer, and that was doubly true when somebody was soaked to the skin.

"Morgan, we need some blankets," Breckinridge said.

Like most of the others, Morgan was staring at the aftermath of the battle. Breckinridge's words broke through to him. He nodded and said, "Sure, Breck," then hurried to fetch a couple of blankets from their bedrolls.

Breckinridge lowered Dulcy to the log where they had been sitting a few minutes earlier. When Morgan came up with the blankets, Breck took one of them and draped it around Dulcy's shoulders.

"Wrap up Annie with the other one," he told his friend. "These gals need to warm up."

He sat down next to Dulcy and pulled the blanket tighter around her. What she really needed to do was get out of those wet clothes, but he didn't see how they were going to accomplish that with all these people standing around.

He told Akins, "Roscoe, see if you can build a fire. We need to get some heat goin'."

"Sure." Akins nodded. He hurried off to search for some firewood.

Meanwhile, Morgan knelt next to Annie and wrapped her in the other blanket. Through chattering teeth, she said, "Th-th-thanks."

Finch stalked over to glare at Breckinridge and Dulcy and began, "Now, see here—"

"Stop right there," Breckinridge snapped. "I ain't in the mood for it, Finch, and before you start tryin' to throw your weight around, you'd best remember this ain't your land. Everybody else has got just as much right to be on it as you do. All this stuff about your side of the creek and Mahone's side of the creek is a bunch of damn bull."

Finch's mouth opened and closed like a fish. When he could form words again, he said, "You can't talk to me like that!"

"I just did, you addle-pated musharoo."

Normally, Breckinridge wouldn't talk like that to one of his elders, but tonight's events had pushed his patience to the breaking point.

On the other side of the creek, Mahone leaned on his walking stick and cackled with laughter at the way Breckinridge had turned one of Finch's nonsensical insults around on him.

Mahone's reaction irritated Breckinridge, as well. He drew Dulcy against him and tried to put everything else out of his mind.

"It'll be all right," he told her as she shivered in

the crook of his arm. "We'll get you dried off and warmed up."

"I . . . I could have t-taken her," Dulcy said. "I was going to d-d-drown her."

"I know. I didn't figure you'd want to live with that on your conscience, though. That's why I waded in to stop you."

Actually, Breckinridge hadn't had to stop Dulcy from drowning Annie. The blonde had already fought her way free by the time Breck got there. His main goal then had been to break up the fight as quickly and efficiently as possible before one of the women was badly injured.

A few yards away, Morgan sat on the ground with his arms around Annie. She lifted her head from his shoulder where she had been resting it and told Dulcy, "You couldn't b-beat me on your b-best day, you—"

"Hush now," Morgan told her. "Let's don't go starting the whole thing over again."

Roscoe Akins bustled up with an armload of firewood. He got down to work with it and soon had a nice blaze going in front of the log. Breckinridge and Dulcy stayed where they were, while Morgan helped Annie up and led her over to sit down on the other side of the fire. The women let the blankets fall open so the heat from the flames could reach their wet clothing. They stopped shivering as the fire warmed them.

Finch worked up his courage and came over to them again. He said, "I ain't sure you and your bunch are welcome here anymore, Wallace."

"That's fine with me," Breckinridge said. "We'll just go across the creek, and once the fur company men show up and buy our pelts, we'll spend our money over there."

"Now, hold on, hold on! There ain't no need to be hasty."

"Then why'd you come over and try to run us off?"

"I started to say, you ain't welcome here as long as you're talkin' ugly to me. Promise you'll keep a civil tongue in your head, and you can stay."

"And you can go to hell," Breckinridge said. "I'll stay or go, whichever I please, and it'll be my decision, not yours."

Finch glared at him some more but didn't say anything else. After a few seconds the scrawny old-timer turned and stomped off again.

A few more minutes went by as the women basked in the heat from the fire, then Dulcy said, "Breckinridge, I think I'd like to go on back to my tent. I'm still damp, but I'm not freezing now."

"Sure, I'll take you." He stood up, and when Dulcy started to get to her feet, as well, and remove the blanket, he went on, "No, you keep that wrapped around you."

As he had done before, he scooped her up in his arms and cradled her against his chest. As he walked toward the creek, obviously intending to wade across it and take Dulcy to her tent, Morgan called after him, "Breck, are you coming back tonight?"

Breckinridge looked down into Dulcy's face, saw that she wasn't angry with him anymore, and said, "I reckon not."

Chapter Thirty

At the edge of the crowd that had gathered on Finch's Point to see what all the commotion was about, Powell stood and watched with great interest as Breckinridge Wallace crossed the creek with the dark-haired whore in his arms.

All evening, Powell had been waiting for a chance to catch Wallace alone, with none of his friends around to help him.

Now it looked like luck—and a couple of battling soiled doves—might have given him that chance.

Otto Ducharme and the rest of the hardcases the vengeful German had hired back in St. Louis would be here by the middle of the day tomorrow, and they could take Wallace anytime they wanted to.

How much better would it be, though, if Powell was able to place Wallace in Ducharme's hands before then, so that Ducharme could take his revenge without having to worry about Wallace's friends or any of the other men who were going to show up for the rendezvous?

If there was any bonus to be paid for this job, Powell wanted to make sure *he* was the one who collected it.

With that thought in his mind, he faded back away from the creek and the crowd, although he stayed close enough to watch as Wallace walked out of the stream carrying that lovely dark-haired burden. Powell took note of which tent Wallace and the whore went to. Once the two of them had disappeared inside the canvas structure, Powell went in search of the men he had brought with him.

There were four of them: Bristow, Harkins, Edgeworth, and Snell. Cutthroats, all of them. Tonight they would have to suppress their tendency to murder, though, since Ducharme had insisted that the object of his hatred be taken alive.

Each of the four men had taken quite a bit of punishment during the fight with Finch's men earlier. They were sitting under some trees near where the horses were picketed, passing around a jug and commiserating with each other over their bruises. They barely looked up to acknowledge Powell's arrival when he strode up to them.

"Didn't you fellas hear that ruckus a few minutes ago?" Powell asked.

"Yeah, and we figured it didn't have anything to do with us," Edgeworth answered in a surly voice.

"Well, you were wrong about that," Powell snapped. "Wallace was right in the middle of it."

Bristow said worriedly, "Nothing happened to him, did it? If that bastard was to get himself killed, Ducharme probably wouldn't pay us the rest of what he owes us."

Powell frowned. He hadn't thought about that. Bristow was right. If Ducharme was disappointed in his quest for vengeance, he'd probably take it out on the men he'd hired. So it was in their best interest to keep Wallace alive . . . until Ducharme could kill the big redheaded bastard himself.

"Wallace is fine, but we've got a chance to grab him tonight. He went across the creek with one of the whores who works for that fella Mahone. His friends stayed on *this* side. So if we're quiet enough about it, we can take him prisoner and get him out of here without anyone knowing."

"If he's staying with one of the whores, she'd know," Harkins pointed out.

Powell thought about that for a few seconds and then nodded slowly.

"What we'll need to do is kill her," he decided. "One of us can strangle her, and then when Wallace disappears, it'll look like *he* killed her and ran off so he wouldn't have to answer for it."

The other four men considered that plan, then nodded and muttered their agreement. The potential death of a soiled dove meant less than nothing to them. It was convenient, that was all that mattered.

"When are we gonna do this?" Bristow asked.

"We'll wait until it's closer to morning. Give both camps plenty of time to settle down and go to sleep. That'll give Wallace a chance to wear himself out with the whore, too." An ugly grin stretched across Powell's rugged face. "I hope he enjoys it, since it'll be his last time on this earth."

Cots weren't really made to support Breckinridge's weight, but several blankets spread on the grassy earth were plenty comfortable for him and Dulcy. She got out of her still-damp clothes and so did Breck, and by the time she sighed in contentment and snuggled against him as he wrapped the blankets around them, they were pleasantly warm and sleepy. Their lovemaking had been very satisfying for both of them.

He fell into a deep, dreamless slumber almost right away, and he had no idea how long he had been asleep when something roused him. He had always been a light sleeper, and he didn't know if he had heard something or if it was just instinct that had awakened him.

But he was instantly alert as soon as his eyes opened. He lay there in pitch darkness and let his senses do their work as they searched for any sign of potential danger.

He didn't hear anything except the soft, regular pattern of Dulcy's breathing as she slept in his arms, nor did he smell anything except the scent of her hair as she pillowed her head on his chest.

She was sleeping so peacefully that he didn't want to disturb her, but if trouble was lurking around, there was a good chance her slumber was going to be interrupted anyway. Breckinridge began sliding out from under her as gently and carefully as he could.

The movement caused her to murmur in her sleep. Because of that, Breckinridge almost missed the slight sound of the canvas being brushed aside as somebody came into the tent. It wasn't pitch-black in here after all, he realized. Enough light from the moon and stars came in for him to make out a looming shape just inside the entrance.

Instead of trying to slide out from under Dulcy, he tightened his left arm around her now. At the same time, his right hand shot out and closed around the butt of the pistol he had placed beside the bedroll.

He shifted his weight and threw himself to the left as he kicked off the blanket. Only half awake and startled by the sudden movement, Dulcy cried out. Breckinridge rolled on top of her, shielding her body with his own.

He brought his right foot sweeping up and around in a kick that impacted hard against the intruder. The man let out a pained grunt and doubled over. An unfamiliar voice rasped, "He's awake! Get him!"

That told Breckinridge more than one man was stealing into the tent. He was pretty damn sure they didn't mean him any good, either.

He looped his thumb around the pistol's hammer and pulled it back as he raised the weapon. When he squeezed the trigger, the *boom* as the charge of powder exploded was deafening. Flame spurted from the muzzle, lighting up the inside of the tent for an instant.

In that instant, Breckinridge saw a man thrown backward as the ball slammed into his body. He got tangled up with two more men in the tent's entrance. Another man lay crumpled to one side, laid low by the kick Breck had landed in his belly.

Cursing, the two men flung aside the one who had been shot and charged into the tent. The muzzle flash had faded, and Breckinridge could see them now only as vague shapes.

"Stay down," he told Dulcy. He started to surge to his feet, but something crashed into his back. The intruders had clubs that they swung with brutal strength, hammering Breckinridge to the ground.

So far he'd been lucky and none of the blows had landed on his head. If they had, he probably would have been knocked out, and then there wouldn't be anything he could do to stop the men from carrying out whatever plan they had. If they kept whaling away at him like that, though, they were bound to connect with such a blow sooner or later.

Breckinridge's hands shot out in the darkness. He closed them around a pair of ankles and heaved. A man cried out in surprise and alarm as his legs went out from under him. Breck heard the heavy thud as the man crashed down on his back.

Something brushed his shoulder and arm as it fell. The man he had just upended had dropped his club. Breckinridge grabbed it and came up swinging blindly. He hit something, and then suddenly he was tangled in the canvas side of the tent. He staggered back and forth, trying to free himself, but succeeded only in wrapping more of the flapping stuff around him as he dragged the tent loose from its moorings.

Men shouted somewhere nearby, more than likely Mahone's men reacting to the shot Breckinridge had fired. Breck heard a man's pained voice gasp, "Let's get out of here!" Booted feet slapped against the ground as the intruders retreated.

Dulcy cried, "Breckinridge!" as he finally got hold of the canvas and ripped it away from his face. He threw the demolished tent aside and looked around, his eyes adjusting to the moonlight. He saw Dulcy with a blanket wrapped around her. She rushed to him and clutched at his arm as she asked, "Are you all right?"

"I'm fine," he told her. "How about you?"

"I'm all right, too," she said, causing a wave of relief to go through him.

He looked down at his hand and saw that he was holding a section of thick tree branch. He checked the ground nearby, ready to swat any of the attackers who'd been left behind.

He didn't see anybody, though, and realized that the men had taken their wounded with them.

More men approached, one of them carrying a lantern. As its yellow glare washed over him, Breckinridge became aware that he was standing there stark naked, holding a club in one hand like some sort of primitive savage. He tossed the club aside and picked up another blanket to wrap hastily around his waist.

"What the blue blazes is goin' on here?" Mahone demanded. It was one of his men who held the lantern aloft. Others clustered behind him, some of them holding rifles.

"Somebody snuck into Dulcy's tent and jumped us," Breckinridge explained.

"Finch's men! He sent them over here, damn his eyes!"

"Maybe," Breckinridge allowed, "but I heard a couple of 'em talkin', and they didn't sound like any of the fellas I know work for Finch."

"Who else could it have been?" Mahone demanded.

Breckinridge could only shake his head. He didn't have an answer for Mahone's question.

Somebody shouted from across the creek, "What's all the commotion over there? Breck, are you all right?"

Breckinridge recognized Morgan Baxter's voice. He called back, "Yeah, I'm fine, Morgan. Just a little ruckus. Nobody hurt."

Except one of the intruders, he thought. He was sure his shot had winged one of them.

Come morning, he was going to have to have a look around and see if he could spot any sign of an injury like that.

In the meantime, he said, "Reckon some of you fellas could help me put this tent up again? It's still a while until dawn. Might get some more sleep."

And as fetching as Dulcy looked with the blanket wrapped around her like that, they might do a little more than just sleep, too, he thought.

Chapter Thirty-one

Powell and the other men departed from Finch's camp very early that morning, well before dawn. Powell wanted to get away from there while most of the people around were still asleep. They might get too curious if they saw the bloody bandage tied around Bristow's shoulder.

Bristow wasn't the only one who'd been injured during the fight with Breckinridge Wallace. Edgeworth had been spitting up blood and complaining that the kick Wallace had landed in his belly had busted something inside him.

That was certainly possible, Powell thought. Wallace had torn into them like a wildcat. Powell had hung back and let the other four men go first and run the most risks, and he was glad he had, otherwise Wallace might have injured him, too.

It was too bad Otto Ducharme wanted to take his revenge on Wallace personally. Wanted to look Wallace in the eye in the instant before the big man died. Otherwise it sure would have been easier to ambush Wallace and kill him that way.

Ducharme was paying well enough to make some risks acceptable, though.

Powell and the others saddled their horses in the dark and led the animals a good distance away from the camp before mounting and riding off. Their early, stealthy departure might puzzle some people, but that was better than letting Wallace lay eyes on the injured Bristow and Edgeworth and realize that Powell's men were the ones who'd attacked him in that whore's tent.

When they met up with Ducharme and the rest of the bunch and returned to the rendezvous, they would do so without the injured men. Bristow and Edgeworth would have to fend for themselves.

Edgeworth rode hunched over in the saddle as he muttered curses to himself. An ashen-faced Bristow swayed and had to clutch the saddle horn with his good hand from time to time to keep from falling off his horse. The shot from Wallace's pistol had broken his shoulder, and Powell doubted if he would ever be good for much of anything again.

Might be kinder just to shoot him in the head and put him out of his misery. The same went for Edgeworth. If Wallace's kick really had broken something inside him, his death would probably be a lingering, agonizing hell.

That was their lookout, though, Powell decided. Both men had pistols if they wanted to end their suffering.

Powell knew the route Ducharme and the others would be following. It wasn't hard to backtrack along the trail. Around midmorning he sighted the wagon and the other riders coming toward him and his companions.

Powell reined in and told the others, "We might as well wait here and let them come to us."

They sat there on horseback as Ducharme's party approached. The wealthy German was handling the reins of the wagon team himself this morning, instead of having one of the other men do it. His beefy face wore a scowl as he brought the vehicle to a halt about ten feet from Powell.

"That man is wounded," Ducharme snapped, pointing to the bandaged Bristow. He nodded in Edgeworth's direction and went on, "And that one looks sick. What happened? Is that devil Breckinridge Wallace responsible for this?"

"That's right," Powell said as he sat with his hands crossed and resting on his saddle. "We tried to grab him last night and bring him to you, but he turned out to be too much for us to handle."

"Too much for you to handle! Five against one?"

"Tackling Wallace is sort of like trying to corral a grizzly bear," Powell drawled. He wasn't going to let Ducharme intimidate him. "We'll get him, though, don't you worry about that, Mr. Ducharme. Even if it takes all of us."

Ducharme's glare didn't go away as he ordered, "Tell me what happened. All the details."

Powell did so, not glossing over anything or trying to paint himself in a better light. He had put this group of hardcases together and was their leader, so he'd had a right to order the other men to try to capture Wallace.

Ducharme seemed not to see things that way, however. When Powell was finished with the story, Ducharme let out a contemptuous snort and said, "So you remained out of harm's way, eh, Powell, while your minions failed at their task?"

"I'm not sure I like what you're hintin' at there, boss," Powell said with an icy hint of anger in his voice.

"And I'm certain I do not care what you like or don't like," Ducharme replied. "All that matters to me is that Breckinridge Wallace must pay with his life for the great evil he did to my son. I will settle that debt with my own hands, looking him in the eye so he knows why he is about to die. Nothing else means a thing to me."

"You'll have your revenge," Powell promised. "We'll head on to the rendezvous, and when we get there we'll come up with another plan for separating Wallace from his friends so they can't interfere with us."

"Do not delay too long," Ducharme warned. He swept a pudgy hand toward the other riders. "We have enough men. If it becomes necessary, we will deal with Wallace's friends, as well, along with anyone else who stands in our way."

"Are you saying—"

"I am saying," Ducharme intoned flatly, "that we will kill everyone at that rendezvous if we have to in order for me to take my vengeance on Breckinridge Wallace."

Chapter Thirty-two

The sun was already up when Breckinridge woke the next morning, which was mighty unusual. Right off hand, he couldn't recall the last time he had slept that late. Out here on the frontier, a man had to be up before dawn if he was going to get the day's work done.

He stretched, opened his eyes, and realized that he was alone in the tent. As he pushed himself into a sitting position and yawned, though, the entrance flap opened and Dulcy came in carrying a tin cup. Steam curled up from what was inside it, and a delicious aroma drifted to Breckinridge's nose.

"I thought you might like some coffee," she said. She handed him the cup and then sank to her knees on the blanket in front of him.

Breckinridge sipped the strong black brew from the cup. It was scalding hot, and it cleared away almost instantly the cobwebs that lingered in his brain from sleep.

"That's mighty good," he told Dulcy. "I'm obliged to you."

"And *I'm* obliged to *you*," she said. "That was the

best night I've had in a while. Well, if you ignore that blond harpy trying to drown me and those men busting in here for whatever they were after, that is."

Breckinridge took another sip of the coffee and frowned in thought. It was sort of early in the morning to try to figure things out, but he couldn't help himself.

"From what I heard one of 'em say, I'm pretty sure they were after me. I don't think they were tryin' to kill me, though. From the way they were actin', lambastin' me with clubs and all, it seemed more like they wanted to knock me out so they could carry me off somewhere."

"Who in the world would want to do that?" Dulcy asked with a frown of her own.

Breckinridge could only shake his head and say dolefully, "I don't know."

His thoughts went back, though, to the battles of the past few days. He and his friends had assumed that the men who'd jumped them had wanted to kill them and steal their furs. But all along, Breckinridge had had the nagging feeling that there was something more to it than that.

One thing was certain, however: the men with whom he and his friends had fought had been trying to kill them. Breckinridge had felt the hot breath of too many rifle balls coming too close to his face to doubt that.

So unless they had changed tactics, the survivors from that bunch weren't the same men who had invaded Dulcy's tent the night before.

Was it possible there were two separate groups after him, one that wanted him dead and the other that intended to capture him for some unknown reason?

That theory seemed crazy to Breckinridge, but it

would go a long way toward explaining things. But even if it were true, two vital questions remained.

Who and why?

Breckinridge had no answers. Maybe when he had woken up a little more, he told himself.

"I reckon we'll worry about it later," he told Dulcy. "Any grub left out there to go with this coffee?"

"There is," she said, "but I thought there was one other thing we should do before having breakfast."

"What's that?" Breckinridge asked.

"This," she said as she leaned forward. She put her arms around his neck and pressed the soft curves of her body against his bare chest as she kissed him.

Breckinridge set the coffee cup aside without spilling a drop of the liquid that remained in it, then put his arms around Dulcy and lay back on the blanket, pulling her on top of him.

When they emerged from the tent later, Breckinridge looked around and saw that the camps on both sides of the creek were already larger than they had been the day before. More trappers were arriving for the get-together. A low buzz of conversation and laughter hung in the air.

After Breckinridge and Dulcy had had a breakfast of biscuits and bacon cooked by the soiled dove called Emma, Breck said regretfully, "I reckon I'd better go hunt up my pards and see how they're doin' this mornin'."

"I understand," Dulcy said. "You'll stop back by later, though, won't you?"

Breckinridge grinned as he said, "Just let anybody try to stop me!"

He started to turn away when she stopped him by saying, "Breck . . . you know what I'll be doing today, don't you?"

He frowned as he answered her question this time, saying, "Well, sure. I'd have to be a fool not to know."

"I hope it doesn't bother you too much. It's just a job, you know."

"We all do what we've got to do," he said. "I sort of wish you'd never been put in the position of havin' to work for Mahone. I don't know the story, and I ain't askin'. But I'm sure things could've worked out a whole heap better for you." He shrugged. "On the other hand, if you weren't workin' for Mahone, I'd never have met you, and that'd be a shame, too. So I don't hardly know what to think."

"That's all right, Breckinridge." She came up on her toes, and he bent down so she could brush a kiss across his cheek. "I think you're a nice young man, and we'll leave it at that."

"Sounds good to me," Breckinridge agreed. He smiled and lifted a hand in farewell as he headed for the creek.

He found the rocks Dulcy had mentioned using as stepping-stones, and with his long legs he had no trouble crossing the stream that way.

It might not be as easy for others, though, he realized, and he wondered if there was some better way to span the creek. There were quite a few logs around, and if he found one long enough, he and some of the other men might be able to lift it and place it across the creek so it would serve as a bridge.

Finch and Mahone probably wouldn't be happy if it was easier for their customers to cross back and forth—doubtless they would prefer that the mountain men pick a side and stay there—but Breckinridge didn't really care what the two feuding old-timers thought about it.

He put that plan out of his mind for the moment as he approached the spot where Morgan, Akins, and Fulbright had camped near the canoes. The lightweight craft loaded with pelts was still sitting on the bank, apparently undisturbed since the men had arrived the day before. Fulbright and Akins sat nearby on a log, smoking pipes. Breckinridge didn't see Morgan Baxter.

"Mornin', Breck," Fulbright greeted him between puffs. "How are you this mornin'?"

Akins said, "What in hell happened over there last night? We heard all sorts of commotion."

"I'm fine," Breckinridge said, answering Fulbright's question first. "As for that ruckus, some fellas tried to bust into the tent where Dulcy and me were sleepin'."

Both of the other men exclaimed in surprise. Breckinridge told them about the fight, concluding, "I didn't really get a good look at any of 'em, so I don't know who they were or what they wanted, other than it seemed like they were tryin' to grab me and carry me off."

"No offense," Akins said, "but why would anybody want to do that?"

"Ransom, maybe?" Fulbright suggested.

"That don't seem likely," Breckinridge said. "It ain't like I'm worth anything. Morgan's pa had money, so I guess that means Morgan does, too, once he goes back home and collects his inheritance, but my pa's just a hardworkin' farmer. Anybody who wanted to sell me back would wind up mighty disappointed."

"Well, it beats me," Akins said, "but I'm glad you're

all right. It's a damned shame when you can't even come to a rendezvous without runnin' into a bunch of trouble."

Breckinridge sighed and nodded.

"Hate to say it, but the blamed stuff seems to follow me around wherever I go."

Chapter Thirty-three

Morgan sauntered up a short time later with a pleased expression on his face. Breckinridge took one look at him, grinned, and said, "I reckon you had a good night."

"Annie is quite a woman," Morgan said with a sigh.

"I thought you already bedded that skinny Francesca."

"Well, hell, I'm young, aren't I? Fellas our age bounce back quick."

With a sour look on his face, Akins said, "I don't remember that far back."

Morgan's expression grew more serious as he asked, "What happened over there last night, Breck?"

Breckinridge had to tell the story yet again. At least this was the last time, he thought. Anybody else asked him, he would tell them it was none of their damn business.

Morgan couldn't come up with an explanation for the attack, either. He shook his head and said, "It almost sounds like somebody with a grudge against you followed you out here, but that's kind of crazy."

"Yeah, it is, isn't it?" Breckinridge said.

A frown creased his forehead, though, as he thought about what Morgan had said. He had left some enemies back home, and he had made more on the way west. It seemed unlikely to think that any of them would come this far simply to seek revenge on him, but he supposed he couldn't rule it out until he had more evidence to go on.

For the time being, he was going to try to enjoy the rendezvous. With the fur business shrinking, it was only a matter of time until these annual affairs wouldn't take place anymore. He wanted to experience all this one had to offer.

The first order of business was to dispose of their pelts. Around midday, a couple of wagons rolled in. A short, bald man incongruously outfitted in a tweed suit and a coonskin cap was on the seat of the lead wagon, and many of the trappers greeted him with friendly shouts of "Hey, Stubby!"

"Who's that?" Breckinridge asked Akins as they were drawn to the commotion like the others.

"One of the fur buyers," Akins answered. "I never did business with him myself, but I've heard of him. Name's Blaine, I think, but everybody calls him Stubby."

The newcomer didn't waste any time getting down to business. A couple of the men who'd come with him took a table from one of the wagons and set it on the ground. Blaine placed a chair behind it and declared himself ready to deal, adding in a gravelly voice at odds with his small stature, "I'm the first one here, gents, so you know what that means. I get the pick of the pelts, and I pay the best prices. So grab your furs and let's get started."

Morgan held their place in line while Breckinridge
and Akins went to fetch the pelts. They brought Fulbright back with them. Once the furs were sold, he
wouldn't have to stand guard over them anymore. That
would be the responsibility of Stubby Blaine and
his men.

Quietly, Breckinridge asked Morgan, "Do you know
what a good price is for a load of pelts like this?"

"No," Morgan admitted, "but Roscoe does. We'll let
him handle the dickering."

"I'll do the best I can, boys," Akins promised.

When their turn came, Breckinridge lifted the heavy
bales onto the table. Stubby Blaine pawed through the
furs, examining some of them closely, seemingly
paying little attention to others. After several minutes,
he nodded, looked up at Breck and the other three, and
announced his offer.

Akins frowned and said, "No offense, but that
seems a mite on the low side to me."

One of the big, burly men who had come to the
rendezvous with Blaine made a low growling sound in
his throat and started to step forward.

Blaine lifted a hand to rein in his assistant and gave
Akins a friendly smile.

"None taken," he said, "but you haven't dealt with
me before, have you, friend?"

"Nope," Akins said. "I've always taken my pelts to
a tradin' post or down the river to St. Louis."

"All right, because of that I'm not going to be insulted by your comment. I'll just tell you that no one
who comes to the rendezvous pays as well for furs as
Hobart Blaine. If you don't believe that, you're free to
go and ask around." A touch of steel came into the little

man's voice as he went on, "But if you take these pelts off the table now and come back with them later, after you're satisfied with my bona fides, I can promise you that the offer won't be as high. These are good pelts, and I've offered you a good deal."

Akins glanced nervously at his partners.

"What do you boys think?"

Before the others could answer, Blaine said, "Tell you what. I'll sweeten the deal a little and add . . ." He appeared to think about it. "Ten more dollars to the price."

Breckinridge caught Akins's eye and nodded. He had seen a lot of horse trading going on back in Tennessee, and he figured Blaine had been prepared to pay that price all along. It was possible they could nudge him up a little more if they were stubborn about it. But Breck's pa had taught him it was better to cultivate a good relationship with those a fella did business with, rather than trying to gouge every single nickel out of them. That way it was more likely there would be another deal to do next time.

"All right," Akins said. "We're obliged to you, Mr. Blaine."

"Oh hell, call me Stubby," Blaine said with a grin. He gestured to his men to take the pelts and load them in one of the wagons. While they were doing that, Blaine took a buckskin pouch from inside his coat and counted out coins from it until he had the agreed-upon amount lying on the table. He pushed them across to Akins. "Pleasure doin' business with you."

"Likewise," Akins told him.

As the four trappers walked away, Akins split up the gold and silver pieces among them. With that taken care of, there was nothing left for them to do during the rest of the rendezvous except enjoy themselves.

"Reckon I'll go see Annie," Morgan declared.

"You owe her some for last night, I expect," Fulbright said. "These gals ain't in it for fun, you know."

"Annie wouldn't charge me. Not after the way we hit it off so well." Morgan shrugged and ignored the grins the other men gave him. "But I'll pay her some anyway, just so she won't get in trouble with that crazy old Nicodemus Finch."

"And I'd better square things with Dulcy," Breckinridge said. "Before I do, though . . ."

He told the other three his brainstorm about making a log bridge across the creek. They agreed it was a good idea.

"You find a good log," Akins told Breckinridge. "I'll go round up enough fellas to lift it."

"You come with me, Morgan," Breckinridge said. "Annie won't mind waitin' a while before she sees you again."

"I don't know about that. She seemed mighty taken with me."

Breckinridge doubted if Annie was completely sincere about that, but he supposed it was possible. Soiled doves could fall for a fella same as any other gal. Morgan came along with him as he searched for a suitable log, albeit a little grudgingly.

It didn't take them long to find a fallen cottonwood with a straight, fairly thick trunk. All its limbs had been chopped off and used for firewood, leaving only the bare trunk. Breckinridge tried to pick up one end by himself. Even his prodigious strength could barely budge it.

"This one ought to do fine," he said. "Go find Roscoe."

Morgan came back a few minutes later with Akins, Fulbright, and half a dozen other roughly dressed men. With the exception of Fulbright, who couldn't lift because of his wounded arm, they all spaced themselves at intervals along the trunk and bent to get hold of it.

"Ready, boys?" Breckinridge said. "Heave!"

With grunts of effort they lifted the long, heavy tree trunk into the air and started carrying it toward the creek.

They hadn't gotten there yet when Nicodemus Finch rushed up to them with an agitated look on his billy-goat face.

"Here now!" Finch cried. "What're you moss-brained weehawkers doin' with that log?"

"They're gonna make a bridge out of it," Fulbright explained. All the men carrying the log were straining too much under its weight to spare the breath for an answer.

"A bridge to where?" Finch asked. "That pitiful bunch o' spavined, ragtag varmints on the other side o' the creek?"

"That's the general idea."

"No! No, you can't do that! You fellas don't need to be goin' back and forth. You'll go over there and drink Mahone's pathetic excuse for likker and associate with his unclean whores, and there ain't no tellin' what kind o' damn pox you'll bring back over here!"

Attracted by the yelling, Mahone had appeared on the other side of the stream and came close enough to hear Finch's ranting. He shouted, "My whiskey's a lot better and my gals a lot cleaner than anything you'll find over there in Finch's camp, boys! Put that log right across the creek there! It'll make a fine bridge!"

That was no surprise, thought Breckinridge as he carried the front end of the log toward the creek. If Finch didn't want something, Mahone was bound to insist vehemently on it. It would have worked the other way around if Finch had been in favor of the makeshift bridge.

"Damn it, I say don't do it!" Finch howled.

Breckinridge and the other men ignored him. Breck waded into the creek at a spot he thought was narrow enough that the log would span it. The water was cold through his boots and buckskins, but he ignored it. The other men splashed into the stream behind him.

The log was long enough to reach the opposite bank with several feet to spare on each end. Breckinridge turned his head and called to the men Akins had recruited, "All right, fellas, let's set 'er down nice and easy!"

They lowered the log into place, then climbed out onto the bank to check out their handiwork. Morgan walked to the center and turned to grin at Breckinridge and the others.

"Works just fine," he proclaimed. "I think we ought to name this the Breckinridge Wallace Memorial Bridge, since it was your idea, Breck."

"I don't want any credit," Breckinridge said. "Just figured it might make things a little easier for everybody, that's all."

"And it was a fine idea, too," said one of the men who had helped carry the log. He stuck out his hand and went on in a voice that held a trace of a British accent, "It's good to meet you, Wallace. My name's Harry Sykes."

Chapter Thirty-four

With the log bridge in place, Morgan set off to find Annie, as he had mentioned before. Akins returned to the side of the creek unofficially dubbed Finch's Point, too, since he was smitten with the strawberry-blond Siobhan. Fulbright went with them. Freed of his duty watching over the pelts, he could find one of the doves who suited his fancy now.

"Careful of that ventilated wing o' yours, Amos," Breckinridge called after the big, bushy-bearded man.

Fulbright just grinned back at him confidently and said, "I reckon I can manage."

Breckinridge headed for Dulcy's tent. As he approached, the man called Danny got in front of him, blocking his path.

"Hold on there, Wallace," he said. "If you're lookin' for Dulcy, she's sort of busy at the moment."

Breckinridge frowned, discovering to his surprise that the idea of Dulcy carrying on with her job bothered him more than he'd thought it would. He didn't want to cause a scene and embarrass her or make her mad, though, so he said, "Reckon you could do somethin' for me?"

"What's that?" Danny asked.

Breckinridge took out one of the coins Akins had given him as his share of the money from the pelts. He said, "Here," and slapped it into Danny's outstretched palm. "Give that to her, will you?"

"Sure."

Breckinridge's scowl darkened as he added, "Don't go puttin' it in your pocket and forgettin' about it, you hear? I'm gonna ask her about it later."

"I like Dulcy," Danny protested. "I'm not gonna try to cheat her. And I'm sure as hell not gonna try to cheat Mahone. That wouldn't be a safe thing to do."

Breckinridge nodded and said, "Just don't forget."

He turned away, at a loss as to what to do now. He wasn't really interested in any of the other women anymore, even the gorgeous Annie. Morgan had staked his claim on her, and Breckinridge wasn't going to interfere with his friend.

It was a little early in the day to be getting drunk, too, so he steered clear of the big tent taverns as he wandered around both camps.

Some of the trappers appeared to be playing a game of some sort. They ran around carrying sticks, swatting at a rolled-up leather ball, and whooping in excitement. Breckinridge watched for a while with a puzzled frown on his face, then asked a man who was also watching, "What in the blue blazes are they doin'?"

"It's a game the Injuns play," the man explained. "Some of the fellas picked it up whilst they was winterin' with friendly redskins."

"What's it called?"

"Blamed if I know."

"I've been tryin' to figure it out but can't make head nor tails of it," Breckinridge said. "Does it have any rules?"

"I reckon it must, but I sure don't know 'em."

One of the players walloped the ball with his stick and sent it flying across the open area where the game was going on. Some of the other men yelled and shook their sticks in the air. Breckinridge couldn't tell if they were excited or mad. He didn't really care which it was, either. He watched the nonsense for a few more minutes and then moved on.

He came across a card game taking place on a spread-out blanket with half a dozen men grouped around it, and that was more to his interest. One of the men was Harry Sykes, the fella with the English accent who had helped put the log bridge in place over the creek.

Sykes looked up from his cards, grinned, and asked, "You want to sit in on the game, Wallace?"

Breckinridge started to say yes, then hesitated. He was a pretty good poker player, or at least he liked to think he was, but he could just see himself joining this game and then losing all the money he had earned from the past weeks of trapping. That would be a plumb waste.

And if he was broke, he couldn't very well ask Dulcy to spend much time with him, either. That realization made up his mind for him.

"Reckon I'd better not," he said.

"I've lost just about enough money, too," Sykes said with a chuckle, "and my old mum taught me never to throw good money after bad." He tossed his cards onto the blanket. "I'm out, boys."

Sykes stood up, dusted off his hands, and nodded toward the tent serving as the tavern on Finch's side of the creek.

"How about a drink?" he asked Breckinridge. "I'm buyin'."

Maybe it wasn't too early after all, Breckinridge decided. Anyway, Sykes would buy him a drink, then Breck would buy one for the Englishman, and that would be it.

"Sure," he said. "I'm obliged."

As they started toward the tent, Sykes asked, "Where are you from, Wallace?"

"Place back in Tennessee called Knoxville," Breckinridge replied. "Well, not from the town itself, mind you. My pa has a farm not far from there, in the foothills of the Smoky Mountains. How about you?"

"I was born in London," Sykes said.

"I could tell that from the way you talk. You've been over here for a while, though, haven't you?"

"That's right. My mum came over to the colonies and brought me with her when I was just a wee tyke. Well, they weren't still colonies then, of course. In fact the war had been over for quite a while. But that's what she always called 'em, so I reckon I picked it up from her. We landed in New York, stayed there for a while, and then started movin' around a lot."

"What about your pa?"

"Never even knew the bastard. I ain't sure my mum knew who he was, to tell you the truth."

"Sorry," Breckinridge muttered.

Sykes waved a hand, grinned, and said, "Oh hell, I don't care. I don't have any illusions to shatter or naught like that. She traded me to a fella who owned a tavern when I was twelve. Worked me like a dog around the place, the bastard did. I never saw my mum again." He pulled aside the canvas flap that served as a door into the big tent. "Here we go."

Breckinridge couldn't help but feel a mite sorry for his companion. He had clashed with his father and brothers on numerous occasions, and his mother had always been a little cool toward him because he wasn't the daughter she'd been hoping for, but he'd never had the least bit of doubt that his family loved him. He couldn't imagine growing up in the sort of hard, grim existence that Sykes had just described.

Since trappers were still arriving at the rendezvous, the makeshift tavern wasn't very busy at the moment. Half a dozen men clad in buckskins or rough homespun or linsey-woolsey were scattered around the place. Nicodemus Finch stood behind the crude bar, along with his man Moffit.

Finch glared at Breckinridge as he said, "There he is, the fella that's tryin' to ruin my business."

"Not hardly, Mr. Finch," Breckinridge said. "I wish you well, I really do."

The old-timer ignored what Breckinridge had said and went on, "I should've shot you and that no-good friend o' yours the first time I had you in my sights. I knowed you was workin' for Mahone just by lookin' at you. You ain't done nothin' but try to sabotage me ever since."

"By puttin' a log across the creek? Is that what you're goin' on about?"

"Aidin' and abettin' the enemy, that's what they call it. Treason, pure and simple."

Under his breath, Sykes said, "Somebody's simple around here, I'm thinkin'."

"I heard that!" Finch yelped. "Who in the doodle-buggin' hell are you, mister?"

Sykes took a coin out of his pocket, tapped it on the plank bar, and said, "I'm the man who's about to buy a drink for me and my friend here."

"Well, why didn't you say so!" Finch exclaimed. "Moffit, get the jug and pour these fine gents a drink!"

Chapter Thirty-five

Breckinridge and Sykes took the tin cups Moffit filled for them and carried the drinks over to one of the tables, where they sat down on benches on opposite sides.

The whiskey was raw stuff that burned all the way down Breckinridge's gullet. He coughed a little, even though he tried not to.

Sykes grinned across at him and said, "Aye, it'll open your eyes for you, won't it?"

"And burn a hole in your belly," Breckinridge said hoarsely. "I've had some pretty potent whiskey in my time, but this stuff may be the worst."

"Don't let our host hear you say that. He's liable to start with that crazy jibber-jabber again."

Breckinridge knew what Sykes meant. Nicodemus Finch had calmed down a little, and Breck would just as soon he stayed that way while they were here.

Sykes went on, "You make it sound like you've had an adventurous life, Wallace. Why don't you tell me about it?"

"There ain't that much to tell," Breckinridge said as

his broad shoulders rose and fell in a shrug. "I grew up on a farm, like I told you. It was really a normal life until about a year ago."

"What happened then?"

"I ran into some Chickasaw renegades while I was out in the woods, huntin'."

"Huntin' for redskins?"

"No, I was after deer. I'd always gotten along pretty well with the Injuns around home until then." Breckinridge's face took on a grim cast. "But these fellas jumped me, and I didn't have any choice but to kill a couple of 'em."

Sykes leaned forward slightly and asked, "You never killed anybody before that?"

"Nope," Breckinridge replied with a shake of his head.

"How about since then?"

That seemed like sort of an odd question for his new friend to ask, but Breckinridge always tried to be honest, so he said, "I've had to kill a few, red and white. I tangled with river pirates on the Mississippi and the Missouri both, and I've been in a few Injun fights. Had fellas get crosswise with me and try to shoot me, and I had to shoot back at 'em. I don't like it, though. I'm a peaceable man."

"Yes, I can see that. So am I. Circumstances have a way of forcin' us into violence, though."

"They sure do," Breckinridge agreed solemnly. He took another sip of the whiskey, which was starting to seem not quite as raw as it had earlier.

Sykes said, "Listen, I thought I'd enjoy this rendezvous, but I guess I'm a bit of a solitary man, too. Havin' this many people around sort of gives me the fantods. Think I might have myself a tramp in the woods once we've finished these drinks. Care to come along?"

"Thought you just said you was a solitary man."

"Yes, but a walk with one friend is hardly the same as bein' in a crowd."

Given the life Sykes had described, he was probably a pretty lonely gent, thought Breckinridge. And he didn't really have anything else to do until he could see Dulcy again.

"All right," he said. "I'll have to stop by my camp and get my rifle. I never go off into the woods without it."

"That's fine. Maybe you can teach me a little about fur trapping."

"You're not a trapper?" Breckinridge asked in surprise.

"Well, that's what I came out here for, but I arrived just in time to come to this rendezvous. Thought maybe I could partner up with some experienced fellas and learn the ropes from them."

"It's a mite late in the season to be startin' . . ."

Sykes spread his hands and said, "Yes, but we can only do what we can do, eh?"

Breckinridge chuckled.

"That's the truth, I reckon." He tossed back the rest of the whiskey in his cup. "Now I got to buy you one, and then we can go."

"Why don't you just owe me the drink until later?" Sykes suggested. "I feel the need to stretch my legs."

Breckinridge considered the idea and then nodded.

"All right, I reckon we can do that. It's a mite early in the day to be drinkin' too much, anyway."

They left the empty cups on the table and got to their feet. Breckinridge turned and led the way to the entrance. As he pushed through the canvas flap and stepped outside, he saw a wagon and a large number of riders approaching Finch's Point. The man on horseback leading the group had white hair under his pushed-back hat.

"Hold on a minute," Breckinridge said to Sykes. "That looks like another friend of mine. Now that I think about it, I haven't seen him around all day. Reckon he must've gone to lead the rest of his bunch to the rendezvous."

"You can see them later, surely," Sykes said with a frown.

"Won't take but a minute to say hello," Breckinridge promised.

He started toward the newcomers with his long-legged strides. Sykes lagged behind him.

Powell reined in as Breckinridge met the group at the edge of Finch's camp. Breck lifted a hand in greeting, smiled, and said, "Howdy."

"Hello, Wallace," Powell said in his gravelly tones. "Anything happen while I was gone?"

"Hard to say. I don't know when you left."

"Pulled out early this morning to go meet the Colonel."

Powell inclined his head toward the wagon that had come up behind him. Breckinridge glanced in that direction and saw a short, broad, rusty-haired man with a beefy face. He was well-dressed, and Breck figured he had to be the Colonel.

"Well, then, no, it's been pretty quiet around here, except for the games and the get-together," he said. "Oh, there's a log bridge over the creek now, so fellas can go back and forth from Finch's to Mahone's easier."

"That's a good idea," Powell said. "Who came up with that?"

"Reckon I did," Breckinridge admitted with a note of pride in his voice.

Powell got a thoughtful look on his rugged face and said, "You know, a fella who shows that sort of smart thinkin' ought to meet the Colonel. He could use a man like you, Wallace."

"I'm not lookin' for a job," Breckinridge said with a shake of his head, "but I don't mind meetin' the Colonel."

He strode toward the wagon while Powell turned his horse and fell in alongside him. From behind Breckinridge, Sykes called, "Wallace, where are you goin'?"

"I'll be back in a minute, Harry," Breckinridge said over his shoulder.

When he reached the wagon, he extended his right hand to the ruddy-faced man on the seat. Powell said, "Colonel, this here is Breckinridge Wallace. You know, I told you about him?"

The Colonel grunted and said, "Of course." His piggish eyes didn't look very friendly, but he briefly clasped Breckinridge's hand with his pudgy one. He gave Breck a curt nod. "Mr. Wallace."

"I'm pleased to meet you, Colonel," Breckinridge said. "Heard a lot about you from Powell here."

That wasn't strictly true. Powell had said only that the Colonel intended to build a trading post somewhere out here in the mountains. Breckinridge didn't even know the man's real name, not that it mattered. He was trying to be polite, though, as he greeted the Colonel.

"Wallace, come on," Sykes urged. "You were going to show me some things about settin' traps, remember?"

"Sure, sure," Breckinridge said easily. To Powell, he went on, "You boys gonna be around for the rest of the rendezvous?"

"I reckon we will," the white-haired man replied.

"I'll see you later, then."

Breckinridge turned and started to rejoin Sykes.

He hadn't gotten there when he heard his name being called urgently and looked around to see Morgan hurrying toward him.

Chapter Thirty-six

Breckinridge's first thought was that something was wrong, but then he realized that Morgan didn't look upset, just excited.

"What is it?" Breckinridge asked as his friend came up to him.

"Some fellas are going to have a tug-of-war," Morgan said. "We need to get in on this. There's a prize for the winning team."

"What sort of prize?"

"A five-dollar gold piece. Finch is putting it up."

Breckinridge frowned and asked, "How are a bunch of fellas gonna split up one gold piece?"

"Well, they won't, of course. They'll buy as much whiskey as that amount will cover and then split *that* up."

Breckinridge supposed that might work. And Finch would wind up getting the prize money back, which came as no surprise. Breck said, "How are they gonna do this tug-o'-war?"

Morgan waved a hand toward the creek and said, "They'll stretch a rope from one bank to the other, line up on either side, and start pulling. First team where all the men either let go of the rope or fall in the water loses."

"Wallace . . ." Sykes said peevishly.

"Sorry, but we'll have to talk about trappin' some more later, Harry," Breckinridge said. "I got to help out my friends for a while."

Sykes scowled in evident disappointment, but he didn't say anything else. Breckinridge turned back to the wagon, said, "Pleasure meetin' you, Colonel," then lifted a hand in farewell to Powell and started toward the creek with Morgan.

"Roscoe's getting in on this, too," Morgan said. "And there'll be some side bets going on, I'm thinking."

"Just be careful," Breckinridge warned him. "You don't want to go losin' all that money you've worked for."

"I won't lose," Morgan said, "because I'll bet on the side you're on."

"I ain't the only big fella here at this rendezvous, you know," Breckinridge pointed out.

"Maybe not, but you're the only one who could pass for Hercules!"

"Never heard of him."

"How about Samson, then?"

"The fella from the Bible?" Breckinridge asked. "The one with the long hair?"

"That's right." Morgan grinned. "The scriptures don't say anything about him having red hair, as I recall, but other than that you're a dead ringer for him!"

"Speakin' of dead, that's the way Samson wound up, if I recollect the Bible story right."

"Well, there's no temple to fall on you out here, so I don't think we have to worry about that. The worst that can happen is that you'll get dunked in the creek."

Breckinridge supposed Morgan was right. And the contest sounded like it might be entertaining, too.

"All right, we'll give it a try," he said. "I thought you'd be spendin' most of the day with Annie, though."

Morgan laughed ruefully and shook his head.

"I may be young," he said, "but I'm not made of iron! A man's got to have a little bit of a break, no matter how beautiful the woman is."

Breckinridge supposed that was true.

As they approached the creek, he saw that crowds had gathered on both sides of the stream. Finch and Mahone were both there, and so were a number of the soiled doves, including Dulcy. She smiled across the creek at Breckinridge, which made his heart seem to swell up a mite in his chest.

"Who'd you say was offerin' that prize?" he asked Morgan quietly.

"Finch put up the five dollars. Why?"

"Just wait," Breckinridge said.

One of Finch's men brought a long, coiled rope to the creek's edge. He threw one end of it across the stream to where one of Mahone's men waited. They played out the rope until there were roughly equal lengths of it on each side of the stream. The men who were going to participate moved in to take hold of the rope.

"Remember, boys, you're battlin' here for five dollars, American!" Finch shouted.

"I'll make it ten!" Mahone yelled from the other bank.

Finch glared at him and demanded, "Tryin' to make me look bad, are you?"

"I just matched what you're puttin' up," Mahone replied. "But now that you mention it—"

"No, no, five dollars apiece it is!" Finch snatched his coonskin cap off his balding head and with surprising agility scampered out onto the log bridge, which was about ten yards downstream from where the rope was stretched across the creek. He waved the cap with its long tail over his head and went on, "When I throw this cap in the air, that'll be the signal to commence! You boys get ready!"

Morgan said, "Breck, you need to be at the back. You're our anchor."

"All right," Breckinridge said. He had already seen that he was the largest man on this side of the rope. None of the men on the other side of the creek were as big as he was, either, he had noted, but quite a few of them were pretty burly, anyway. The teams appeared to be evenly matched.

"Everybody ready?" Finch called.

Excited shouts of agreement sounded from both sides of the creek.

"Go!" yelled Finch, and the coonskin cap rose into the air.

Powell knew how much being civil to Wallace had cost Otto Ducharme. He had seen it in the way Ducharme's face had flushed even more than usual as he was shaking hands and talking with Wallace. Tiny beads of sweat had broken out on the German's forehead as he struggled not to give in to the fierce hatred that filled him.

The shotgun lay on the floorboard of the driver's box, right there at Ducharme's feet. Wallace wasn't expecting any trouble. Ducharme probably could have reached down, picked up the shotgun, and blown Wallace's head off before anybody could stop him.

Of course, if he'd done that he wouldn't have gotten to gloat, and Powell and his men would have had to shoot their way out of this rendezvous in order to protect Ducharme from Wallace's friends. Powell was just as glad that the man hadn't acted so recklessly.

They could still afford to take their time and handle this discreetly.

And something that might interfere with that was nagging at Powell now as the tug-of-war got underway. Cheers and shouts of encouragement from the crowds on both sides of the creek filled the air. Powell intended to the get to the bottom of whatever was bothering him, so as he sat on his horse next to the wagon he said quietly to Ducharme, "You handled that really well, boss."

Ducharme pulled a bandanna from his pocket and mopped his forehead with it.

"I wanted to kill him," he said in a low, strained voice. "I really wanted to kill him."

"I know you did. And you'll get your chance. For now, though, I want to look into something else, so why don't you find a good spot to park the wagon?"

"You are giving me orders now, instead of the other way around?" Ducharme snapped.

"Nope. You're still in charge. But there's something I need to find out, and I want to be sure there's not gonna be any trouble while I'm lookin' into that."

"Very well," Ducharme said with ill grace. "Go on and do whatever it is you need to do."

Powell nodded and turned his horse away from the wagon. He rode slowly after the man who had been with Wallace when they first came up, the one Wallace had called Harry.

Instead of going over to the creek to watch the contest, Harry seemed to be drifting toward the trees. That was where he and Wallace had been headed, and Harry had been upset and even a little angry when first the arrival of Powell and the others and then the announcement of the tug-of-war had interfered with those plans. Powell had seen the anger in the man's eyes.

He wanted to know why Harry had reacted that way.

With all the noise coming from the creek, Powell hoped that Harry wouldn't hear him coming up from behind. Harry glanced over his shoulder, though, perhaps warned by some instinct, and then started walking faster. He turned away from the woods and went behind the big tent instead.

Powell bit back a curse and quickly swung down from the saddle. He left the reins dangling and hurried after Harry on foot. He didn't want to draw attention by galloping across the camp in pursuit.

He rounded the tent's rear corner, expecting to see Harry up ahead, but nobody was back here. Powell took several steps and frowned as he came to a stop. The only explanation was that Harry had ducked *under* the tent's rear wall. He started to turn back in that direction when something hard and metallic pressed against his neck from behind.

"You just stand right where you are, mate," a menacing voice warned, "or I'll blow a pistol ball right out through your throat."

Chapter Thirty-seven

As Nicodemus Finch shouted, "Go!" and sailed his coonskin cap in the air, Breckinridge planted his booted feet solidly on the ground and threw his weight and strength against the rope. He felt the shock as the weight of the men on the other side of the creek hit his muscles, but he didn't budge. In fact, he was able to take a short step back as the other team gave a little ground.

Morgan was right in front of Breckinridge. He glanced back over his shoulder at Breck and grinned.

"We've already got them losing!" he called.

Breckinridge didn't waste breath or energy replying. He put his effort into pulling on the rope instead.

Huge, corded lengths of muscle in his back, shoulders, and arms stood out against the buckskin shirt. Those muscles bulged and shifted as he poured more and more strength into the competition. At first he heard the crowds shouting and cheering, but after a short time all he could hear was the pounding of his own pulse inside his head.

He was able to move back another step, but then the

resistance from the other side stiffened. The men over there were no lightweights. They were trappers, too, many of them hard, seasoned veterans of the frontier. They had fought for their lives in the past, and while they might only be vying for a couple of gold pieces now, they still fought to win. That was the only way they knew how.

A sudden surge in the other direction took Breckinridge by surprise. Before he could stop himself, he had lost the two steps he had gained, plus another. Then he got his feet braced again and heaved, but he and the men with him couldn't regain the ground they had lost.

Panting, Morgan let out a couple of curses. Through clenched teeth, Breckinridge asked him, "Did you . . . bet on us?"

"Of course . . . I did," Morgan replied. "I bet . . . everything I've got!"

Breckinridge wanted to admonish his friend. Morgan had done the very thing Breck had warned him against. But again, he didn't want to waste his breath, so he remained grimly silent and tried to summon up some more strength.

Finch danced around on the log as he watched the contest. Even though the terms of the competition hadn't been framed as being between him and Tom Mahone, that was an instinctive reaction on the part of both men. Each wanted the men on his side of the creek to emerge triumphant. Finch yelled, "Pull, you dadgum flibbertigibbets, pull!"

"Come on, boys!" Mahone exhorted the men on his side of the creek. "Special deals for all of you if you win!"

Finch wasn't going to let his old enemy top him. He waved his cap in the air and shouted, "Free drinks and half-price for the gals! All you gotta do is beat those Mahone varmints!"

Another surge from the men on Mahone's side pulled Breckinridge and his teammates forward. The man at the front was perilously close to the creek, and suddenly he lost his balance and toppled forward with a yell as he lost his grip on the rope. He went into the water with a splash that was swallowed up by the noise welling up from the other side.

Now Breckinridge and the men on this side were outnumbered by one, and before they could recover, another man went into the creek. This was fixing to be a rout, Breck thought, unless they could stem the tide. His lips drew back from his teeth in a grimace as he hauled on the rope.

Outnumbered or not, the massive strength of Breckinridge Wallace as their anchor made a difference. Breck took one stomping step back, then another. An inarticulate cry escaped from his throat. He dug in, leaned back, heaved. His boot heels sunk into the ground. He leaned more and more, the angle becoming extreme. Another step, another . . .

The lead man on the Mahone side went into the creek, followed almost instantly by the second in line. That tipped the balance where it had failed to do so the other way. Breckinridge kept backing up, aided by the other men on his side but in truth doing most of the work himself. As the resistance lessened, he was able to turn, put the rope over his shoulder, and bull forward now, away from the creek.

Suddenly the rope was slack as the rest of the other team floundered and splashed into the creek. Breckinridge lost his balance and staggered for several yards before he was able to catch himself. He turned, grinning, and saw Morgan and the other men on this side jumping up in the air and shouting in excitement.

Out on the log bridge, Nicodemus Finch capered so enthusiastically that he slipped and fell into the creek. He came up sputtering and shouting incoherently, which to be honest didn't really sound that much different from what usually came out of his mouth. A couple of his men waded into the stream to fish him out.

Morgan, Akins, and the other men crowded around Breckinridge, whooping and pounding him on the back in congratulations.

"You did it, Breck!" Morgan said. "We never could have won without you! You did it practically single-handed!"

"We were all workin' at it," Breckinridge said, trying to be fair. "We all won."

With creek water pouring off of him, Finch came up and slapped a coin into Breckinridge's hand.

"Looks like I was wrong about you, son!" he said. "You sure took care of those black-hearted musha-roos! Drinks are on me!" He started toward the tent, then stopped short and added, "One drink! One drink on me!"

Breckinridge handed the gold piece to Morgan and said, "You take care o' this."

"Don't you want your share of the bet, Breck?"

"I didn't bet anything," he said. "That was all your doin', remember?"

"Well, maybe, but you deserve something . . ."

Breckinridge looked across the creek to where Dulcy was standing by herself now as the disappointed crowd began to break up. He told Morgan, "Don't worry, I intend to collect some winnin's . . ."

* * *

The mule team from Ducharme's wagon had been unhitched and picketed by the time Powell walked up with Harry Sykes beside him. Sykes had put away his pistol, but anger still smoldered inside Powell. He didn't like to have anybody pull a gun on him, and any time that happened, normally he made sure the son of a bitch who did it soon regretted his action.

So he wasn't going to forget that he had a score to settle with Sykes over that, but for now it made more sense to swallow his pride and let the Englishman talk to Otto Ducharme.

At the moment Ducharme was sitting on a stool that had been taken out of the wagon. He still looked angry, but it was hard to tell for sure since that was his regular expression most of the time.

Ducharme glared at Sykes and demanded, "Who is this?"

"His name's Harry Sykes, boss," Powell said, "and he's got something in common with us."

"And what is that?" Ducharme asked with a sneer.

Powell glanced around to make sure no one except the rest of Ducharme's men was in hearing distance, then said, "He wants Breckinridge Wallace dead, too."

Ducharme's eyes widened. He sat up straighter and said, "*Was ist los?*"

"I don't speak your language, mister," Sykes said, "but I reckon I understand. You heard right. I'm after that redheaded bastard Wallace, too."

Powell and Sykes had been cautious about revealing their true goals, but after a few tense minutes of feeling each other out it had become obvious they were after the same thing.

Something else was obvious, and that had led Sykes to seriously consider pulling the trigger of the gun he held. Powell had seen that indecision in the other man's eyes when Sykes realized that Powell's bunch had jumped them the day before, during the ambush at the camp on the bluff several miles upstream.

That meant Powell and his men were responsible for the deaths of Sykes's companions. The ones who hadn't been killed in the fighting had cut and run, leaving Sykes to go after Wallace by himself. Sykes had explained that to Powell once they'd decided it was in their best interests to call a temporary truce despite the previous bloodshed.

Now Ducharme stared at Sykes and rasped, "Why do you want to kill Wallace? What did he ever do to you?"

"To me?" Sykes shook his head. "Nothing. I never laid eyes on the man until a few days ago. But he took away plenty from the man who hired me. The way I heard the story, Wallace tried to shoot my employer but wound up hittin' the fella's wife instead. Damn near killed her, and caused her to lose the babe she was carryin'."

Ducharme grunted and said, "I can believe that. The man gunned down my son in cold blood."

Powell knew that wasn't exactly the way things had happened, but Ducharme could tell himself whatever he wanted to. The old man could even believe it if that made him happy. It was nothing to Powell either way.

"So you see, my loss is greater than yours," Ducharme went on. "I have first claim on Wallace."

"We don't have to argue about this," Sykes said. "You see, I don't care *who* kills Wallace, as long as he winds up dead. The gent who's payin' me is more than a thousand miles away. If I go back and tell him that Wallace is dead and that I done the deed, he'll never know the difference."

"Why not just tell him that anyway?" Ducharme asked.

Sykes frowned. Powell understood the reaction. A man with the sort of money that Ducharme had didn't know anything about honor. Powell and Sykes might both be hired killers, but if they took on a job, they did their best to see it through. Sykes might shade the truth a little about who actually killed Wallace, but he wouldn't go back to his boss and report the big man's death unless it was true.

Powell stepped in and said, "I suggested that Sykes throw in with us, boss. It makes more sense to work together than it does to be competin' against each other."

Ducharme thought about it and nodded slowly.

"I suppose this is true," he said. "If you join forces with us, what value can you offer, Herr Sykes?"

"Wallace and I are friendly. He thinks I came out here to learn how to be a fur trapper. He agreed to show me some of the tricks of the trade."

Powell said, "I figure we can use Harry to lure Wallace away from his friends. I would have come up with a way to do that myself, but this one's ready-made."

"That could work," Ducharme said. Then, as his frown deepened, he went on to Sykes, "I suppose you will wish to be paid."

"That makes it an even better deal for you," Sykes said. "I'll collect from the fella who hired me back in Tennessee. You won't be out anything extra."

Ducharme nodded again and said, "I must confess, I am coming to like this proposal more and more."

"It's workin' out for me, too." A savage grin spread across the Englishman's rugged face. "I won't have to split the rest of the payoff with anybody else. It's startin' to look like you boys did me a favor by killin' or runnin' off the rest of my bunch."

That was one way of looking at it, thought Powell. But he had seen what lurked in Sykes's eyes and knew the truth. Sykes might play along with them until Wallace was dead, might even help them accomplish that goal as he'd said . . . but then he would double-cross them at the earliest opportunity.

Powell meant to see to it that Sykes never got the chance. As soon as Breckinridge Wallace was dead, Harry Sykes would be following him straight down to hell.

Chapter Thirty-eight

Tom Mahone was waiting when Breckinridge crossed the log bridge a short time later. He leaned on his walking stick with one hand while holding out a five-dollar gold piece with the other.

"I promised this prize to the winnin' team," Mahone said, "and from where I was standin' it looked like you were pretty much the whole team by yourself, Wallace."

Breckinridge hesitated, then took the coin and stowed it in his poke.

"The whole team won, not just me," he said. "But I'll see to it that the other fellas get their share later."

"Right now you want to go see Dulcy, is that right?"

"Well, yeah," Breckinridge admitted.

Mahone scowled as he said, "Damn a man who'll get a whore smitten with him. Makes her pert' near useless for her job. I wish you and her had never laid eyes on each other."

"But we did," Breckinridge said, "and there ain't nothin' that can change that."

He left Mahone there and walked along the creek until he came to Dulcy's tent. She had disappeared after he'd seen her watching him from across the creek, so he figured she had to be here. He called her name, quietly.

The flap was pulled back. He couldn't see her, but she said, "Come on in, Breckinridge."

He stooped and did so, and was quite pleased with what he found waiting for him.

Breckinridge and Dulcy didn't emerge from the tent until after nightfall, and then it was to find a huge bonfire burning across the creek on Finch's Point. Some of the trappers had shot a couple of elk, and elk steaks were roasting on the flames. Men were passing around jugs and a couple of old-timers had gotten out their fiddles, so a general air of hilarity and celebration filled the camp.

Breckinridge and Dulcy passed a gloomy Black Tom Mahone sitting on a keg with his chin resting in his hand. He seemed to be the only one around.

"Where is everybody, Tom?" Dulcy asked.

"I gave 'em all leave to go across the creek and join in on the fandango," Mahone said as he lifted his head and draped both hands over the walking stick. "There was no reason to keep 'em here. No customers. They're all over there at . . . *Finch's.*"

The utter disgust in his voice couldn't have been more plain.

"They'll come back after a while," Breckinridge said. He wasn't sure why he would go to the trouble of trying to cheer up Mahone. He didn't like the man. But he didn't like Finch, either, and the origin of the feud between the two old-timers was too far in the past to be sure who was really in the wrong.

"I don't care if they come back," Mahone said. "It was a mistake to come out here. I should've stayed where I was, runnin' a tavern back in Missouri. I just heard that Finch was braggin' about how much money he was gonna make at this rendezvous, and I couldn't stand not tryin' to do him one better."

Dulcy suggested, "Maybe it's time to just forget about all those old grudges, Tom."

Mahone sighed, and without taking his eyes off the bonfire on the other side of the creek, he said, "You might be right about that. That old scalawag's never gonna change, and neither am I. What does it really matter?" He lifted a gnarled hand from the head of his walking stick and waved it toward the creek. "You two young folks go on over there and have a good time. Dulcy, you and me are quits."

"What?" she exclaimed. "Tom, I never said I didn't want to work for you—"

"I know you didn't," he broke in. "But any debt between us for me helpin' you out when you were in bad shape, that's long since squared away. Don't worry, I'll take you back to Missouri with us when we go, if that's what you want, but while we're here . . . you don't have to work for me no more."

"But you're already shorthanded, what with Poppy being hurt . . ."

"Doesn't matter. You're still done workin' for me. You just ain't cut out for this kind of life, Dulcy. You deserve better."

Dulcy was clearly at a loss for words. She said, "Why, that's just . . . just . . ."

"Don't say nice. It's been a long time since I fit that description. No, I'm just a whoremongerin' old scoundrel, and you know it. But I'd rather see you do somethin' else with your life, and I reckon you're ready to do it now." Mahone pushed himself to his feet with the help of the walking stick. "Now, go on, I tell you! Go get you one of them elk steaks and somethin' to drink and dance a jig with this big redheaded galoot! Go over there and enjoy yourself, damn it."

"Thank you, Tom," Dulcy whispered. She started to lean toward him, but he lifted a hand to stop her.

"Don't waste any kisses on me. Git!"

Breckinridge took hold of Dulcy's hand and said, "Reckon we'd best do what he says 'fore he changes his mind."

"Ain't gonna change my mind," Mahone insisted. "I'm just too old and tired for all of it."

He sank back down on the keg with a sigh.

Breckinridge led Dulcy toward the creek. She glanced back once with a sad smile on her face, visible in the light from the leaping flames.

"What's wrong?" Breckinridge asked her.

"Even when you know it's for the best," she said, "sometimes it's hard to put a whole part of your life behind you. Like Tom said, though . . . maybe it's time."

Without looking back again, she crossed the log bridge ahead of Breckinridge, and they plunged into the celebration.

They found Morgan dancing with Annie, and for a moment Breckinridge worried about the earlier clash between Dulcy and the blonde.

The spirit of truce seemed to extend to both women, though. The nods that they gave to each other were rather cool, but there were no angry words. They didn't speak at all, in fact.

"This is quite a shindig!" Morgan said excitedly as he and Annie paused in their dancing. "It's finally starting to seem like a real rendezvous. Breck, did you know there are Indians here?"

"Friendly ones?" Breckinridge asked as he glanced around.

"Well, sure. They're Shoshone, I heard somebody say. They brought furs to trade. Stubby Blaine brought cloth and beads and other gewgaws, and the Indians were lined up at his table making deals."

"That's good, I reckon."

Annie said, "I'm not so sure. Those squaws may take some of our business away."

Morgan laughed and slapped her on the bottom.

"There's going to be plenty of business for you ladies," he said. "I reckon I could keep you occupied the rest of the time all by myself."

Annie laughed and told him, "You just keep on dreaming, son!"

He clasped her in his arms and twirled her away again as the fiddlers struck up another sprightly tune. Breckinridge and Dulcy watched them disappear into the crowd of dancers. Since there were only a limited number of women here at the rendezvous, some of the trappers were dancing awkwardly with each other, unwilling to let the lack of female companionship keep them from having a good time.

Dulcy said, "I hope Morgan doesn't get too taken with her. He'll get hurt if he does."

"What makes you say that?"

"Because I've seen too many of her kind, Breck. She doesn't really care about him. And honestly, you can't blame her. This sort of life hardens a woman pretty quickly. She doesn't have to be part of it for very long before it changes her."

"Did it change you?" he asked.

"My life was in tatters before I ever . . . I mean, you can't go by what happened to me. I was a little older . . . different . . ."

"Stronger," Breckinridge said.

"I don't know about that."

"I do. That's the way it seems to me, anyway, and I'm a pretty fair judge of character."

She laughed softly and said, "Are you really?"

Breckinridge thought back over his life and had to say, "Well . . . if I'm bein' honest about it . . . maybe not all the time . . ."

Dulcy laughed again, took his hand, and said, "Come on. I'm not too old to enjoy some dancing."

Chapter Thirty-nine

The party went on most of the night, so as a result there were a lot of sleepy, groggy, hungover gents in both camps the next day.

Breckinridge wasn't one of them. He'd had some whiskey the night before, but with his size it took a lot to get him drunk. His iron constitution meant that he threw off liquor's effects pretty quickly, too.

And he wasn't sleepy because after eating, drinking, and dancing for a while, he and Dulcy had gone back to her tent, made love again, and then Breckinridge had fallen into a deep, dreamless slumber that left him rested and refreshed when he woke up early the next morning.

Dulcy claimed she was still tired, so he promised he would see her later and then kissed her on top of the head and left her curled up in the blankets with a small, satisfied smile on her face. Breckinridge walked out into a beautiful morning and followed the smell of coffee to the cook fire.

Fortified by some breakfast, he crossed the log bridge and went in search of Morgan. He found Akins and Fulbright sitting on a log near their canoes but didn't see any sign of Morgan. Both men looked a little green around the gills.

"Too much to drink last night?" Breckinridge asked them cheerfully.

"Maybe," Akins admitted.

"How come you look so damn chipper?" Fulbright wanted to know.

"Clean livin', boys," Breckinridge replied with a grin.

Fulbright snorted and said, "Clean livin', hell! I'll bet you spent the night with that Dulcy gal."

"Don't go makin' insinuations, Amos. Matter of fact, I did spend the night with Dulcy, but she don't work for Mahone anymore, so it wasn't exactly like what you're thinkin'."

"Maybe not, but you oughta be wore out anyway."

Breckinridge changed the subject by saying, "Where's Morgan? Have you seen him this mornin'?"

"Haven't laid eyes on the boy since last night," Akins said. "Reckon Finch could probably tell you. Accordin' to Siobhan, he keeps pretty close track of what his girls are doin'. He don't want 'em cheatin' him out of any of the money he's got comin'."

Breckinridge nodded. He said, "I'll go hunt up Finch, then."

He wanted to find Morgan and give him the other gold piece, the one Mahone had given him the night before. Breckinridge didn't figure he needed his share of the prize. Morgan could split it up with the other men who'd been on their end of the rope.

"That crazy-talkin' old coot's probably in the big tent," Fulbright said. "I think I saw him goin' in there a while ago, but I'm so cross-eyed this mornin' I can't guarantee it." He used his good hand to massage his temples. "I'll never guzzle down that much who-hit-John again." Then a grin spread under the bushy whiskers. "Until the next time."

Breckinridge left them there and headed for the big tent. When he went inside, he saw that nobody was drinking this early in the morning, and none of the soiled doves were there. The only two men Breck saw were Moffit, who was behind the crude bar, and Nicodemus Finch, who sat at one of the tables sorting through a pile of coins in front of him.

A pistol lay on the table, as well, and Finch put his hand on it and glared as Breckinridge approached him.

"Place is closed right now," Finch snapped. "If you've come to rob me whilst I count last night's profits, I'll blow a hole clean through you, you gold-plated gazoon."

"I'm not here to rob you or anybody else," Breckinridge told the old-timer. "I'm just lookin' for my partner. Thought you might know whether he's with Annie."

Finch appeared to relax a little. He said, "Yeah, I reckon so. He paid for the whole night. Cost him nearly ever'thing he had left after he settled up with those other fellas, but Annie Belle, she's worth it!"

Breckinridge hated to hear that Morgan had spent most of his money, but that came as no surprise. Morgan seemed to have fallen head over heels in love with Annie.

Which meant that Dulcy was probably right. Morgan was going to wind up getting hurt when Annie headed back East with Finch and the rest of the bunch. Breckinridge figured there was no way she would be willing to give up the life she was leading and stay out here with Morgan.

That thought made him consider the question of what Dulcy was going to do. Mahone had told her she wasn't working for him anymore, but he'd also said he would take her back to Missouri with them when his group left. Was that what she intended? Breckinridge wasn't sure he could ask her to endure the hardships of life on the frontier, even if she was willing to do so.

And it was possible that he was taking things a lot more seriously than she was, he reminded himself. He liked Dulcy enough that he'd started thinking about spending the rest of his life with her, but she might not feel the same way at all. He hadn't asked her about it.

A part of him was afraid to do so, he realized.

Nicodemus Finch broke into Breckinridge's reverie by demanding, "What the hell are you standin' there and frownin' about, boy? You'll scare off my customers."

"I thought you said the place was closed."

"Well, maybe it is, but that don't mean I'm gonna turn away customers."

That didn't make any sense to Breckinridge, but not making sense was pretty common where Finch was concerned. Breck nodded and said, "All right, I'll move on, but if you see Morgan, tell him I'm lookin' for him."

"Just go on over to Annie's tent if you want to find him that bad. She won't mind."

Breckinridge shook his head, which was now full of murky thoughts about Dulcy and the possible future they might have together. Or the *im*possible future, depending on how she felt about the idea.

Anyway, he wouldn't want to interrupt Morgan and Annie. That might embarrass Morgan, whether Annie would care or not. And Breck knew that *he* would be embarrassed.

Instead he pushed past the tent's entrance flap and stepped back out into the morning sunshine, unsure of what to do next.

That question was answered for him in the person of Harry Sykes, who came up to him and said, "There you are, Wallace."

"Mornin', Harry," Breckinridge said. "You're up and about early. Not really surprised, though. I didn't see you at the big bonfire last night."

"I didn't come out here to get drunk and dance with whores," Sykes said. "I take what I do seriously, and I came to be a fur trapper."

Breckinridge slapped the Englishman on the shoulder and said, "That's the best way to look at it, I reckon. Since neither of us is sleepin' it off today, why don't we go on over to where my partners and me got our canoes? I'll introduce you to 'em."

"I was hopin' you could show me how to set a beaver trap."

"Sure! In fact, we could paddle upstream a ways and I'll let you watch while I check one of our traplines. We left 'em baited and ready so that if any beaver come along while we're here at the rendezvous, they'll find themselves caught."

"That's why they make traps, ain't it? To catch unwary creatures?"

"That's the way of it, all right," Breckinridge agreed.

He led Sykes over to the creek where Akins and Fulbright were still sitting and recuperating from the previous night. They shook hands with Sykes, but they were too hungover to be very friendly.

"I thought I'd show Harry one of our traplines," Breckinridge said. "You fellas want to come along?"

Fulbright shuddered and said, "Good Lord, no. The thought of bein' out on the creek today, 'specially in some of the rougher stretches, that don't sit well with me at all."

"Hush up," Akins croaked. "I don't even want to think about it."

"That's fine," Breckinridge said. "I'm sure that if I need a hand with anything, Harry'd be glad to pitch in."

"Of course," Sykes said. "After all, you're doin' me a favor, takin' me along with you like this, Wallace."

"Glad to do it. Come on, help me get one of these canoes in the creek."

A couple of minutes later the two men were paddling upstream, Breckinridge in the back of the canoe, Sykes in the front. The Englishman was a little awkward at first when it came to handling the paddle, but he soon got the hang of it.

"Is there anybody else up there where we're goin'?" he asked Breckinridge.

"Shouldn't be. Everybody else in the valley ought to be here at the rendezvous. Unless we should happen to run into some Injuns, that is. If we do, there's a chance they might be unfriendly, so keep your rifle handy."

"I don't intend to let it out of my reach," Sykes said.

In the shadows under some trees about a hundred yards away, Powell watched as Wallace and Sykes climbed into one of the canoes and paddled away upstream.

It looked like the plan he and Sykes and Otto Ducharme had hatched was working to perfection.

Sykes had lured Wallace away from his friends so that Powell and his men could deal with the big bastard on his own. If the other trappers had gone along, Powell would have cut their throats and got them out of the way, but he didn't believe in spilling blood for no good reason.

Besides, he wasn't getting paid for killing those other fellas, and money was the best reason of all for spilling blood.

He didn't wait until the canoe carrying Wallace and Sykes had gone out of sight. Instead he turned and moved deeper into the trees where Ducharme and the rest of his men waited. Powell nodded to the German and said, "Wallace took the bait, just like we hoped he would."

"Good," Ducharme said. "And soon he will be gutted like a fish."

"I thought you were gonna blow his head off with that scattergun."

"And so I am," Ducharme said. "Eventually. When he has suffered enough to pay me back for what he did to my Rory. It may require a great deal of time . . . and blood . . ."

Chapter Forty

It took an hour or so to reach the area where Breckinridge and his partners had placed their traps along the creek and the smaller brooks that ran into it. Finch's Point and the rendezvous were far behind them, and as Breck and Sykes paddled along, they might as well have been the only men within five hundred miles. The majestic mountains all around them conjured up that feeling of beautiful isolation.

"How far are we from the rendezvous?" Sykes asked.

"Don't know for sure. Three or four miles, I'd say."

"Would the sound of a shot carry that far? If we were to run into trouble and needed help, I mean."

"It might. Might not. And dependin' on how hungover those fellas are, they might not hear it. But I wouldn't worry, Harry. I don't expect to run into anything we can't handle. Out here a man learns how to take care of his own problems."

Sykes grunted and said, "That's good to know."

Breckinridge lifted his paddle from the water, pointed to a smaller stream branching off to the right, and said, "We'll head that way. Got a few traps up there."

Sykes nodded that he understood. Their paddles cut into the water, and the canoe angled into the tributary.

About fifty yards farther on, they came to the first of the traps. Submerged as it was, Sykes probably would have paddled right past without ever seeing it if Breckinridge hadn't pointed it out.

"There's no beaver in it, but let's haul it out anyway," Breckinridge suggested. "I'll spring it and reset it so you can see how it's done."

"I appreciate this, Wallace," the Englishman said. "Not every man would take the time and trouble to teach the competition like this, you know."

"Oh, I don't think of you as competition, Harry. I reckon there's plenty of beaver out here for all of us. At least there will be for a while yet. Some of the old-timers say the end of the fur trade is comin', but when you look around it's sort of hard to believe."

"Everything comes to an end sooner or later."

"Well, that's the truth," Breckinridge agreed. "There's no denyin' it."

Breckinridge showed Sykes how to set the trap, then they moved on. As they paddled upstream, the banks rose higher on both sides of them. The trees grew thicker.

Suddenly, Breckinridge lifted his paddle from the water and said, "Hold on a minute." Sykes stopped paddling, too, and the canoe drifted to a halt.

Breckinridge stared at the mouth of a ravine that cut into the left-hand bank, which was about thirty feet tall at this point. The ravine was like a gash in the earth, penetrating about a hundred yards before it tapered down to nothing.

Sykes looked back over his shoulder and asked, "What's wrong?"

"Didn't really realize where we were until just now, since we come at it from a different direction," Breckinridge muttered. "And somethin' ain't right. I need to go take a look up yonder in that ravine, Harry."

Sykes shrugged and said, "All right. Whatever you need to do is fine with me."

"Let's pull this canoe ashore . . ."

Once they were out of the lightweight craft, Breckinridge picked up his rifle and frowned worriedly up at the ravine, which began only a few paces away. Although the day was bright with sunshine, gloom hung over the area at the bottom of the slash in the earth.

"You want me to come with you?" Sykes asked.

"No, stay here," Breckinridge told him. "And keep an eye out."

"Are you expectin' trouble?"

"Maybe," Breckinridge said grimly.

With his hands clasped tightly on the long-barreled flintlock, he started up the ravine, weaving through the rocks that littered the bottom of it.

The last time he'd been here, Morgan, Akins, and Fulbright had been with him, and they'd been toting the bodies of those Blackfoot warriors they had been forced to kill. They had dropped the corpses from up above and then pushed rocks down to conceal them.

The memory of that day put a bad taste in Breckinridge's mouth. He was perfectly willing to kill to defend himself or someone he cared about, but ending another human being's life wasn't something he took lightly, even when it was necessary. Thinking about it made a solemn feeling come over him.

A few minutes later he stopped short as the smell of death drifted to his nose and made his stomach twist.

Something had been messing with those Blackfoot corpses, and he could only hope it had been scavengers.

Breckinridge forced himself to go on. He could see the heap of rocks now that marked the resting place of those dead warriors. He wasn't sure, but it looked like some of those rocks had been tumbled aside . . .

Again he stopped. He saw an arm sticking out, with decay already setting in on the flesh that was visible. He knew the patches of white he saw were bone showing through rotted flesh. His stomach lurched, and the breakfast he had eaten a couple of hours earlier threatened to come up.

He forced himself to control that and turned his attention to the ground at his feet. He knelt and brushed away leaves and pine needles. The light wasn't good here at the bottom of the ravine, but his eyes were keen. He spotted the tracks left by previous visitors, but they weren't animal prints as he had hoped.

They were human.

Moccasin tracks.

Could have been left by other trappers, he supposed, since some of the white men in these mountains preferred Indian footgear.

But they could have just as easily been left by Indians, and if they were then the question became, were they friendly, like the Shoshone, or . . .

Or had another Blackfoot war party discovered what had happened to their lost brothers?

Strain carved bleak trenches into Breckinridge's cheeks as he rose to his feet. He had no way of knowing for sure who had found the bodies, but as long as there was a chance it was the Blackfeet, he needed to get back to the rendezvous and warn folks. It seemed unlikely that Indians would attack such a large gathering of seasoned, well-armed frontiersmen, but since there were women there, Breck couldn't afford to take the chance.

Since Dulcy was there . . .

He swung around to start back along the ravine toward the stream, and once again surprise stopped him in his tracks. He had told Harry Sykes to stay with the canoe, but he saw now that Sykes had followed him into the ravine. Breckinridge had been so engrossed by what he'd found that he hadn't heard the Englishman's approach.

Sykes wasn't alone, either. A frown of confusion creased Breckinridge's forehead as he recognized the white-haired gent named Powell, who stood beside Sykes. Close behind them were half a dozen other men, all bristling with rifles and pistols.

"What the hell?" Breckinridge exclaimed.

"Don't get jumpy, Wallace," Powell said. His voice was cold with menace, not friendly like before. "You're outnumbered and outgunned."

"What is this?" Breckinridge demanded. "If you're plannin' to rob me, you're gonna be disappointed. I don't have a damned thing anybody would want."

"You're wrong about that," Powell said. "You've got your life."

Breckinridge didn't know what the man meant by that, but clearly it couldn't be anything good. And yet there was more going on here than any of the others knew about.

"Listen to me," he said, and he tried to make his voice as urgent as he could. "We've got to get back to the rendezvous right away. We have to warn the folks there—"

"You're not going back to the rendezvous," Powell interrupted. "And neither are we. We've got what we came to the mountains for. Now, drop that rifle and come with us."

"Damn it, you don't understand!" Breckinridge burst out. "There's liable to be trouble!"

Sykes chuckled and said, "There's gonna be for you, no doubt about that."

Breckinridge saw that he had misjudged the Englishman. Sykes wasn't a friend, and he probably had no interest in becoming a trapper. From the looks of it, Sykes and Powell were working together, and they didn't have his best interests at heart. Breck suddenly wondered if they might have been responsible for the earlier attacks on him and his partners . . .

That didn't really make sense, since Powell had helped them during one of those fights, but Powell sure wasn't on his side now. In fact, the white-haired man raised the cocked pistol he held and pointed it at Breckinridge, saying, "Drop the rifle, Wallace. I won't tell you again. I'm not supposed to kill you, but I can make you wish you were dead."

Maybe it would be best to play along with them for the moment, Breckinridge thought. That would give him a chance to tell them about the possible threat from the Blackfeet. No matter what the men were after, the chance of a war party in the vicinity could mean danger for them, too. If Breck could convince them of that, he might get them to postpone whatever it was they had in mind for him.

"All right," he said. "Sykes, here's my rifle."

He tossed the weapon to the Englishman, and for a

second he considered lunging after it and tackling Sykes.

He didn't want a bunch of shooting, though. If there really were Blackfoot warriors around, that could draw them back to the ravine. The most important thing was to get out of here and warn the folks at the rendezvous.

Sykes caught the rifle. Powell motioned with his pistol for Breckinridge to walk out of the ravine. As he did so, his captors parted and then formed a ring around him, making sure he couldn't run.

As they came back out into the open, Breckinridge saw the short, thick figure of the Colonel standing there with a double-barreled shotgun in his hands. Maybe he could talk some sense into him, Breck thought. He said, "Colonel, you need to tell your men—"

"I am not a colonel," the man interrupted in his guttural voice. "I am a grieving father. My name is Otto Ducharme."

As soon as he heard that, Breckinridge knew there was no chance of persuading him to go back and warn the others. If Ducharme would come all this way, go to all this trouble, then there was no room in his brain for anything except hate.

Which meant Breckinridge had to find some other way to escape—

Before that thought was even fully formed, what felt like a mountain crashed down on the back of his head and buried him under a ton of darkness.

Chapter Forty-one

When Breckinridge came around, he had no idea how long he'd been out cold. Pain throbbed unmercifully inside his skull, and as he forced his eyes open, the world blurred and shifted around like it would have if he'd been underwater.

He groaned, then realized he probably shouldn't have. That would just let his captors know that he was awake again.

Someone stepped in front of him as his vision began to clear. After a few seconds he recognized the squat figure of Otto Ducharme.

"So, you are awake, Herr Wallace," said the man Breckinridge had first known as the Colonel.

The German's right hand, with fingers as fat as sausages, came up and cracked across Breckinridge's face. The impact jerked Breck's head to the side and made his eyes go blurry again for a second.

"You know me," Ducharme said. "You know the great crime you committed against my family."

Instinct tried to send Breck surging forward in retaliation for the craven blow, but he couldn't budge. He felt the rough bark of a tree trunk against his back and looked down to see ropes wound around his torso and arms, binding him to the tree. He was as helpless as he'd ever been.

But he wasn't gagged, and his mouth still worked just fine.

"I know your son did his dead-level best to kill me, Mr. Ducharme," he said. "That's the only reason I shot Rory. I took no pleasure or pride in what happened."

"But my son is still rotting in the ground, regardless."

"Yes, sir, I reckon that's true. But it was his own doin'."

Breckinridge looked past Ducharme at the other men. There were at least a dozen of them, counting Powell and Sykes. The sight of those two was especially galling to Breck, since he had considered them friends.

Obviously, what he'd told Dulcy about being a pretty good judge of character wasn't anywhere near right.

"So you two have been workin' for Ducharme all along," he said as he glared at them.

Sykes was leaning against a tree stump. He straightened from the casual pose and said, "I'm workin' *with* the fella now, but not *for* him." He looked at Ducharme. "You mind if I talk to Wallace for a minute before you go to work on him?"

Go to work on him. That sounded pretty ominous, thought Breckinridge. He expected nothing less from Otto Ducharme, though.

The German nodded curtly and told Sykes, "Go ahead and speak with him. We have plenty of time."

Maybe less time than they thought, Breckinridge

reminded himself, since it was still possible there were hostile Blackfeet skulking around here.

As Ducharme withdrew slightly, Sykes sauntered over and planted himself in front of Breckinridge. The Englishman sneered and said, "You don't have the slightest idea why I want to see you dead, do you, Wallace?"

"Best I recall I never laid eyes on you until a couple of days ago," Breckinridge said.

"And you're right about that. This is strictly a business deal for me. I was paid to kill you." Sykes shrugged. "Somebody else may do the actual deed, but I helped, and to my way of thinkin' that entitles me to collect the rest of my fee."

Breckinridge was about to ask who could hate him enough to pay someone to kill him, but before the words were out of his mouth, the obvious answer came to him.

"Aylesworth," he said. "That no-good son of a bitch, Richard Aylesworth."

Sykes laughed.

"You're smarter than you look. Not by much, maybe, but a little. Why wouldn't Aylesworth want you dead? You killed his child and almost killed his wife."

Breckinridge seized on one thing Sykes said.

"Almost," he repeated. "Maureen didn't die?"

"No, she's alive, or at least she was when I left Knoxville. Aylesworth didn't tell me all that much about what happened, but I asked around before I set out on your trail. Wasn't hard to find out that you accidentally shot the man's wife while you were tryin' to murder him."

"Yes," Ducharme agreed solemnly. "This man is a murderer and deserves to die."

"The child Missus Aylesworth was carryin' didn't make it, even though she did," Sykes went on. "So you can see why he was willin' to go to any lengths to settle the score with you, Wallace."

"Only problem with that," Breckinridge said, "is that the whole thing is a pack o' lies! Aylesworth's the one who fired that shot, tryin' to kill me. He's responsible for what happened to Maureen and the baby, not me."

For a second, Sykes frowned as if he was surprised, but then his expression cleared. He shook his head and said, "You know what, Wallace? It doesn't matter if I believe you or not. I was hired for a job, and I intend to do it." He shrugged. "Anyway, it ain't me what's gonna kill you. That's up to Mr. Ducharme. I just wanted you to know why I done what I did."

"Betrayed a friendship, you mean."

"We were never friends."

Breckinridge could see now that was right.

Sykes turned and walked back over to Powell and the other men. Ducharme moved in again. He took a razor from his pocket and opened it.

"I am going to see how much of you I can carve away before I finally take pity on you and blow your head off."

Breckinridge tried to summon up his courage. He glared at Ducharme and said, "Do your worst."

"Oh, I intend to, Herr Wallace. I intend to."

Ducharme lifted the razor and stepped closer, and Breckinridge kicked him in the groin.

They had made a mistake by not tying his legs. He couldn't get away, but he could inflict some damage on anybody who came too close, as he had just done to Ducharme. The German screamed and dropped the razor as he doubled over. He fell to his knees and then toppled to the side.

Sykes, Powell, and the other men lifted their rifles and pistols. Breckinridge steeled himself for the volley that was about to roar as they blasted him to pieces. That was better than letting Ducharme torture him to death.

A shot rang out, but it didn't come from any of those men. In fact, Sykes rocked back on his heels and stared down in shock to the hole in his shirt that welled crimson. That stunned reaction lasted only a heartbeat before his eyes rolled up in their sockets and he collapsed.

That first shot came from a rifle. The dull *boom* of a pistol followed it only instants later. A second man was blown off his feet. As Powell and the others started to scatter instinctively, another pistol shot erupted from the trees somewhere behind Breckinridge. A third man stumbled and then pitched forward as blood gushed from his torn throat.

Powell and the other men scrambled for cover along the creek. They had forgotten at least momentarily about Breckinridge. As another pistol shot blasted, Powell yelled, "It's a damn ambush!"

It seemed to be, although Breckinridge had absolutely no idea who might have come to his rescue.

As that thought went through his head, a tall, lithe figure in buckskins drifted past him, almost like a ghost. The stranger scooped Ducharme's fallen razor off the ground with his left hand. His right thrust out a pistol and pulled the trigger at the same time as his left wielded the razor and slashed through the ropes holding Breckinridge to the tree. He didn't really seem to pay that much attention to either of the things he was doing, but the ropes fell free and one of Ducharme's men trying to get behind a log spun around instead with blood spouting from his chest.

"Come on," the stranger said to Breckinridge. "Back this way."

They retreated into the ravine. Breckinridge wanted to tell the man that it was a dead end, that they would be trapped in there, but rifle and pistol balls had started to whip through the trees and brush around them and they had to go somewhere.

As they moved, the stranger darted from side to side and grabbed pistols that were wedged into the crooks of branches. From the sound of the shots a few moments earlier, Breckinridge had thought that several men were attacking Ducharme's party. Obviously, Powell and the others had believed that to be the case, too.

Now it appeared that it had been just this lone man, making it seem like there was more than one of him by setting up cocked and loaded pistols in different places and then dashing from one to the next to fire them.

That was pretty clever, he thought—but they were still about to get boxed up in this ravine that was also the final resting place for those dead Blackfoot warriors.

As they ran past the rocks toward the spot where the ravine played out, Breckinridge noticed something he couldn't have seen until now.

A rope dangled down into the ravine from somewhere up above.

"Shinny up that as fast as you can," the stranger told him as they reached the rope. "Those fellas'll be a mite leery of chargin' in here, and if they try it I'll give 'em a warm reception to slow 'em down. Don't just stand there, big'un. Get movin'.""

The man began reloading his rifle and pistols. Breckinridge thought he was pretty good at reloading, but this stranger's hands moved almost too fast for the eyes to follow, as if they were doing something they had done thousands of times before.

He was almost as tall as Breckinridge but not as massively built. There was an air of strength and power about him, but it was more like a wolf rather than a bear. His face was rugged and weathered and looked like he hadn't spent much time indoors for years, perhaps decades. Under his broad-brimmed brown felt hat was a shock of graying dark hair that matched his thick mustache and the stubble on his lean cheeks.

Breckinridge saw all that in a glance as he grasped the rope and lifted a foot to plant it against the wall of the ravine. Before he started to climb, he glanced over his shoulder and asked, "Just who in blazes *are* you, mister?"

"They call me Preacher," the man said as he lifted a pair of pistols, one in each hand ready to deal out death. "Now, move!"

Chapter Forty-two

Breckinridge started climbing. The ravine wall was rough enough to provide numerous footholds, so as he leaned back against the rope, hoping it was tied securely at the top and would support his weight, he began "walking" up the wall.

Rifles cracked from the direction of the creek. A couple of balls smacked into the earth not far from Breckinridge. Below him, Preacher's pistols roared as the man tried to discourage any more potshots at Breck.

As he got closer to the top, urgency gripped Breckinridge and made him scramble like an ape. Finally he was able to lunge over the brink and roll away from the edge.

He came up on his knees and looked around. The rope was tied around the trunk of a nearby pine. As he watched, it grew taut again, and he knew that Preacher was climbing out of the ravine now.

Breckinridge didn't have any guns, so he couldn't cover the other man's ascent as Preacher had done with his.

But he had something else to use as a weapon, he realized as his eyes fell on a pile of rocks left from when he and his friends had built the cairn for the fallen Blackfoot warriors. They had judged these rocks too small, but now they would work just fine. He scooped up an armful of them and ran along the ravine.

When he reached a spot where he could see Powell and some of the other men firing toward Preacher, Breckinridge stopped and dropped all the rocks except one that was about as big around as a man's head. He lifted it above his own head with both hands and heaved it toward the would-be killers below.

Breckinridge's aim was good and his strength was formidable. The rock landed on the head of a man who seemingly never saw doom descending on him from above. Even from where he was, Breck heard the ugly sound as the man's skull and brain were crushed like a melon.

That drew excited, angry shouts from the other men, who pointed their weapons at the top of the ravine and opened fire. Breckinridge dropped back rapidly so that they couldn't hit him from that angle. He knew from his first throw that he had the range, so he scooped up another rock and let fly with it, then another and another.

The angry shouts turned to frightened ones as those deadly missiles rained down. The guns fell silent, probably because the men were looking for shelter from the falling rocks.

Breckinridge looked along the ravine and saw Preacher pull himself over the edge. He leaped to his feet and pulled the rope up behind him, then waved for Breck to join him.

"Come on," Preacher said as he coiled the rope. "My horses are back yonder in the trees."

After a minute they came to the spot where a large, rawboned gray stallion was tied, along with a smaller but still powerful-looking packhorse. Standing in front of the horses was what Breckinridge took at first to be a wolf, all bristling fur and snarling teeth.

"Dog!" Preacher snapped at the big cur. "This fella's a friend." He glanced over at Breckinridge. "I reckon that's true?"

"After the way you saved my life, Mr. Preacher, it sure is," Breckinridge declared.

"Just Preacher. No mister. Get up on Horse there. He's strong enough to carry double, at least until we put some distance between us and those fellers."

"I don't know," Breckinridge said dubiously. "I weigh a whole heap."

"You don't know Horse," Preacher said. "Let's get movin'. No time to lollygag."

The man was right about that. Not only did Breckinridge want to get away from Ducharme, Powell, and the others, but it was urgent that he get back to the rendezvous and warn everyone there about the possible threat from the Blackfeet.

Preacher swung up into the saddle and Breckinridge climbed on behind him. As Preacher heeled the stallion into motion and brought the pack animal along with a lead rope, the big wolf-like cur loped out well ahead of them.

"If we're fixin' to run into any trouble, Dog'll let us know," Preacher said over his shoulder.

"You call your horse Horse and your dog Dog?" Breckinridge asked.

"Can you think of any better names for 'em?"

Preacher had a good point, Breckinridge supposed. He hadn't told his rescuer his own name yet, so he said, "I'm Breckinridge Wallace."

"Yeah, I heard those fellers talking to you and sort of figured out what was goin' on."

"How'd you manage to get so close and set up those guns without anybody noticin' you?"

Preacher snorted.

"I ain't inclined to brag, but the simple fact o' the matter is, more than once I've slipped into Blackfoot villages at night, cut the throats of half a dozen warriors whilst they was sleepin', and got back out again without anybody knowin' I'd been there until the next mornin'. I don't reckon a bunch of greenhorns like those are likely to see me unless I want 'em to."

"Wait a minute," Breckinridge said. "I think I've heard of you. Folks talk about you like they talk about mountain men like John Colter and Jim Bridger."

Preacher nodded and said, "Good men, both of 'em."

"What are you doin' here?"

"You mean besides savin' your hide?" Preacher chuckled. "I heard tell there was a rendezvous goin' on and decided to pay it a visit. I heard voices and indulged my natural-born curiosity. Good thing for you I did."

"I'll say," Breckinridge agreed. "How'd you know those fellas didn't have a right to do what they were fixin' to do to me?"

"I recognize a bunch of no-goods when I see 'em," Preacher said simply, and Breckinridge thought that unlike himself, the mountain man really was a good judge of character.

They had been angling away from the creek as Preacher kept both horses moving at a fast pace, but now Breckinridge said, "You need to head back the other way and follow the main branch of the creek. That'll take us to the place where the rendezvous's goin' on."

"In a hurry to get there now that you ain't bein' tortured to death after all, eh?"

"It's not that. I think there's a Blackfoot war party that might have its sights set on those folks."

Preacher turned his head to show Breckinridge a surprised frown. He said, "You'd best explain that."

Breckinridge did, as quickly as he could. He concluded by saying, "I saw moccasin tracks down in the ravine, and somebody had been messin' with the rocks where those warriors were buried, so I got to think there's a chance some other Blackfeet discovered 'em."

"There's a good chance of it," Preacher agreed. "A damned good chance. And if they did, they're gonna be on the lookout for some white folks to kill, just as soon as they can."

"So you can see why I want to get back."

Preacher was already turning the horses to the west, the direction they needed to go. He said, "Yeah. Hang on. I don't want to run Horse into the ground, but we need to move as fast as we can."

The gray stallion stretched out his legs into a ground-eating lope. The packhorse struggled to keep up. After a while, Preacher let go of the lead rope and told Breckinridge, "He won't wander far, loaded with supplies and pelts like that. I can come back for him later, once we've made sure those folks at the rendezvous ain't in any trouble."

"I'm obliged to you for your help, Preacher—for savin' my life and for carryin' the warnin' about the Injuns this way."

"I been gettin' along out here in the mountains for

more'n twenty years, son. Folks got to help each other out ever' now and then." Preacher paused. "Were you tellin' the truth back there? You didn't shoot that gal back wherever it is you come from?"

"The Great Smoky Mountains of Tennessee," Breckinridge said. "And no, sir, I never did shoot her. I wouldn't hurt that little gal for anything in the world."

"Sweet on her, are you?"

"I was," Breckinridge answered honestly. He thought about Dulcy. "I reckon I'm not anymore, but I still wouldn't want to see any harm come to her. Maybe I shouldn't care. It was her decision to go and marry a fella who's lower than a snake's belly. But I wish her well anyway."

"Sign of a good man," Preacher said. "It was her husband who shot her, you said?"

"Yeah. He was aimin' at me."

"Sounds like somethin' outta one o' them old Greek tragedies my friend Audie's always talkin' about. He used to be a professor 'fore he gave it up to be a mountain man, if you can picture that. Knows all sorts of things from books."

"I'd like to meet him someday."

"You stay around out here long enough, chances are you will. If you *live* long enough. I can tell you ain't exactly a greenhorn, but you ain't got all the moss knocked off yet, neither."

"I'm learnin'," Breckinridge said grimly.

"The frontier's a hard teacher."

Breckinridge couldn't argue with that.

He waited for Horse to start faltering under the great weight of him and Preacher, but the stallion's stride never broke. The muscles that moved smoothly under the rough gray hide might as well have been made of steel cable.

They had reached the creek now and were following it toward the rendezvous site. Breckinridge recognized plenty of landmarks and knew they were getting close, probably no more than half a mile away.

Preacher suddenly hauled back on Horse's reins and brought the big stallion to a halt.

"Why are we stoppin'?" Breckinridge asked anxiously.

"Listen," Preacher said.

Breckinridge listened and heard the same thing his newfound friend had. Somewhere not far away, round after round of gunfire shattered what should have been a peaceful late morning.

The rendezvous was already under attack.

Chapter Forty-three

Preacher heeled Horse into motion again, urging the stallion into a gallop this time. Breckinridge could sense that Horse was finally beginning to tire, but they didn't have far to go and the big gray poured what was left of his strength into this last run.

Breckinridge spotted smoke billowing into the sky up ahead. Preacher had seen it, too, and called, "Somethin's on fire up yonder!"

It had to be one or both of the big tents, Breckinridge thought. Nothing else would produce that much smoke. Setting the tents ablaze would provide a mighty good distraction for the Indians, too, as they launched their attack.

A *boom* sounded, and suddenly the clouds of smoke became thicker and darker. Breckinridge knew the flames must have reached some barrels of whiskey.

They rounded a bend in the creek and came in sight of Finch's Point. As Breckinridge expected, both of the big tents were burning. So were some of the wagons. Breck saw muzzle flashes coming from behind the wagons that weren't on fire. Some of the defenders had taken cover there, he realized.

Confusion reigned in both camps. Painted and feathered warriors dashed here and there, some armed with rifles, others with bows and arrows or tomahawks. Every trapper they caught in the open was either gunned down, skewered with arrows, or had his brains dashed out by a 'hawk.

White men weren't the only ones dying, though. Quite a few warriors' bodies were scattered around, too. The Blackfoot war party was a large one, though. It must have numbered at least a hundred, Breckinridge estimated. There were only fifty or sixty trappers at the rendezvous.

Breckinridge took in all that at a glance as Horse thundered toward the battle. He saw a gray, furry streak up ahead and realized it was Dog. The big cur flew through the air in a leap that ended with his razor-sharp teeth sunk in the throat of a Blackfoot warrior. The man went down under the impact and shuddered in his death throes as Dog tore out his throat.

Fear for Dulcy was uppermost in Breckinridge's mind, but he was also worried about Morgan, Akins, and Fulbright. He didn't see any of them and hoped that his friends were among the men behind the wagons, trying to fight off the attackers.

Right now, more than anything else, he wanted to get across the creek and find Dulcy. Over the pounding of Horse's hoofbeats, he called, "If I don't see you again, Preacher, I'm mighty obliged for your help!"

The mountain man twisted his head and began, "What're you—"

He was too late. Breckinridge had already dived off the stallion.

His leap carried him into one of the warriors. Breckinridge wrapped his arms around the Blackfoot and drove him to the ground. Momentum made both of them roll over and over.

They came to a stop with Breck on top and the warrior on the bottom. Breck brought his right fist up and around in a looping, sledgehammer blow that landed in the center of the man's face and collapsed it as bones shattered and crunched. The Indian spasmed and then lay still.

Breckinridge scooped up the tomahawk the man had dropped, then leaped to his feet.

He would have charged directly into the creek and waded across, but he spotted Nicodemus Finch in the middle of the log bridge, struggling with one of the Blackfeet. The warrior had a big hunting knife clutched in his fist and was doing his best to bury it in Finch's scrawny chest. Finch had hold of his enemy's wrist and was keeping the blade away for the moment, but Breckinridge could tell that Finch's strength was about to give out. Breck had to help him.

Before Breckinridge could get there, Tom Mahone limped out onto the log from the other direction, raised his walking stick, and brought it crashing down on the warrior's head from behind with skull-crushing force. The Indian dropped the knife and pitched off the makeshift bridge.

That left the two old enemies standing there facing each other, but only for a second. Then an arrow ripped into one of Mahone's withered thighs and lodged there. Mahone yelled, flailed his arms in the air, and toppled into the creek.

"Tom!" Finch yelled. "Hold on, you frazzle-livered gafftop!" He leaped into the stream, as well.

Breckinridge didn't take the time to help them. The creek was shallow enough that they shouldn't drown. He bounded across the log instead, his feet barely touching it twice.

Gripping the tomahawk tightly, he headed for Dulcy's tent. There was no guarantee she would be there, but he figured it was the best place to start looking. Also, he didn't see any Blackfeet around there at the moment, so maybe if she was hiding there no one had bothered her yet.

He ran up to the tent, ripped the entrance flap aside, and plunged in. Instantly, something crashed against his back with enough force to make him stumble. He dropped to one knee but caught his balance in time to keep from falling all the way down.

"Breckinridge! Oh my God! I'm sorry!"

The startled cry came from Dulcy. Breckinridge was so relieved to hear her voice he didn't care that she had walloped him with something. From where he knelt, he looked around and saw her as she dropped the piece of firewood she had used to hit him.

She rushed into his arms as he turned and came to his feet. He held her tightly against his broad chest, encircling her with his arms. She sobbed a little, whether from pain or fear, he couldn't tell.

"Dulcy, are you all right?" he asked as he stroked a hand over her raven hair.

"I . . . I'm fine," she said without lifting her head. "When . . . when you rushed in, I didn't know it was you. I thought it was . . . was one of those savages. When all the yelling and screaming started, I ran outside and grabbed that piece of firewood from one of the stacks, then came back in here to hide . . ."

"You done the right thing," he told her.

"Who are all those Indians?"

"Blackfeet," he said grimly. "They hate whites more'n any other tribe in this part of the country."

He didn't mention that his own actions had played a part in causing this attack. He didn't feel like he had done anything wrong—he and his friends had only been defending themselves from that earlier war party—but it was doubtful that these warriors would have attacked the rendezvous if the previous clash hadn't happened.

"What's going to happen to us?" Dulcy asked.

"I don't know. Depends on how the fight goes, I reckon."

He should have tried to reassure her and tell her that everything was going to be fine, he thought, but he generally tried to tell the truth. Anyway, Dulcy was smart enough to know just how bad the situation was without Breckinridge telling her.

All of them would stand a better chance in the long run if he was out there in the middle of the fracas. He let go of her, bent, and picked up the piece of firewood. As he pressed it back into her hands, he said, "Hang on to this. You might need it again. Best aim for the head next time, though."

Even in these perilous circumstances, she was able to summon a smile.

"I *was* aiming for where a normal person's head would be," she said. "It's not my fault you're as big as Goliath."

Breckinridge had to laugh. He said, "Stay here, keep your head down, and don't come out until somebody you know tells you it's all right."

"You come back and get me, Breckinridge. You hear me? *You.*"

"Do my best," he promised her.

Still carrying the tomahawk, he ducked out of the tent and looked around for somebody to fight.

Several strident whoops erupted from his left. He wheeled in that direction to see three of the Blackfoot warriors charging at him. Two of them brandished knives while the third man carried a 'hawk like the one in Breckinridge's hand.

The one with the tomahawk hung back a little and let his knife-wielding companions lead the attack. Breckinridge ducked under one of the slashing blades, then lowered his shoulder and rammed the warrior into the man beside him.

While both of the Indians stumbled, Breck whipped the tomahawk back and forth. The first strike shattered one man's jaw, then the return buried the head in the second man's temple.

Breckinridge jerked the weapon free and leaped back just in time to avoid a vicious downstroke from the third Indian's tomahawk that would have caved in his skull. The 'hawk's stone head brushed the front of Breck's shirt.

With his free hand, he grabbed the front of the warrior's buckskin shirt and heaved him off his feet. The Blackfoot crashed to the ground and rolled over, and as he did, Breck pounced, bringing his tomahawk down between the man's eyes with such terrific force that it split the warrior's head in two.

Whirling away from the man who had met that grisly fate, Breckinridge almost caught an arrow in the throat. It missed by inches, and the shaft bounced off his shoulder instead. The warrior who had fired it was about fifteen feet away, about to nock another arrow. Breck let fly with the tomahawk.

It cracked into the man's forehead and dropped him either dead or out cold. Breckinridge bounded past him, pausing for a split second to retrieve the tomahawk, and then he plunged back into the melee.

There was no way to keep track of time in the bloody swath of violence that followed. Breckinridge waded through his enemies, hacking right and left with the 'hawk. Somewhere he picked up a knife with his left hand and slashed and thrust with it, as well. The ground was sticky with blood under his feet, and gore splattered both arms up past the elbows. It was slaughter the likes of which he had never experienced. He didn't even feel the minor wounds he suffered in return. He was moving so fast it seemed that none of the Blackfeet could get a decent shot at him.

In reality the battle probably lasted less than half an hour, but to Breckinridge the killing seemed endless. Finally, though, there was no one left for him to fight. He stood rooted to the ground, chest heaving, shaking his head as if to clear away the bloodred haze that had descended over his eyes, and looked around to see the bodies heaped around him.

"Breck! Breck!"

The shout made his head jerk around. It wasn't Dulcy calling his name this time, but rather Morgan Baxter. Morgan hurried toward him, face smeared with blood from a gash on his forehead. He grabbed Breckinridge's arm.

"Breck, are you all right?" Morgan asked. Aghast, he looked up and down his friend's giant frame. "My God, you're covered with blood!"

"Most of it ain't mine," Breckinridge said. "I reckon I'm fine. How about you?"

"A few scrapes. Nothing to worry about."

"What about Roscoe and Amos?"

A bleak expression settled on Morgan's face. He shook his head and said, "Roscoe got an arrow in the side, but I think he'll be all right. Amos is dead. One of those red bastards shot him through the heart."

Breckinridge sighed. It was hard to believe Amos Fulbright was gone. The big, bearded man had been so full of mirth and vitality.

"I'm sorry," Breckinridge muttered. "He was a good man."

Morgan was starting to look anxious now. He said, "I've got to go find Annie. Come with me, Breck."

Breckinridge hesitated. He wanted to get back to Dulcy, but Morgan seemed really worried, and who could blame him? Anyway, it shouldn't take them more than a few minutes to locate Annie, Breck reasoned. Finch's Point wasn't that big.

They set out searching, and as they did Breckinridge looked around them. The big tents had burned to the ground, the infernos fueled by the whiskey that had been inside them. For the most part, the fires were out now. Only a few small flames danced here and there.

The Blackfeet had wreaked a considerable amount of bloody havoc, but the trappers were better armed and they were good shots, to boot. The abundance of rifles and pistols had taken a deadly toll. Breck didn't know if any of the attackers had escaped with their lives. Considering the number of Blackfoot corpses littering the ground, not many could have.

"Hey, youngster!"

Breckinridge looked over and saw Preacher approaching them. Dog padded along at the mountain man's side, his muzzle stained with the blood of his enemies. Preacher seemed to be unharmed, which

came as no surprise to Breck. From what he had heard
of the man, Preacher was the deadliest Indian fighter
west of the Mississippi.

"Glad to see you made it," Preacher said as he joined
them.

"You, too," Breckinridge said. He introduced
Preacher and Morgan, then went on, "We're lookin' for
a gal that Morgan's right fond of."

"One of the doves?" Preacher asked. He nodded to
their right. "I just saw some of 'em over yonder outside
a tent."

Morgan broke into a trot in that direction.

Breckinridge and Preacher followed and caught up
in time to see Morgan hugging Annie for all he was
worth. The blonde clutched him with equal intensity.
Breck saw several of the other young women nearby,
then frowned as he spotted Francesca and Bonnie lying
motionless on the ground behind them. Both had
arrows protruding from their bodies, and there was no
doubt they were dead. The other soiled doves, including Annie, didn't appear to be hurt, so there was that
to be thankful for, anyway, while mourning the two
who were lost.

Since Morgan and Annie had been reunited, at least
for now, and since there was nothing he could do here,
Breckinridge told Preacher, "I'm headin' back across
the creek. I left somebody over there."

"That gal you told me about?"

"Yeah. I saw her earlier and she was all right then. I
told her to keep out of sight until I came to get her."

"I'll come with you," Preacher said with a shrug.

They walked to the log bridge. On the far bank sat
Nicodemus Finch and Tom Mahone. Both of the old-
timers were soaked from being dunked in the creek.

Finch must have taken the arrow out of Mahone's leg, because he was tying a torn piece of cloth from his shirt around the wound.

Breckinridge didn't figure the two of them would ever give up their feud, but maybe they didn't hate each other quite as much as they let on, he thought.

Then he and Preacher were on the far side of the creek heading toward Dulcy's tent. They were still about twenty feet from it and Breckinridge was about to call her name when the entrance flap was thrust back and she stepped out.

She wasn't alone, though. Right behind her with his left arm looped around her neck and his right hand holding a pistol to her head was the white-haired killer called Powell.

Chapter Forty-four

Breckinridge started to lunge forward, but Powell stopped him by grinding the gun's muzzle against Dulcy's head hard enough to make her gasp in pain.

"Don't do anything crazy, Wallace," Powell warned. "I got nothin' against this woman, but I'll sure kill her if I have to."

"You let her go," Breckinridge raged. "Your fight's with me, not her."

"I don't have a fight with you. Ducharme does. You're nothin' to me but the promise of some gold, Wallace."

"You son of a bitch. You hurt her, you'll be dead two seconds later."

"Maybe. But that won't bring her back to life, will it?"

Preacher said, "Mister, you better make sure I'm dead when you leave here, otherwise you're gonna be lookin' over your shoulder for me from now on."

"Who the hell are you?" Powell asked with a frown.

"Friend of the boy's." Preacher inclined his head toward Breckinridge.

"You're the one who pulled him out of that ravine!"

"Yep. And killed a goodly number of your bunch in the process, I'm thinkin'."

"There's enough of us left," Powell said ominously.

As if to prove his point, half a dozen men came out of the trees nearby, including Otto Ducharme. The German was disheveled and more red-faced than usual, but his beefy face was still etched with lines of hate as he glared at Breckinridge.

"Kill the woman," he snapped at Powell. "If Wallace cares for her, let him know the pain of loss as I have."

"Not a good idea, boss," Powell said. "This gal's our way outta here. She and Wallace are comin' with us, and once we're good and away from here, you can do whatever you want to the big bastard."

"I'll come with you," Breckinridge said without hesitation, "but you got to let Dulcy go."

"Not until we know we're safe," Powell insisted. "Then sure, she can go. Nobody'll hurt her."

Breckinridge knew beyond a shadow of a doubt that he was lying. As soon as they had no further use for Dulcy, they would kill her.

Well, maybe not right away, he amended. First they would have their sport with her, like the craven animals they were.

Dulcy must have known that, too, and more than that, she had to realize that Breckinridge had just volunteered to give up his life in an attempt to save hers. Her lips formed a word, and Breck realized she had just whispered, *"No."*

He cried, "Dulcy, wait—"

It was too late. She twisted in Powell's grip and grabbed at the pistol he held. Somehow, she was fast enough to get her hands around the barrel and jerk it away from her head before he could pull the trigger.

But pull the trigger he did, and as the pistol boomed Dulcy cried out and doubled over. A howl of rage tore itself from Breckinridge's throat as he leaped at Powell.

The white-haired man slashed at Breckinridge's head with the empty pistol. The blow glanced off Breck's head but didn't slow him down. His momentum carried him into Powell with an impact that drove Powell off his feet. Breck's hands found Powell's throat as the two of them crashed to the ground next to Dulcy's sprawled body. He was vaguely aware of guns going off, an ear-numbing roar of black powder fury, but the rest of his attention was focused on the man who had just shot Dulcy.

He clamped down harder with both huge hands around Powell's throat, planted a knee in the middle of the man's chest, and heaved. The crack of Powell's neck snapping was as loud and sharp as if a tree branch had broken. The man's eyes glazed over as he went limp.

Breckinridge knelt there, breathing heavily, for a couple of seconds before an inarticulate cry was wrenched from deep inside him. He turned his head and saw Dulcy's bloody, motionless form.

Then his head swung the other way, and his eyes fixed on Otto Ducharme, who stood there quivering as if in rage.

It wasn't anger that made Ducharme shake now, though. It was fear. The men with him were all down, a couple wounded, the others dead. Smoke still curled from the barrel of Preacher's rifle, as it did from the pistols held by Morgan Baxter, who had come up in time to join in the brief gun battle. Nicodemus Finch was there, too, with his old-fashioned blunderbuss clutched in his gnarled hands. The wide-barreled weapon might be old, as was its owner, but it had done some damage.

Breckinridge pushed himself to his feet. Slowly, deliberately, he started toward Ducharme. The man's blubbery lips spilled what had to be frightened curses in his native tongue as Breck approached him. The young man's face was set in lines as hard as stone.

"You . . . you got what you deserved!" Ducharme stammered in English.

Preacher drawled, "I reckon you're the one who's about to get what's comin' to him, mister."

Ducharme's eyes suddenly got wider. They bulged until they seemed like they were about to pop from their sockets. He lifted a trembling hand and pressed it to his chest as he took a couple of reeling steps to the side and then pitched forward, landing with his face in the dirt.

Breckinridge stopped. He shook his head a little, as if he were puzzled by what he had just witnessed.

Finch said, "Looks like the sumbitch's ticker give out."

Morgan looked over at him and said, "You didn't call him some crazy names."

Finch snorted.

"Fella like that ain't worth makin' up fancy words over," he said.

Morgan hurried forward and dropped to a knee beside Ducharme. He rolled the German onto his back and then said, "Looks mighty dead to me."

"Me, too," Preacher agreed.

That was all Breckinridge needed to hear. It was over.

All but the grieving, he thought as he turned toward Dulcy.

* * *

The black maid called Ophelia answered the heavy knock on the door of Richard Aylesworth's house in Knoxville. When she saw who stood there, her eyes got big and her mouth formed an O of surprise. She took an involuntary step backward.

Breckinridge Wallace said, "I know he's here. I want to see him."

Ophelia stammered, "You . . . you can't—"

Breckinridge stepped into the foyer, brushing her aside easily but being careful not to get too rough about it. He smelled the smoke from a pipe and moved into the entrance to the lamp-lit parlor.

Aylesworth sat smoking in an armchair near the fireplace, with a snifter of brandy on a small table beside him. He had a leather-bound book open in his lap. He gave every appearance of being a fine young gentleman enjoying a peaceful evening at home.

He didn't *look* like the monster he was.

Nor was he alone in the parlor. Maureen sat on a divan across the room, needlework in her lap. She gaped at Breckinridge, apparently as astounded by his arrival as her maid had been.

"Wallace," Aylesworth grated. His jaw had clenched tightly at the sight of the big, redheaded young man.

"Didn't expect to see me alive, did you?" Breckinridge asked. "Not after you hired Harry Sykes to round up a bunch of men, track me down, and kill me."

Aylesworth's lips thinned even more. He said, "I don't know what you're talking about."

"I reckon you do. So does the law, since Sykes told all about it to try to save his hide."

That was a lie, but Aylesworth didn't have to know that. Not yet, anyway.

"Richard, what . . . what is this?" Maureen asked

anxiously as she leaned forward. "Did you really send someone to hurt Breckinridge?"

"Wallace is insane," Aylesworth snapped. "He always has been. You know that, Maureen."

Breckinridge shook his head and said, "I ain't the crazy one. I'm not the one who fired off a pistol in here and nearly killed my own wife. You couldn't stand knowin' what really happened, could you, Aylesworth? And you couldn't take the rightful blame for it yourself, so you twisted things around and made it all my fault, at least in your head. You figured if I was dead, that'd put an end to it." Breck's voice hardened even more. "But it won't. The four of us here"—he gestured to indicate himself, Maureen, Aylesworth, and Ophelia— "we know the truth and we always will."

Aylesworth flung the book aside and surged up out of the chair. He took a step toward Breckinridge and raged, "You bastard! *You* should have died that night, not my child! You were the one I was aiming at, not Maureen—"

Aylesworth stopped short as three more men appeared in the foyer, just outside the parlor. One was the stolid lawman, Sheriff Parley Johnson, who had tried more than once to arrest Breckinridge for things he hadn't done. Just behind him were Morgan Baxter and the lawyer Morgan had hired, using some of the considerable estate he had inherited from his late father. The three of them had come in while Breck was distracting Aylesworth, and the ploy had worked. They had heard Aylesworth's declaration that he was the one who had wounded Maureen and caused her to lose the baby, not Breckinridge Wallace.

Sheriff Johnson, convinced of Breckinridge's guilt because of Aylesworth's false testimony, hadn't wanted to go along with the plan at first, but Morgan and the lawyer had talked him into it. Now the lawman stepped into the room, his face dark with anger, and said, "You lied to me, Mr. Aylesworth. All of you did. You let me go after an innocent man."

Aylesworth stared wildly around the room, looking a little like a trapped animal now. He struggled to find his voice, then said, "Wallace isn't innocent! He . . . he caused the whole thing. He came to see my wife—"

"Breckinridge was saying good-bye, Richard," Maureen said. "It was your own jealousy that caused . . . that caused . . ."

She couldn't go on. She lifted her hands, put them over her face, and sobbed.

With a visible effort, Aylesworth regained some of his usual arrogant bravado. His jaw jutted out defiantly as he asked, "Are you going to arrest me, Sheriff?"

"For lying to me?" Johnson shrugged. "Maybe I should, but we all know the judge'd just throw it out. For shooting your wife? Well, as bad as that might be, I reckon it really was an accident."

"How about for hirin' somebody to kill me?" Breckinridge asked.

"Since Sykes is dead, that's your word against Aylesworth's. Can't prove it either way."

Aylesworth glared at Breckinridge and said, "You told me Sykes was alive!"

"Nope, that's just what you figured." Breckinridge looked at the sheriff. "You heard him admit that he knew Sykes."

"No crime in knowing somebody," Johnson said. "You better be satisfied with what you got, Wallace. I'll see to it that all the charges against you are dropped. Your name is clear again."

Breckinridge thought about it, but only for a second. Then he nodded and said, "All right. I guess I got what I came for, anyway." He looked at the woman crying on the divan. "I'm sorry, Maureen, I truly am. Sorry for the way it all worked out for you more than anything else. I hope you'll be happy someday, one way or another."

"Breckinridge!" she said brokenly as he turned to leave.

"Good-bye, Maureen," he told her without looking back. He strode out of the house. Morgan, the lawyer, and Sheriff Johnson followed him.

Johnson said, "Everybody's going to know what really happened that night, Wallace. The gossip's gonna be mighty hard on that poor woman."

Morgan said, "It seems to me she made her own bed, Sheriff. You can't expect Breck or anyone else to feel sorry for her."

"Everybody makes decisions they wish they hadn't," Breckinridge said. "Nothin' they can do except carry that with 'em for the rest of their lives and hope they can do enough good to balance out some of the mistakes." He sighed and shook his head, then turned and shook hands with the lawyer, thanking him. Then he took Morgan's hand and pulled the smaller man into a bear hug, slapping him on the back. "See you in St. Louis in a couple months?"

"I'll be there," Morgan promised. "I'll have an outfit waiting and ready for us to head back to the mountains."

"That'll be a good day," Breckinridge said. "Right now, though, I got to head on out to the farm. Got somebody I need to introduce to the folks."

With a smile on his face, he walked toward the wagon where Dulcy waited on the seat, holding herself a little stiffly because she was still recuperating from the deep graze in her side. The joy that had filled him when he realized she was wounded but still alive remained just as strong in him as ever.

Dulcy was well enough to travel and had insisted on coming with him back to Knoxville. She returned his smile as he climbed onto the seat beside her and took up the reins.

"Did everything go like you wanted it to?" she asked.

"Went as well as could be expected," Breckinridge replied. "Lot of pain in that house, though. Reckon there always will be."

He flicked the reins and got the team moving.

As it rolled along the street, Dulcy asked, "Are you sure you want to take me home with you?"

"I want you to meet my folks and my brothers," Breckinridge answered without hesitation. "It's only fittin' that they all get to know you before the weddin'. But the farm's not my home anymore."

She linked her arm with his and leaned her head against his shoulder.

"My home . . . *our* home . . . is in the mountains," Breckinridge said.

*Turn the page for a special excerpt of the next
adventure in the bestselling Duff MacCallister series.*

DAY OF RECKONING
A Duff MacCallister Western

by NATIONAL BESTSELLING AUTHORS
WILLIAM W. JOHNSTONE
with J. A. Johnstone

*The legendary MacCallister clan brought 500 years
of Highlander tradition, honor, and fighting courage
to the American frontier. In an astounding new novel
from the national bestselling Johnstones,
Duff MacCallister rides into the Colorado
mountains with a young girl at his side—and a gang
of stone-cold killers eagerly waiting for them . . .*

DAY OF RECKONING

When Duff MacCallister sees smoke rising from
his neighbor's ranch, he knows that something is
very wrong. But he isn't prepared for what he finds:
smoldering buildings, a rancher and his wife brutally
slaughtered, and a 14-year-old survivor who could
not save her parents. Now Duff is going after
the killers—and his only companion is the
headstrong girl who refuses to be left behind.

Duff and his new companion head into the towering
Gore Range. Up ahead are two convicted murderers
who were about to be hung in Cheyenne, and the
killers who broke them lose. Duff doesn't have a
plan—or a prayer. But the girl will be more help
than he can know, and when the day of reckoning
comes, bullets and blood will prove who is
the bravest and fiercest fighter of all . . .

Available now, wherever Pinnacle Books are sold.

Chapter One

The first rider came into town from the north, stopping in front of Mrs. Steinberg's Boarding House. He tied his horse off at the hitching post, then went inside. He was a large man who had once been a prizefighter, and that occupation had left him with two distinguishing features. His nose had been broken so that the bridge of it lay closer to his face than normal, and he had a cauliflower left ear. He signed his name, Clay Callahan, with tobacco-stained fingers.

"Will you be staying with us for an extended period of time, Mister . . ." Bella Steinberg paused to read the name, "Callahan? The reason I ask is, anyone who stays longer than a month gets a special rate."

"No," Callahan replied. "Just for a few days."

"Oh? Well don't get me wrong, I am most happy to have you, but generally people who stay less than a month take their lodging at the hotel."

Callahan smiled. "I like the homey atmosphere of a boardinghouse," he said.

"Yes," Mrs. Steinberg replied. "All of our residents

regard this as their home, and as you will see when you dine with us, it is as if we are one big family."

"That's exactly the way I like it."

Zeke Manning rode into town two days later, checking in to the Adam's Hotel. Manning and Callahan weren't in the same room at the same time until the next evening after Manning arrived. Manning went to the Cock o' the Walk Saloon, where Callahan, who had already been in town for three days, was joking and laughing with the new friends he had made. And though Callahan saw Manning come in, the two men maintained a separation.

In a town as small as Archer, any new visitor was noticed, and several of the saloon patrons commented on getting two new people coming to town within just a few days.

It created even more attention when two more strangers arrived later that same evening. The two men were laughing and talking loudly as they stepped up to the bar.

"Barkeep!" one of them called. "A beer for me 'n my brother."

The bartender filled two mugs and set them before the brothers. One of the two turned away from the bar and looked out over the ten tables, all of them occupied by from one to four men. A couple of bar girls were hopping from table to table.

"Hello to all here. My name is Dan LaFarge. This is my brother, Don. Anyone here from Texas?"

"Yeah, I'm from Texas," a rather large man said.

"I'm from Texas, too. What about it?"

"We're from Texas, too. Barkeep, give our Texas friends a drink on me 'n my brother."

Dan and Don flirted outrageously with the bar girls

and went from table to table, laughing and talking with the other saloon patrons.

Archer was a railroad town, five miles east of Cheyenne, and it was here that the holding and feeding pens were located for shipping cattle. Earlier that day, Duff MacCallister, Elmer Gleason, and Wang Chow had brought cattle here to be shipped out.

"Here you go, Mr. MacCallister, a receipt for the rail shipment of two hundred Black Angus cattle to the McCord Beef Processing Plant in Kansas City. Your beeves will be there in two days," Bull Blackwell said.

Blackwell was the shipping agent for the Union Pacific Railroad in Archer. He got the name "Bull" because he was a big man, with broad shoulders and a somewhat oversized head that seemed to sit directly on those shoulders, without benefit of a neck.

"Thank you, Bull," Duff replied.

"You know, Mr. MacCallister, you have become one of our largest cattle shippers. You are, by far, the largest shipper of Black Angus, and while I would have to examine all the documents to be certain, I can tell you without equivocation that you are in the top five for all of Wyoming."

"Aye, coming to Wyoming was a good thing for me," Duff replied. "'N I can say, 'tis lucky I have been in introducing the Angus cattle to the American market."

"Luck hasn't had anything to do with it, the way I've heard it told," Blackwell said. "You come to Wyoming and started raising all these black cows that many of the other ranchers teased you about." Blackwell chuckled. "I'd be willing to bet a dollar to a cow turd that nobody is teasing you now."

Duff laughed. "Sure 'n ye meet a lot of people who are willing to bet a cow turd do ye? 'N would be for tellin' me, Bull, what you would do with the cow turd once you won it?"

"Well, I don't really want a cow turd, you understand, it's just . . ." Blackwell stopped in mid-sentence when he saw the twinkle in Duff's eye. "You're funnin' me, aren't you? 'N here I didn't think you Scotsmen had a sense of humor."

"'Tis thankin' ye I am, Bull, for handling the shipping for me. I'll see you next time I come this way."

"You going back home today?" Blackwell asked.

"Nae, I think I'll ride over to Cheyenne before I go back. Cheyenne is only five miles, and 'tis so infrequently that I am this close that I plan to stay for a day or two 'n enjoy all the benefits of a big city."

To anyone from one of the bigger cities back east, such as St. Louis, Chicago, Philadelphia, or New York, Duff's reference to Cheyenne as a "big" city might sound laughable. But compared to where Duff called home, Cheyenne was a metropolis.

Home, for Duff, was Sky Meadow, a very large ranch that was located about eight miles south of Chugwater. He did his banking there, he shopped there, he had very good friends there, most notably Biff Johnson who owned Fiddler's Green.

Biff Johnson was a retired army first sergeant who had served with General Custer. Indeed, Biff had made that last scout with Custer, though he was spared the ultimate disaster because when Custer divided his regiment, Biff was with Captain Benteen.

Biff's saloon, Fiddler's Green, got its name from an

old cavalry legend. The legend claimed that any trooper who had ever heard the sound of "Boots and Saddles" would, when they die, go to a broad, inviting meadow, surrounded by shade trees and bounded by a sparkling brook. Then all the old cavalrymen there gathered would have all they wanted to eat and drink, they would enjoy the music of "Garryowen" and "The Girl I Left Behind Me," and sit around telling drunken war tales until the last day.

Fiddler's Green wasn't just a saloon for men, it was more on the order of what the English called a pub, and thus was of the character that decent women did not have to feel out of place while visiting. One woman who was a patron of the saloon was Meagan Parker. Meagan owned a dress emporium in Chugwater, and she and Duff had what could be referred to as a "special" friendship.

Meagan was also Duff's business partner. She had been an early believer in his idea of introducing a new breed of cattle to the area and had loaned him money at a time when he needed it. Duff, long ago, had gathered the wherewithal to repay Meagan, but she didn't want to be repaid. She preferred, instead, to be a part owner of the cattle, and the nature of their relationship was such that Duff found her interest and participation in his ranch to be agreeable enough that he made no effort to disentangle himself for her involvement.

Though he didn't share the information with Bull Blackwell, one of the reasons Duff wanted to go to Cheyenne was because Meagan would be there on a buying trip for her store. They had already planned their rendezvous.

As Duff left the cattle holding lot, he had absolutely no idea of the drama that was occurring at this very moment just down the street in the Cattlemen's Bank and Trust of Archer. There, Callahan, Manning, and the two LaFarge brothers were about to play out the real reason they had come to Archer, for though the four men had arrived in town separately, that had been a subterfuge. They were about to come together to carry out the nefarious scheme they had planned two days earlier.

It was Callahan who went into the bank first to break a fifty-dollar bill, requesting five and one-dollar bills. Counting out the money, kept the teller preoccupied. Because of that, he paid no attention to Manning who came into the bank shortly thereafter and stepped over to a table, where he began to fill out a bank draft.

A moment later the two LaFarge brothers stepped into the bank as well. It wasn't until then that the teller noticed, with some surprise, that there were so many people in the bank at the same time. But what was even more surprising than the number of customers was the fact that he didn't recognize any of them. And, in his position as bank teller, he knew almost everyone in town.

The two LaFarge brothers raised their guns.

"This is a holdup!" one of them shouted.

"Oh, I'll be damned!" the teller said to Callahan. "I believe they intend to rob the bank!"

"Oh, we not only *intend* to rob the bank, we are going to do it," Callahan said.

"You are a part of this?" the bank teller asked.

"We all four are," Manning said from the table where he had, ostensibly, been filling out a bank draft. Manning, like the two LaFarge brothers, was holding a pistol in his hand.

Callahan handed the teller the pillowcase he had taken from his bed in the boardinghouse.

"Empty the cash drawer and the safe, and put the money in this if you would, please."

"Four strangers in the bank at the same time," the teller said. "I should have realized that something strange was going on."

"Shut up and empty the cash drawer and safe like I told you to," Callahan said, his tone of voice little more than a growl.

Complying with the request, the teller filled the pillowcase with money.

"Get the money," Callahan ordered, and Manning took the money from the teller. Then, just as the four men turned to leave, a man and woman came in through the front door.

"Ernie, this is a wonderful day! The collection in church yesterday was the best we've had in a long time!" The man who called out was wearing a black suit and a low-crown, black bowler hat.

"Run, Reverend Pyle, run! The bank is being robbed!" Ernie, the teller, shouted.

"What?" the reverend replied. He was unable to get another word out, because all four robbers began shooting at them. Both the good reverend and his wife went down under a hail of bullets.

The four men ran from the bank and leaped onto their horses, followed out the door by the teller.

"Bank robbery!" the teller shouted. "These men robbed the bank!"

Callahan and one of the LaFarge brothers turned to fire at the teller, and he went down with one bullet in his heart and one in his neck.

Callahan was the mastermind of the robbery, and

he had researched it quite thoroughly, including the fact that there was no city law in town, only a sheriff's deputy who didn't spend all his time here.

What he did not know, and could not have possibly anticipated, was the fact that Duff MacCallister was in town. Duff was also, at that very moment, no more than one block away from the bank, and he had both heard the teller's shout and seen the teller shot down.

The four men mounted their horses, then started galloping away from the bank. They were bearing down on Duff, who, in contrast to all the others in town who hurried to get out of the way, had stepped out into the street in front of them.

"Who is that crazy son of a bitch?" Dan LaFarge shouted.

"Shoot him!" Callahan ordered. "Shoot him!"

All four of the bank robbers turned their guns toward the man who was standing, like a statue, in front of them.

With bullets whizzing by him, Duff raised his pistol and fired. His first shot took one of the LaFarge brothers from the saddle.

"Dan!" Don LaFarge shouted.

Don LaFarge was taken down by the second shot.

"Hold it up! Hold it!" Manning shouted, pulling his horse to a halt. "Don't shoot, don't shoot! Here's the money!" Manning, who was carrying the money, threw the bag on the ground and put up his hands.

"Manning, you cowardly bastard!" Callahan shouted. Callahan aimed at Duff, but when he saw Duff's pistol being pointed unerringly at him, he had second thoughts and threw his gun down as well.

Now, with two of the robbers lying dead in the street and the other two still mounted but sitting still, with their hands up, an enraged citizenry began to appear from the buildings where they had taken shelter.

"Two of 'em is still alive," someone said.

"They kilt Reverend Pyle 'n his wife," another said.

"An' don't forget Ernie, they kilt him, too," a third added.

"String 'em up!" someone shouted. "String the bastards up!"

"I'll get a rope!" another shouted.

The shouts were interrupted by Deputy Wallace firing a pistol into the air.

"No!" Deputy Wallace shouted. "There's not goin' to be any lynching while I am here."

"What do you mean while you are here? Where was you awhile ago, when the bank was bein' robbed? Where was you when we needed you?"

"I was having lunch," Wallace said.

"Come on, Larry," one of the angry mob said. "You heard what they done! They kilt the preacher 'n his wife."

"And they'll hang for it," Wallace replied. "But I'm takin' 'em to Cheyenne where they'll get a trial, and then we'll hang 'em all legal like." He looked over at the two men who were still holding their hands in the air.

"And this way, they'll have plenty of time to think about it."

Chapter Two

Deputy Wallace had company for the five-mile ride as he took the prisoners from Archer to Cheyenne. Duff was with him, and so were Elmer and Wang.

"I tell you the truth, Duff, I don't know why you didn't shoot these two the way you did the LaFarge brothers," Deputy Wallace said. "If you'd done that, these two men would be back at the undertaker's parlor with the other two."

"The difference is, the other two men were trying to shoot me," Duff said.

"Hell, the way I heard it told, all four of 'em was shootin' at you."

"Aye, but these two changed their mind and threw down their weapons. And I'm for thinking that it would nae be a good thing to shoot an unarmed man."

"You mean the way these two sons of bitches shot down Reverend Pyle 'n his wife?" Wallace asked.

"We didn't know they was unarmed," Manning said.

"A man wearing preacher's garb, 'n his wife standin' right beside him, 'n you didn't know he was unarmed?"

Deputy Wallace asked. "Ha. Try that in court 'n see how far it'll get you."

"What are we goin' to do, Callahan?" Manning asked, his voice on the edge of panic.

"We're goin' to hang I reckon," Callahan replied.

"That's the first thing you've said that's right," Deputy Wallace said.

News of what had happened in Archer had already reached Cheyenne, and more than a hundred people lined up on both sides of the street, watching as the little parade of men rode down Central Avenue. Many of them followed the riders, so that by the time they dismounted in front of the sheriff's office, more than a dozen of the citizens of the town were there.

"Is it true they kilt Reverend Pyle?" someone shouted.

"Yeah," another answered. "Shot him 'n his wife down in cold blood they did."

"You two are goin' to hang, 'n I plan to be there to watch," another shouted.

"Hell, why wait? Let's hang the bastards now!"

"You gotta pertect us," Manning said.

"Why?" Wallace asked.

"Because you do! That's your job!" Manning said, his voice breaking with the terror he was feeling.

By now Sheriff Sharpies had come out of his office, accompanied by two more deputies.

"Don't you worry any," the sheriff said. "I'm not going to let anything happen to you two boys. If you're lynched, I won't have any hand in it. But if you're hung legal, I'm proud to say that I'm the one that'll march you two up those thirteen steps to meet the hangman."

"It's goin' to be a public hangin', ain't it, Sheriff?" someone from the crowd asked.

"Oh, yes indeed, it will be public," Sheriff Sharpies answered.

"Then hell, that's as good as us doin' it our own selves, I mean, if we get to watch it 'n all."

"Sheriff, I think you need to know that it was Duff MacCallister that caught these two, 'n he's the one that kilt the other two," Wallace said.

"Yes, I've already been told." The sheriff smiled at Duff. "There was already a two-hundred-and-fifty-dollar reward on each of these men, even before they tried to rob that bank. Looks like you've got a thousand dollars comin'."

"Sheriff, if it's all the same to you, I'd like you to give that money to the orphanage."

"That's damn decent of you, Duff. I know the orphanage will be most appreciative."

When Sheriff Sharpies took the two prisoners into the jail, Duff, Elmer, and Wang rode out to the railroad depot. Elmer and Wang had helped Duff deliver the cattle to the holding pens at Archer, and even had there not been prisoners to escort to Cheyenne, Duff, Elmer, and Wang would have come anyway.

With a wave, Elmer and Wang started back toward Sky Meadow. Duff, who had arranged to meet Meagan in town, decided that he wanted to be a bit cleaner and smell somewhat better for the rendezvous, so he stopped at Mac's Barbershop for a haircut and bath.

"Is that him?"

"Yeah, that's him. That's the son of a bitch that kilt both my brothers."

Eric LaFarge and Ira York were standing just outside Nippy Jones Tavern, which was across the street from Mac's. Eric had been part of the planning of the bank robbery gone wrong in Archer. He had not gone into the bank with the others because his job was to stay back in town to see what sort of posse was put together, then to meet the others at a prearranged place and give them warning.

But there was no prearranged place for them to meet, and there was no posse. One man, Duff MacCallister, had stopped the bank robbers before they even got out of town. And Eric LaFarge had stood helplessly by as he watched MacCallister shoot down both of his brothers.

Blood was strong, and even Ira York felt the connection because he was a first cousin. And it was the blood connection that brought LaFarge and York to this place and this time.

"The son of a bitch just went into the barbershop," York said.

"Yeah, well, he won't come out alive," LaFarge said.

Drawing their guns and holding them down by their sides, LaFarge and York started across the street toward the barbershop.

Mac was just building up some lather when Duff happened to glance out the window. He saw the two men crossing the street with what could only be described as a purposeful stroll. He also saw that both men had drawn their pistols and were holding them down, tight against their legs.

"Mac, get out of here, go into the back room," Duff said in a stern order.

"What?" Mac replied, confused by the unusual demand.

"Just do what I say!" Duff said, even louder. "There are two men coming in here, and there's going to be shooting." Duff drew his own gun and was holding it under the apron.

Mac didn't need any further persuasion.

"Oh, my!" he said in a worried tone as, holding the lather cup in one hand and the brush in the other, he hurried into the back of the shop.

The bell on the door tinkled as the two armed men pushed it open.

"You gentlemen might want to come back a little later," Duff said in a calm voice. "I'm afraid the barber had to step away."

"Yeah?" one of the two men said. "Good, that'll just make killin' you easier."

"Oh? And why, may I ask, would you want to kill me?"

"My name is LaFarge," one of the two men said. "Eric LaFarge."

"Oh, I see," Duff said. "And you were related to the two men I killed?"

"They was my brothers," LaFarge said.

"And do ye be a LaFarge as well?" Duff asked the second man.

"No, I'm Ira York, 'n Dan 'n Don was my cousins."

"Gentlemen, I'm sorry it came to the point where I had to kill them, but they had just robbed a bank and they were trying to kill me. I had nae choice; 'twas either them or me."

"Yeah, well, now it's down to you 'n us," LaFarge said. He brought his pistol up and pointed it at Duff. York followed suit.

"Aye, so it would appear," Duff said. "'N that bein' the case, I would advise the two of ye to drop your guns now before this goes any further."

"Ha! You would like that, wouldn't you?" LaFarge said.

"Aye, I would like that. I plan to have a good dinner with a beautiful lady tonight, 'n it always puts me off my feed a bit when I have to kill someone. I'd just as soon not have to kill the two of ye, but if I have to, I will."

"I would tell you to say your prayers," LaFarge said. "But you didn't give my brothers time to do even that, did you?"

"Their choice, not mine," Duff replied.

"Now!" LaFarge said, thumbing back the hammer on his Peacemaker. York followed suit.

Duff had cocked his pistol even before the two men came into the barbershop, so when he saw them pull the hammers on their pistol, he didn't hesitate. He pulled the trigger twice, the shots so close together that to anyone who may have heard them, they would think only one shot was fired.

Both Eric LaFarge and Ira York went down with a look of surprise on their faces and a bullet in their hearts.

Duff stepped out of the chair and examined both men. They were dead.

"Mac?" Duff called. "You can come out now."

After explaining the situation to Sheriff Sharpies, with corroborating testimony from Mac the barber, the sheriff had the two bodies removed. Duff finished his shave and haircut, then topped it off with a bath.

An hour later he checked in to the Mixon Hotel on Central.

"Yes, sir?" the desk clerk said, greeting him with a practiced smile.

"I'd like accommodations for the night if such be available," Duff said.

"Yes, sir, we can take care of that," the clerk said, turning the book around to allow Duff to register.

"I'm expecting a lady friend; if she should inquire, please tell her the number to my room," Duff said. "I hope that will nae be a problem."

"No problem at all, sir," the clerk said. "Cheyenne's ladies of the evening are quite familiar with our hotel and need fear no harassment for the practice of their avocation."

Duff looked up from the registration book with a flash of anger in his steel-blue eyes.

"She is *not* a lady of the evening," he said, coming down hard on the word "not" and using the more Americanized negative instead of his more comfortable Scottish "nae" to emphasize his response.

"Of course not, sir, and I beg your pardon for the inference," the desk clerk replied. He took a key down from a marked board on the wall behind him. "Your room is two oh five, sir."

"Very good."

Not long after Duff checked into his room, there was a light knock on his door.

"Duff?" It was Meagan Parker's voice.

Duff opened the door and Meagan stepped inside to an embrace and a kiss.

* * *

After dinner that evening, Duff took Meagan to the Cheyenne Theater to see Annie Mack Berlein in a production of *Oliver Twist*. There was a reception after the play, and the theater director, James Anderson, introduced the star to Duff MacCallister.

"I know you have heard of our 'wild west,'" Anderson said to the actress. "Mr. MacCallister here is a part of that wild west. Why it was just this morning that he broke up an attempted bank robbery in Archer, killing two of the perpetrators and capturing the other two. Then this afternoon, two other outlaws, seeking revenge, tried to kill him, but Mr. MacCallister bested them as well."

"My," Annie said, flashing a broad smile toward Duff. "I have certainly dealt with 'heroes' on the stage, but I'm not sure I've ever encountered such a person in the flesh."

"Sure 'n 'tis not a word I would apply to m'self," Duff said.

"The accent! Scottish born, are you?"

"Aye."

"Then we share a kinship, for I am Irish born."

"We share a connection beyond that," Duff said. "I met ye 'n your husband once before."

Meagan, who had been standing at Duff's side from the time of the introduction, smiled and breathed a bit easier when she heard that the beautiful young actress had a husband.

"We have met before?" Annie questioned.

"Aye. 'Twas working backstage at the Rex Theater I was, for the production of *The Highlander*."

"Ah yes, *The Highlander*. It starred Andrew and Rosanna MacCallister, brother and sister, and two of the most skilled and famous actors in New York. Wait a minute. MacCallister? And would you be kin, Mr. MacCallister?"

"Aye, I would be, for 'tis my cousins they are."

"Oh, how exciting. I'll be seeing them again next month; it will give me a great pleasure to tell them that I met their handsome cousin . . . and to pass on news of your heroic exploits."

The next morning Duff and Meagan rode back to Sky Meadow and Chugwater. Chugwater was some sixty miles north of Cheyenne, but Sky Meadow was only thirty miles, so Meagan would spend the night at the ranch.

"*It will give me a great pleasure to tell them that I met their* handsome *cousin*," Meagan said, mimicking the actress. However, the smile on her face gave evidence that she was teasing, and not jealous or upset.

"Here now, lass. 'N would ye be for saying that I am nae handsome?" Duff replied, his smile as broad as Meagan's.

"You'll do," Meagan said.

Connect with Us

Visit us online at
KensingtonBooks.com
to read more from your favorite authors, see books
by series, view reading group guides, and more.

Join us on social media

for sneak peeks, chances to win books and prize packs,
and to share your thoughts with other readers.

facebook.com/kensingtonpublishing
twitter.com/kensingtonbooks

Tell us what you think!

To share your thoughts, submit a review,
or sign up for our eNewsletters, please visit:
KensingtonBooks.com/TellUs.